For testimonials from law enforcement,
visit Carolyn Arnold's website.

ALSO BY CAROLYN ARNOLD

Detective Madison Knight

Ties That Bind
Justified
Sacrifice
Found Innocent
Just Cause
Deadly Impulse

In the Line of Duty
Power Struggle
Shades of Justic
What We Bury
Girl on the Run
Life Sentence

Brandon Fisher FBI

Eleven
Silent Graves
The Defenseless
Blue Baby
Violated

Remnants
On the Count of Three
Past Deeds
One More Kill

Detective Amanda Steele

The Little Grave
Stolen Daughters
The Silent Witness
Black Orchid Girls

Her Frozen Cry
Last Seen Alive
Her Final Breath

Sara and Sean Cozy Mystery

Bowled Over Americano   *Wedding Bells Brew Murder*

Matthew Connor Adventure

City of Gold
The Secret of the Lost Pharaoh

The Legend of Gasparilla and His Treasure

Standalone
Assassination of a Dignitary
Midlife Psychic

A gripping crime thriller full of heart-pounding twists

TIES
THAT
BIND

A decades-old family secret
has just turned deadly...

CAROLYN
ARNOLD

A Detective Madison Knight Mystery

HIBBERT & STILES
PUBLISHING INC.

2019 Revised Edition

Copyright © 2011 by Carolyn Arnold
Excerpt from *Justified* copyright © 2011 by Carolyn Arnold

Hibbert & Stiles Publishing Inc.
hspubinc.com

This is a work of fiction. Names, characters, places, and incidents are the products of the author's imagination or are used fictitiously. Any resemblance to actual events, locales, or persons, living or dead, is entirely coincidental.

Names: Arnold, Carolyn, 1976
Title: Ties That Bind / Carolyn Arnold.
Description: 2022 Hibbert & Stiles Publishing Inc. edition. | Series: Detective Madison Knight Series ; book 1

Identifiers: ISBN (e-book): 978-0-9878400-1-1 | ISBN (4.25 x 7 paperback): 978-1-988064-09-3 | ISBN (5 x 8 paperback): 978-1-988064-10-9 | ISBN (6.14 x 9.21 hardcover): 978-1-988353-06-7

Additional formats:
ISBN (large print editon): 978-1-988353-95-1
ISBN (audiobook): 978-1-989706-22-0

TIES
THAT
BIND

CHAPTER ONE

Someone died every day. Detective Madison Knight was left to make sense of it.

She ducked under the yellow tape and surveyed the scene. The white, two-story house would be deemed average any other day, but today the dead body inside made it a place of interest to the Stiles Police Department and the curious onlookers who gathered in small clusters on the sidewalk.

She'd never before seen the officer who was securing the perimeter, but she knew his type. The way he stood there— his back straight, one hand resting on his holster, the other gripping a clipboard—showed he was an eager recruit.

He held up a hand as she approached. "This is a closed crime scene."

She unclipped her badge from the waist of her pants and held it up in front of him. He studied it as if it were counterfeit. She usually respected those who took their jobs seriously but not when she was functioning on little sleep and the humidity level topped ninety-five percent at ten thirty in the morning.

"Detective K-N-I—"

Her name died on her lips as Sergeant Winston stepped out of the house. She would have groaned audibly if he weren't closing the distance between them so quickly. She preferred her boss behind his desk.

Winston gestured toward the young officer to let him know she was permitted to be on the scene. She signed in, and the officer glared at her before leaving his post. She envied the fact that he could walk away while she was left to speak with the sarge.

"It's about time you got here." Winston fished a handkerchief out of his pocket and wiped at his receding hairline. The extra few inches of exposed forehead could have served as a solar panel. "I was just about to assign the lead to Grant."

Terry Grant was her on-the-job partner of five years and three years younger than her thirty-four. She'd be damned if Terry was put in charge of this case.

"Where have you been?" Winston asked.

She jacked a thumb in the rookie's direction. "Who's the new guy?"

"Don't change the subject, Knight."

She needed to offer some sort of explanation for being late. "Well, boss, you know me. Up all night slinging back shooters."

"Don't get smart with me."

She flashed him a cocky smile and pulled out a Hershey's bar from her pants pocket. The chocolate had already softened from the heat. Not that it mattered. She took a bite.

Heaven.

She spoke with her mouth partially full. "What are you doing here, anyway?"

"The call came in, I was nearby, and thought someone should respond." His leg caught the tape as he tried to step over it to the sidewalk, and he hopped on the other leg to adjust his balance. He continued speaking as if he hadn't noticed. "The body's upstairs, main bedroom. She was strangled." He pointed the tip of a key toward her. "Keep me updated." He pressed a button on his key fob and the department-issued SUV's lights flashed. "I'll be waiting for your call."

As if he needed to say that. Sometimes she wondered if he valued talking more than taking action.

She took a deep breath. She could feel the young officer watching her, and she flicked a glance at him. What was his problem? She took another bite of her candy bar.

"Too bad you showed. I think I was about to get the lead."

Madison turned toward her partner's voice. Terry was padding across the lawn toward her.

"I'd have to be the one dead for that to happen." She smiled as she brushed past him.

"You look like crap."

Her smile faded. She stopped walking and turned around. Every one of his blond hairs were in place, making her self-conscious of her short, wake-up-and-wear-it cut. His cheeks held a healthy glow, too, no doubt from his two-mile morning run. She hated people who could do mornings.

"What did you get? Two hours of sleep?"

"Three, but who's counting?" She took another large bite of the chocolate. It was almost a slurp with how fast the bar was melting.

"You were up reviewing evidence from the last case again, weren't you?"

She wasn't inclined to answer.

"You can't change the past."

She wasn't hungry anymore and wrapped up what was left of the chocolate. "Let's focus on *this* case."

"Fine, if that's how it's going be. Victim's name is Laura Saunders. She's thirty-two. Single. Officer Higgins was the first on scene."

Higgins? She hadn't seen him since she arrived, but he had been her training officer. He still worked in that capacity for new recruits. Advancing in the ranks wasn't important to him. He was happy making a difference where he was stationed.

Terry continued. "Call came in from the vic's employer, Southwest Welding Products, where she worked as the receptionist."

"What would make the employer call?"

"She didn't show for her shift at eight. They tried reaching her first, but when they didn't get an answer, they sent a security officer over to her house. He found the door ajar and called downtown. Higgins was here by eight forty-five."

"Who was—"

"The security officer?"

"Yeah." Apparently they finished each other's sentences now.

"Terrence Owens. And don't worry. We took a formal statement and let him go. Background showed nothing, not even a speeding ticket. We can function when you're not here."

She cocked her head to the side.

"He also testifies to the fact that he never stepped one foot in the place." Terry laughed. "He said he's watched enough cop dramas to know it would contaminate the crime scene. You get all these people watching those stupid TV shows, and they think they can solve a murder."

"Is Owens the one who made the formal call downtown, then?" Madison asked.

"Actually, procedure for them is to route everything through the company administration. A Sandra Butler made the call. She's the office manager."

"So, an employee is merely half an hour late for work and they send someone to the house?"

"She said it's part of their safety policy."

"At least they're a group of people inclined to think positively." She rolled her eyes. Sweat droplets ran down her back. Gross. She moved toward the house.

The young officer scurried over. He shoved his clipboard under his arm and tucked his pen behind his ear. He pointed toward the chocolate bar still in her hand. "You can't take that in there."

She glanced down. Chocolate oozed from a corner of the wrapper. He was right. She handed the package to him, and he took it with two pinched fingers.

She patted his shoulder. "Good job."

He walked away with the bar dangling from his hand, mumbling something indiscernible.

"You can be so wicked sometimes," Terry said.

"Why, thank you." She was tempted to take a mini bow but resisted the urge.

"It wasn't a compliment. And since when do you eat chocolate for breakfast?"

"Oh shut up." She punched him in the shoulder. He smirked and rubbed his arm. Same old sideshow. She headed into the house with him on her heels.

"The stairs are to the right," Terry said.

"Holy crap, it's freezing in here." The sweat on her skin chilled her. Refreshing, actually.

"Yep, a hundred and one outside, sixty inside."

When she was two steps from the top of the staircase, Terry said, "And just a heads-up—this is not your typical strangulation."

"Come on, Terry. You've seen one, you've—" She stopped abruptly when she reached the bedroom doorway. Terry was right.

CHAPTER TWO

The hairs rose on her arms, not from the air-conditioning but from the chill of death. In her ten years on the force, Madison had never seen anything quite like this. Maybe in New York City they were accustomed to this type of murder scene, but not here in Stiles where the population was just shy of half a million and the Major Crimes division boasted six detectives.

She nodded a greeting to Cole Richards, the medical examiner. He reciprocated with a small bob of his head.

Laura Saunders lay on her back in the middle of a double bed, arms folded over her torso. But the one thing that stood out—and this would be what Terry had tried to warn her about—was that she was naked with a man's necktie bound tightly around her neck. That adornment and her shoulder-length, brown hair provided the only contrasts between her pale skin and the beige sheets. Most strangulation victims were dressed, or when rape was a factor, the body was typically found in an alley or hotel room, not the vic's own bedroom. For Laura to be found here made it personal.

Jealous lover, perhaps?

"Was she raped?" Madison asked.

Terry rubbed the back of his neck the way he did when there were more questions than answers. "Not leaning that way. Her clothes are strewn on main level. Seems like if sex did happen, it was consensual."

"And she's in her own house," Madison added.

The entire scenario caused Madison pain and regret—pain over how this woman's life had been snuffed out so prematurely, regret that she couldn't have prevented it. For someone who faced death on a regular basis, one would think she would be callous regarding her own mortality, but the truth was it scared her more with every passing day. Nothing was certain. And the fact Laura was only two years younger than Madison sank into the pit of her stomach.

Terry kneaded the tips of his fingers into the base of his neck. "There is no evidence of a break-in. Nothing seems to be missing. There's jewelry on her dresser, and electronics were left downstairs. No obvious signs of a struggle."

Madison moved farther into the room to study Laura and the tie more closely. It was expensive, silk, and blue striped. Her eyes then took in a shelving unit on the far wall, which housed folded clothes, an alarm clock, and a framed photograph.

She brainstormed out loud. "Maybe it was some sort of sex game that got out of hand. Erotic asphyxiation?"

"If it was something as simple as that, why not call nine-one-one? The owner of that necktie must have something to hide."

Richards's assistant excused himself as he walked through the bedroom. Madison could never remember the guy's name.

Terry continued. "Put yourself in this guy's place if things had gotten out of hand. You would loosen the tie, shake her, but you wouldn't pose her. You would certainly call for help."

"The scene definitely speaks to it being an intentional act." She met her partner's eyes. "But I'd also guess the killer felt regret. Otherwise, why cross her arms over her torso? That could indicate a close relationship between Laura and her killer."

Their discussion paused at the sound of a zipper as Richards sealed the woman in the black bag.

His assistant worked at getting the gurney out of the room and addressed Richards. "I'll wait in the hall."

Richards nodded.

"Winston confirmed you're ruling cause of death as strangulation," Madison said to the ME.

"Yes. COD is asphyxiation due to strangulation. Her face shows signs of petechiae. Young, fit women don't normally show that unless they put up a fight. And there were also cuts to her wrists."

"Cuts?" Terry asked.

"Yes." Richards glanced at Terry. "Crime Scene is thinking cuffs. I don't think they've found them yet."

Madison's eyes drifted to the bed's headboard and its black vertical bars. The paint was worn off a few of them. "She's bound, and then he uncuffs and poses her." The hairs on her arms rose. "When are you placing time of death?"

"Thirty to thirty-three hours ago, based on the stage of rigor and body temperature."

"So between two and five Sunday morning?" Terry smiled and shrugged his shoulders when both pairs of eyes shot to him.

Madison often wondered how her partner could do math so quickly in his head.

"Of course, the fact that it's cold enough to hang meat in here makes it harder to pinpoint," Richards said.

Madison noticed the light in Terry's eyes brighten at the recognition of the cliché. He knew she didn't care for such idioms, and he had proven himself an opportunist over the years. Whenever he could dish them out, he would. Whenever someone else said them around her, he found amusement in it. She was tempted to cross the room and beat him, but instead, she just rolled her eyes, certain the hint of a smile on her face showed. She hated that she didn't have enough restraint to ignore him altogether.

"I'll be conducting a full autopsy within the next twenty-four hours. I'll keep you posted on my findings. Tomorrow afternoon at the earliest. You know where to find me." Richards smiled at her, showcasing flawless white teeth, his midnight skin providing further contrast. And something about the way his eyes creased with the expression, Madison couldn't claim immunity to his charms. When he smiled, it actually calmed her. Too bad he was married.

"Thanks." The word came out automatically. Her eyes were on a framed photograph of a smiling couple. She recognized the woman as Laura, but the man was unfamiliar. "Terry, who is he?"

CHAPTER THREE

He sat in his 1995 Honda Civic, sweating profusely. Its air conditioner hadn't worked for years. The car was a real piece of shit, but perfect for the crappy life he had going. He combed his fingers through his hair and caught his reflection in the rearview mirror.

He lifted his sunglasses to get a better look at his eyes. They had changed. They were dark, even sinister. He put the shades back in place, rolled his shoulders forward to dislodge the tension in his neck, and took a cleansing breath. With the air came a waft of smoke from the cigarette burning in the car's ashtray.

He had parked close enough to observe the activity at 36 Bay Street, yet far enough away to be left alone. At least he hoped so. Cruisers were parked in front of the house, and forty-eight minutes ago, a department-issued SUV had pulled to a quick stop.

All this activity because of his work. It was something to be proud of.

He picked up the cigarette and tapped the ash in the tray.

Statistically, the murder itself was nothing special. Another young lady. People would move on. They always did.

It was the city's thirtieth murder of the year. He was up-to-date on his statistics. But he was always that way; he was a gatherer of facts, of useless information. Maybe someday his fact-finding and attention to detail would prove beneficial.

He wiped his forehead, and sweat trickled from his brow and down his nose. The salty perspiration stung. He winced. His nose was still tender to the touch. That crotchety old man at the bar had a strong right hook.

He rested his eyes for a second, and when he opened them, a Crown Vic had pulled to a stop in front of the house. He straightened up.

A woman of average height—probably about five foot five—with blond hair walked toward the yellow tape. But it wasn't her looks that captured his interest. It was her determined stride. And something was familiar about her.

He smiled when he realized why.

She was Detective Madison Knight. She had made headlines for putting away the Russian Mafia czar, Dimitre Petrov, but the glory hadn't lasted long. People like Petrov had a reach that extended from behind bars, and the rumor was that Petrov had gotten the attorney who had lost his case killed.

He must have hit the big-time to have Knight on *his* investigation. An adrenaline rush flowed over him, blanketing him in heat. Energy pulsed in his veins, his heartbeat pounding in his ears. He strained to draw in a satisfying breath.

Tap, tap.

Knuckles rapped against the driver's-side window.

His heart slowed. His breath shortened. Slowly, he lifted his eyes to look at the source of the intrusion.

A police officer!

Stay calm. Play it cool.

He drew the cigarette to his lips. Damn, his nose hurt so much when he sucked air in that he had to fight crying out in pain. He left the cig perched between his fingers, and the cop motioned for him to put the window down.

"I need you to move your vehicle."

Thank God for his dark-tinted glasses or the cop might see right through him. "Sure."

The police officer bent over and peered into the car. "Are you all right, sir?"

Following the officer's gaze to his unsteady hand holding the cigarette, he forced himself to raise it for another drag. His hand shook the entire way. "Yeah, I'm—" Her lifeless eyes flashed in his mind. He cleared his throat, hoping it would somehow dislodge his recollections. "Sure. I, uh…I'll get out of your way immediately, Officer…Tendum." He read the cop's name from his shirt.

The cop's gaze remained fixed on him, eye to eye.

Can he see through me, sunglasses and all? Is my guilt that obvious?

"All units confirm a secured perimeter." The monotone voice came over the officer's radio.

The cop turned the volume down without taking his eyes off him. "What happened to your nose?"

What is this uniform out to prove?

He forced another cough and then took yet another drag. He tapped the cigarette ash out the window. The officer stepped to the side, but based on the look in his eyes, he wasn't going anywhere.

He needed to give the cop an answer. His words escaped through gritted teeth. "Bar fight."

The officer nodded. His eyes condemned him. "I need you to move your car—" he drummed his flattened palm on the roof "—and try to keep yourself out of trouble."

Too late, Officer. Too late.

CHAPTER FOUR

Madison studied the photograph. Both Laura and the man were smiling. The reflection in their eyes indicated a history. She tapped the photograph and asked Terry, "Are there any other pictures of him around the house?"

"Not that I've seen."

"They look like a happy couple. Maybe next of kin will know who he is. From there, we'll ask neighbors and people where she worked. See if anyone can help us find out more about her social life."

"Detective Knight." A young CSI stood in the doorway. "I noticed that the body's been removed. Can I come in?"

"Just give us a few more minutes."

He nodded and left the room.

"Maybe there was no forcible entry because the killer lived here," Madison said.

Terry slipped on a pair of gloves and opened the bi-fold closet doors. "Only women's clothing. There's certainly nothing to indicate that a guy was living here or even staying here. There are no male clothes or touches."

"Male touches?"

"What?"

"You talk strangely sometimes."

"What's that supposed to mean?"

"Just that." She smiled while facing the interior of the closet. "Laura was an organized woman, liked order. I mean, look at this." Madison gestured to the many pairs of shoes on racks, sorted according to color.

She put on a pair of gloves and opened the top drawer of a dresser that was beside the closet. At quick assessment, there appeared to be a hundred matchbooks, all embossed with the name *The Weathered Rose.*

"Look at these." She scooped a handful of matchbooks and let them filter through her fingers back into the drawer. "No phone number or address on them." She rummaged further and discovered a pair of metal cuffs. She looped a finger in them, dangled them in front of Terry. "Look what I found. Maybe we'll get lucky."

She looked back at the headboard. "I'm going to guess this wasn't Laura's first time being tied up. The paint's worn off from more than two bars. She obviously wasn't a traditional girl."

"They're not even cozy cuffs," Terry said.

"Cozy cuffs?"

"Yeah, they're covered with fur. Popular in black and pink." Terry scrunched up his face at mention of the latter color.

That was more insight than she needed into his sex life. "Maybe the killer suggested bondage and erotic asphyxiation, and she was into it."

"It's possible."

She worked through the drawer with one hand while the other held the cuffs. What was with the matchbooks?

"Could you get that kid back in here?" she asked.

Terry leaned through the doorway and yelled out for him. Back to Madison, Terry said, "His name is Mark Andrews. He's worked cases with you before."

"Yeah, I know." Was it her fault Mark struck her more as an "Eddy"?

"Maddy, you'd think since he loves you, you could at least—"

Madison waved her hand. Mark stood in the doorway, and she pointed to the framed photograph. "Please log that into evidence."

"Sure." He took a picture of it, bagged and tagged it, then scribbled on the evidence log.

"Thank you, Mark." She deliberately said his name in an effort to aggravate Terry, but he wasn't even paying them any attention. He was examining the contents of the closet.

"Do you want me to bag the cuffs?" Mark pointed at them. She handed them over. "Thanks."

"Don't mention it." He smiled and left the room.

"See, he loves you."

"Oh shut up, Terry. I'm not even sure if he's into women." She knew Mark enough to know he was outnumbered in the lab three to one. The other ladies picked on him, and if anything went wrong, he took the blame. But the man's sexual preference was a mystery.

"He at least seems into you," Terry mumbled.

"I'll take that as a compliment."

"Take it how you wish."

"We'll need to get a copy of the photograph to show around, too..." She called Mark back into the room and told him her request. "And the sooner, the better. Please make sure to get what's in the dresser drawer, too." She patted his shoulder as she headed out of the room. He nodded and blushed as if flattered by her acknowledgment. "Thanks, pal."

"I've always admired that about you." Madison's eyes snapped to Terry, and he added, "Just the power you have."

"What power?"

"The power of turning hot or cold depending on your mood."

She smiled and shrugged. "I don't know what you're talking about."

"See, there you go again. Playing all nice and innocent until I turn my back on you."

"Guess since I'm always one step ahead of you, you won't have to worry about that." She left him to trail behind her down the stairs.

She planned to look for evidence that Laura had a steady man in her life, but first she focused on the mud in the front foyer. She had noticed it when she entered but was in a hurry to get to the victim.

Terry must have read her mind. "Crime Scene photographed a shoeprint from the bottom step. Men's size twelve, and based on directionality, the person was headed up the stairs. The mud on the tile had nothing more to offer."

As confirmed by Richards, the time of death was estimated between two and five on Sunday morning. If she recalled correctly, she had been about to go to sleep at that time, and it was pouring. It hadn't rained since.

Her eyes scanned the home starting from the front door. The staircase was to the immediate right, and to the side of that was a hallway table with six long-stemmed calla lilies in a vase. The home had an open layout with the living room to the left of the entry, the dining room straight ahead, and the kitchen to its left.

She noted a couple glasses and a wine bottle sitting on an oval coffee table. One wineglass had lipstick marks and was empty. The other one was full. Crime Scene already had markers placed in front of them.

She turned to Terry. "Well, she probably wasn't drugged or poisoned. Richards mentioned she fought back. It's worth checking out, though. Or maybe it did all start as an experiment with choking. She thought it was all for fun, but he planned to take it all the way?"

"If that's the case, we're looking at premeditation."

"That would make him one scary son of a bitch. Especially scary because he was someone who had earned Laura's trust. At the least, she had let him into her home."

"Hey, Maddy." It was Cynthia Baxter. She was the CSI supervisor, but more importantly, a good friend. Cynthia possessed qualities most men found attractive. Physically, she was eye-catching with her long hair and black-framed glasses. She gave "Sexy Librarian" a real-life translation. But, whatever *it* was, she never had a shortage of interest. Her only downfalls were succumbing too easily to their one-liners and smoking a pack of cigarettes a day. The latter Madison was determined to help her quit.

Madison pointed toward the glass with the wine.

"Don't worry. It's already been processed, and we pulled fingerprints." Cynthia softly rolled her eyes and returned to evidence collection. Her specialties included documentation analysis, fingerprints, and other patterned evidence.

Two shelves in the living area were full of fiction books. Madison recognized some of the authors, and she pulled out a couple paperbacks by their spines.

"Mysteries," Terry said.

Madison nodded and pushed the books back into place. "Ironic, though tragic, but she reads them for fun and becomes a victim in real life."

She worked her way through the room. There were no more pictures of the man that had been in the photograph upstairs. In fact, there was only one of Laura with an older couple. Her parents? The looks didn't hold a striking resemblance, but the warmth coming from the photograph gave that impression, and the couple was about the right age.

A jab of pain resonated in her chest. No doubt she'd be meeting them in person soon. She felt her partner's eyes on her and fought to maintain her emotional balance. "We better get some uniformed officers out there. See if any neighbors noticed anything over the weekend. We'll also have to make sure Laura's name and house aren't all over the news before next of kin is notified."

Terry nodded. "I'm on it."

CHAPTER FIVE

Laura Saunders's parents died in a car accident when she was five. Her father's brother and his wife had taken her in and cared for her. According to the records, their names were Albert and Helen Saunders, and they had no biological children of their own.

Madison and Terry were in the Crown Vic, parked outside the Saunderses' house. Madison was behind the wheel. She told him it gave her a queasy stomach to be chauffeured. The truth was she liked being in control—preferably of everything.

The air conditioner couldn't compensate for the sun beating through the front windshield, yet she refused to move. She asked Terry to get a Hershey's bar out of the glove box, which he did reluctantly.

"It'll be melted at this point."

Madison shrugged her shoulders. "I wish I could delegate this off to you." By *this*, she was referring to notifying the next of kin. She took a large bite of the chocolate and washed it down with a gulp of coffee.

He glanced at her mouth, back to her eyes. "I'm not going to comment about that today."

"Good choice."

"What is that? Two bars in three hours?"

"Shut up, Terry." She wasn't eating because she was hungry. She was eating for emotional comfort. Pacifying with chocolate had started back in her teen years and stuck with her.

"I'm not going to feel bad for you and volunteer to take care of this. I'm keeping track, and it's your turn."

"Come on, Terry. For the team."

"Nope."

"Lucky me." She hated this part of the job. She would rather be doing anything else—having her legs waxed or getting a root canal.

"I'm sweatin' my bag off. Can we get this over with?"

Madison stuffed the rest of the bar into her mouth. Her cheeks bulged to capacity, but she managed to siphon the rest of the coffee in there.

"I should put in for a new partner. One with better habits," Terry said.

"You're complaining about bad habits? You're the one sitting over there talking about your bag!" She laughed. "Besides, what would you do without me? I add excitement to your life."

"I'd find a way to cope."

In front of the Saunderses' door, Madison said, "I'll give you one more chance to step in."

"Not doing it."

"Maybe I should be the one to put in for a new partner."

"You wouldn't survive without me."

She heard the smile in his voice, but she couldn't allow herself to look at him right now. His eyes would detract from the inner strength she needed to carry out this task. She had to somehow convince herself that she was doing them a favor.

The door opened barely wide enough for the man's head to squeeze through. She recognized him from the photograph on Laura's bookshelf. "Mr. Albert Saunders?"

"I am." He opened the door wider, and there was a woman beside him. She was also familiar from the photo, though markedly shrunken. She was wrapped in a shawl and wearing flannel pajamas.

Madison felt hotter just looking at her.

The woman stepped into the sunlight, and her eyes were dark and sunken. The marks of chemotherapy.

Madison's stomach tightened. She hated how memories of her grandmother would seize her, but feared if they ever stopped, it would mean she was gone forever.

Albert put an arm around his wife. She shook violently underneath his touch, seemingly frozen.

"We have some bad news. May we come in?" Madison asked.

The first priority was to make sure the family had a place to sit. The shock alone caused some to collapse under the weight of the news.

Helen looked up at her husband, further dwarfing her stature. She nodded her approval to him.

Madison and Terry followed the couple to their front sitting room. Two sets of eyes steadied on her. It was quiet enough that Madison could hear the faint sound of whooshing water—a running dishwasher?

"You said you had bad news. It might be too much for us to handle." Albert squeezed Helen's hand. She sat tightly beside him.

Helplessness set in. There was no way to stop their suffering. This poor man, having lost the niece he raised, may soon lose his wife to cancer. The woman not only faced her own mortality, she lost someone so young before her.

Focus, Maddy.

The second priority: be direct and to the point. "Your niece Laura was found dead this morning," she said.

Helen gasped, the expulsion of air sucking life from the room. Her eyes enlarged while Albert's eyes went vacant.

Madison relayed the generalities as to the cause of death and how it was being treated as a homicide. She explained they would release the body as soon as possible—the same old spiel she was sick of saying. But the selfish thought occurred to her: if people stopped killing one another, what would she do? She tried to shake it from her mind, but the judgmental glint in Albert's eyes made her question herself.

She always put everything into solving a case, but his eyes begged the question: *why my little girl?* Somehow, she had to stop allowing cases to have such power over her emotions.

"Please be assured we're doing all we can to find your niece's killer," Terry said.

"So that was her...in the news?" Albert asked. "There was a brief piece on at noon. They said a young woman..." He flattened a hand over his chest. "I had a bad feeling."

Madison glared at Terry. He was supposed to have taken care of the media. "Again, I'm sorry for your loss." Her words grew stale in the air.

Seconds later, Albert spoke. "Enough with the damned apologies. It's not your fault." He shook his head. "No, it's Laura's fault."

Helen's shaking stopped. "How dare you, Albert?" Her eyes burned with a fire even chemotherapy couldn't diminish.

"Well, it is, Helen." He clenched his jaw, his focus on a place behind them.

"If there's something you know that could help us..." Madison coaxed.

"She'd always get herself into trouble. Boyfriends." He waved a hand in the air. "They'd come and go. She'd wind up brokenhearted."

"Do you think any of these boyfriends would have wanted to hurt her?"

"Lady, your guess is as good as mine. But your evidence... I'm assuming it leads you to a man, doesn't it?" His eyes searched hers.

She swallowed dryly. Her thoughts flashed back to the murder scene, to Laura's naked body. Her words would belie the communication in her eyes. "We're leaning that way." She thought of pulling out the photo found in Laura's room now, but the Saunderses seemed inclined to continue speaking. She didn't want to discourage them.

"You see, Helen? A *man* killed her. She finally got herself in too deep. Probably someone from that bar she'd frequent."

"Maybe it was *that* man." Helen's voice was low.

Madison didn't overlook her comment, but first latched on to Albert's reference to a bar. The name from the matchbooks sounded like it could be one. "Which bar?"

"Some old bar. More like a pub. It was a rundown place, but she insists...well, guess I should say *insisted*." Helen paused, wiped her nose with her fingers. "I think it was how she tried to stay in touch with her father."

Albert picked up where Helen left off. "She didn't have a chance to know her parents well. But when she went through their stuff years ago, she came across a bunch of matchbooks from this bar. Her father's addiction came to light. My brother was a boozer." He added the last part with a roll of his eyes. "Anyway, ever since she turned legal age, she's been there every night. Guess it was her way of trying to hold on." The man shrugged his shoulders, and despite the body language, his eyes misted with tears.

"Do you know the name of this bar?" Madison asked.

Helen rested her hand on Albert's leg. "Something Rose."

"The Weathered Rose?"

"That's it." Helen pulled a tissue from the waist of her pajamas, dabbed her nose.

"You also mentioned you have suspicions about a specific man, Mrs. Saunders?"

The couple shared a gaze, communicating hesitation.

Albert answered. "There was this one man she told us about. She'd been with him for a while. Now keep in mind that anything past a week was monumental for her. I can't remember his name." He turned to Helen.

"Jeff." Her voice was scarcely above a whisper.

Madison leaned in. "Jeff?" She put a hand over the pocket that contained the photograph of the man with Laura.

"Yes."

"Why would you think it could be him?"

Helen went quiet.

"She broke it off with him. He wasn't too happy about it. He'd show up at her home uninvited. She was thinking about getting a restraining order," Albert said.

"Do you know if Laura got one?" Terry asked.

Albert reached for his wife's hand again. "Knowing Laura, I doubt it. She thought she could handle anything."

"So this Jeff guy…do you know a last name?" Madison asked.

"No, I don't. I only remember her saying something about him working where she did."

Madison pulled out the photo and extended it to them. "Does he look familiar to you?"

Albert took it from her, holding it so Helen could see it as well. Both of them shook their heads.

"Sorry. We never met Jeff, so we can't say if that's him in the picture," Albert said.

"And you've never seen this man?" Madison asked for clarification.

Both of them shook their heads again.

The call came when Madison and Terry got back to the car.

"What have you got for me, Knight?" Winston asked.

She envisioned the sergeant glancing impatiently at his watch. Sometimes she wondered why she didn't strive for a promotion. If she had, she'd likely be boasting three chevrons on a uniform sleeve herself by now and bossing around detectives. But no, she claimed to be happy where she positioned herself in life.

"We're leaning toward Laura Saunders's murder being an isolated incident. We have a reason to feel an ex-boyfriend is involved."

"That's your final answer? In less than four hours, you're positive the rest of the city sleeps safe tonight?"

What did this man want from her—a guarantee? It was always black-and-white with him. She operated within the shades of gray.

She steadied her breath. "Evidence seems to be pointing us in that direction."

"I want this wrapped up, Knight, sooner than later. Keep me informed."

He never spoke the words, but the implication was there: *don't let this case go cold like the other one.* Didn't he know she tortured herself enough over that possibility?

Madison tossed her cell in the air, nearly hitting the car's ceiling, and then caught it when it came back down.

"Are you all right?" Terry asked.

"Pull up Laura's background, and check for anything that stands out. Any restraining orders. I'll get us over to Southwest Welding Products, see if they have anything to say. Maybe we'll get lucky and meet Jeff."

"Sure." He drew out the word and kept watching her.

"Don't say it like that. You're trying to play shrink on me, and I don't like it."

"Maybe it's time you started talking about it."

"Let's just close this case." She held eye contact with him as she put the car into gear.

It wasn't like she'd set out with the desire to save the world, but she did want to impact people's lives. Working as a lonely hero, under the cover of the Major Crimes Division, wasn't what she had originally planned for her life.

Terry clicked away on the keyboard. A few minutes later, he spoke. "Well, nothing stands out on her record, and there are no open restraining orders."

"Maybe she didn't hate the attention from Jeff," Madison said.

Terry didn't respond. His gaze had drifted to the road ahead of them.

"What's wrong with you?" she asked.

"You don't want to talk about your problem. I don't want to talk about mine. Fair enough?" He glanced over at her.

"Not really."

"Good."

Apparently, it didn't matter how she responded. Why was he being difficult? And how could he compare his problem with hers? Then again, her baggage was professional, but she was getting the feeling his was personal. She turned to face him and fulfilled her natural instinct to pry.

"Everything all right at home?" she asked.

"Watch!" Terry's ass came off the seat. He pointed frantically out the front windshield and then gripped the dash.

She turned around and slammed on the brakes.

A street person was walking across the road, pushing a shopping cart full of bottles.

Madison had stopped just shy of impact.

The man was in the middle of the street, yelling in another language. Despite the language barrier, facial contortion indicated what he was saying contained numerous expletives. All doubt was erased when he took his hands off the cart and held up both middle fingers.

"You could have killed him. Dang it, Maddy, would you pay attention to the road?" Terry's face was red, and a pulse had developed in his cheek.

"If you would have just talked to me, we wouldn't be in this position."

The man cleared the road but glared at her from the sidewalk, keeping his eyes trained on Madison as she drove past.

CHAPTER SIX

Southwest Welding Products was a single-story, glass building. Its grounds were surrounded by a wire fence with gated entrances to the front and the side. Two bulk propane tanks, at least twenty feet tall, stood like watchtowers in the parking lot.

"You wouldn't want a fire to start here, or the east end of the city would explode," Terry said.

"That's for sure." The words exchanged between them earlier, her prying into his business, the near accident were all behind them now. Their focus was back on the case. "Let me take the lead on this."

"As always. I'm not as good at playing…hmmm, how do I put this?"

"The bitch? That's not what your wife tells me." She turned, smiling at him, but he had already moved to get out of the vehicle.

They entered the door labeled *Employees Only* and headed to a long reception counter, where Laura Saunders would have sat. Stress and uneasiness permeated the air. It was hard to say if their presence caused it, or if it was because of what had happened to Laura, or if it was always this way. A couple uniformed officers, "unies," would have notified Laura's workmates while they were breaking the senior Saunderses' hearts.

"Hi." The woman at the desk addressed them but avoided direct eye contact. No smile lightened her face. She seemed to view the receptionist position as below her.

Even with just that one word, her voice held an accent, but Madison couldn't place it. She wasn't good with them despite the fact that skill would have proved useful in her career. She recalled her parents' admonition that she couldn't be good at everything, but she'd wished to prove them wrong.

Madison made a brief introduction. "We'd like to speak with Sandra Butler." They needed to talk to the guy named Jeff too, but they didn't have a last name yet and didn't want to scare him off.

"Just a moment." She picked up the telephone to make a call but quickly lowered it as a woman appeared in the reception area. "Sandra, these are—"

"Can I help you?" The redhead was maybe mid-twenties, tall and slender, and regarded them with disdain. Something about her made Madison think she was used to getting her way.

Sandra extended a hand to Madison. "Detective Knight, wasn't it? I overheard you speaking with Janice. I'm Sandra." She offered Terry a brief, insincere smile.

"Is there someplace we could talk?" Madison asked.

"Sure, come with me." She started walking away, but halted in mid-step and addressed the woman at the front desk. "Put all my calls to voice mail."

For a manager who just lost an employee, she seemed unaffected. There was no real sadness in her eyes, only the seeming interest to take care of business.

"We'll also want to speak to a few of her fellow employees to get a rounded view of Laura's life." Madison spoke to the back of Sandra's head as she had resumed walking.

"Of course." Sandra stopped at the door to the conference room and gestured for them to go in ahead of her. Once inside, she closed the door.

Madison sat on one of ten leather chairs that surrounded a table. As she leaned back, the chair kept tilting with her. She started to topple backward and grabbed the edge of the table to stabilize herself.

Crap! How far back will the chair go?

Terry, who sat beside her, was grinning like he was trying to suppress a laugh.

There was the spark of a condescending smirk on Sandra's lips, but it faded when she said, "It is tragic what happened to Laura. I hired her." She was seated across from them, but she spoke loudly enough to address a conference room full of people. Madison tried to hide her irritation. "There will be no good replacement for her. Hard worker," Sandra added, but her words sounded prepared.

"You're the one who called in about Laura?" Madison asked.

"Yes, it's part of our safety policy. If an employee doesn't show up or call—"

Madison raised a hand to stop her. "We've heard that line already. How was your relationship with Laura?"

The directness of the question seemed to surprise Sandra. "I don't understand."

Madison remained silent.

"I'd say our relationship was the same as I have with the rest of my employees."

"So there's no animosity or situation that existed between you?"

"No, absolutely not." Her voice rose in pitch, disproving Madison's assumption that she couldn't talk louder without crossing the line to a yell.

"Do you know of anyone who would have wanted to harm Laura or had a conflict with her?"

Sandra shook her head—too hastily to have given the question any consideration.

Madison reached into a pocket and pulled out the photo of Laura with the man. She slid it across to the woman. "Does he look familiar to you?"

Sandra picked it up and took her time looking at it. The way she had reached for the photo, the expression on her face, and the reflection in her eyes told Madison she had expected to recognize the man.

Sandra's face fell, and she lost all color in it. "No, I don't know him." She let the picture fall to the table, sadness emanating from her.

Maybe Madison's first impression of the woman had been wrong. She could care. Then again, she could be hiding something or protecting someone.

"Are you sure you don't recognize him?" Madison pressed. "You took the photo like you expected to know who the picture was of."

Sandra didn't say anything.

"Is his name Jeff?" Madison took a shot in the dark.

Sandra met Madison's gaze. "That's not Jeff," she said. "What does he have to do with—"

"So you know Jeff?" Madison jumped in.

"Yes, of course. He works here."

"Terrific, we'd like to speak with him once we're finished here," Madison said. "But is there something you should be telling us? I get the feeling that…"

Sandra leaned back and ran her hands along the top of her thighs. Her hands were shaking. Madison let her question hang in the air. Hopefully, the quiet would make Sandra uncomfortable enough to speak.

"I shouldn't say anything," Sandra eventually said. "It's none of my business really. And maybe it was just a rumor." Her eyes darted to the floor.

"Does this rumor involve Jeff?" Madison asked.

Silence.

Evidence at the crime scene suggested a man, but it could have been staged to appear that way. Sandra appeared to be physically stronger than Laura. Could Sandra and Jeff have orchestrated Laura's murder together?

"Maybe you were jealous of Jeff's relationship with Laura," Madison put out there.

"Absolutely not." Sandra's eyes steeled over. "I would never hurt anyone."

"But Jeff would?"

Sandra shook her head.

"It's in your best interests to tell us what you know," Terry said. "It may help us catch Laura's killer."

"We can charge you with aiding and abetting," Madison added. "Is that how you want this meeting to end?" She leaned across the table, closing in on Sandra. She hoped the intrusion into the woman's personal space and the verbal threat would be enough to shake her.

"You and I both know the likelihood of that happening is slim to none, Detective." Her voice was calm. "I don't know that man, like I said." She pushed the photo across the table and folded her arms.

"What do you know about Laura's relationship with Jeff?"

"Apparently, their relationship became quite serious, but Laura wanted out."

"What is his last name?" Madison asked.

"Layton," she huffed out with a sigh as if she'd betrayed a confidant. "He's the general manager, but you can't speak with him."

"And why's that?"

"He's at a conference this week. He'll be back next Monday."

"We'll need his number and the details of where he's staying."

"He asked not to be disturbed unless it's an emergency."

"And you don't consider the murder of an employee an emergency?"

"I'm only relaying what he clarified at least two times on Friday. 'Don't call unless it's really important.' But, of course, I tried reaching him. I left a voice mail on his cell the moment I found out."

"How nice of you." Madison sensed Terry's eyes reprimanding her. If it hadn't been for his silent prodding, the glorified paper-pusher would have gotten a mouthful about how happy making that phone call must have made her. The competition was now out of the way.

"Is it normal for him not to accept calls when he goes away on business?" Terry asked.

"Well, he doesn't like to, but he never stressed it as much before."

Layton could have killed Laura and been on the run. And if that was the case, he had a head start.

"We're going to need his cell number, where he is, where he's staying," Madison said.

"I'll give you his business cell number." Sandra scribbled it down on a yellow sticky note and peeled it off the pad. She extended it to Terry, and then looked defiantly at Madison. "Will that be all?"

"For now."

Sandra stood. "You said you wanted to speak with others? I'd start with Cheryl in AR. They were close. I'll get her for you."

With Sandra out of the room, Terry turned to Madison. "AR?"

"Accounts receivable. Hopefully, you've paid your bills. Those types have a way of smelling money."

"Well, she won't sniff any from this man. You're the one who should worry."

People circulated the rumors, even the ones who didn't consider themselves gossipers. Two years ago when Madison's grandmother passed away, she left her everything she had. It amounted to a slightly padded bank account—nothing close to enough to retire on—but people had the tendency to believe what they wanted. "You have no clue what you're talking about."

The door opened, and a woman of about thirty entered. "I was told you wanted to speak with me." She sat in the chair Sandra had left.

"Cheryl, we understand you and Laura were pretty close. Do you recognize this man?" Madison slid the photograph back across the table.

Cheryl examined the picture where it came to rest, not touching it. She pressed her lips together and shook her head. "No, he doesn't look familiar to me. I don't remember her talking about anyone. At least not anyone that significant. I mean, she appears quite happy in this picture." She swallowed hard. "She had been dating Jeff, the general manager here, for a while, but that ended months ago. She wanted a serious relationship. He wanted to fool around."

Her statement contradicted what Sandra had said—that Laura wanted out because Jeff was getting too serious. If it went the way Cheryl indicated, Madison imagined Photo Guy could be the type to settle down with. "You're sure she wanted it to be serious, and not the other way around?"

"Yes, but I'm not sure if she got into that reason with Jeff."

"You said their relationship ended months ago. How long has it been?" Madison said.

"Two months, maybe a little longer."

"Is it possible she found someone new and didn't tell you?"

"I guess anything's possible." A single tear slid down her cheek, and she was fast to wipe it away.

"Were you friends outside of work?"

"No." She paused, reached for a tissue, and dabbed her nose. She bunched it up in her hand afterward.

"How did Jeff handle the breakup?"

Cheryl's eyes rose then fell. "Not well."

That coincided with what the Saunderses had said.

"Jeff couldn't handle the rejection. He'd show up at her house to drive her to work and bring in vanilla lattes, even though she asked him to stop. On one occasion, she took the drink he handed her and put it directly into her garbage bin."

"How did Jeff react to that?" Terry asked.

"He said she was making a big mistake. He was so loud that the entire office heard him. He picked up her phone and threw it on the floor."

"Was that normal for him?" Madison asked.

"To lose his temper? Yeah. But he's the kind to keep it bottled up and then explode."

"Sandra mentioned that he's away on business. Do you know where?"

Cheryl curled her lips and then licked them. "I'm not sure. Sometimes, management meetings are held at the head office. But I think sometimes they rent places, too."

Cheryl kept speaking, but Madison's interest was on what had already been said. Jeff Layton possessed a temper, which brewed beneath the surface. That elixir made for a dangerous and volatile type of person. Madison had to wonder if, translated, that meant murderous.

CHAPTER SEVEN

They had called on Layton's residence regardless of the fact they were told he was out of town, but no one appeared to be home. Even the purple Taurus registered to him wasn't in the driveway. Madison had blocked her number and tried his cell a few times, but it kept ringing to voice mail. They were now back at the station exploring other avenues to find him.

Terry fidgeted with a pen, snapping it against the top of his desk. "I think the guy's made a run for it."

"He doesn't handle rejection well." Madison reiterated what they already knew but kept the next thought to herself. *Maybe Jeff knew that Laura had moved on and got jealous and killed her over it.*

"I tried contacting Southwest Welding Products' head office, but they closed a couple of hours ago. They're ahead of us by one."

Madison consulted the clock. It was six.

She shared her findings. "And all his background shows is a DUI charge back in '96. Nothing violent, no assaults—" Her cell rang, and she answered. "Knight...okay...I'll be right there." She hung up. "I'm going to see Cyn for a sec."

"I'll come with you."

"No, I need you to stay here and keep digging. Find out more about this guy, see if there's anything online about this conference he's supposed to be attending. Call the local hotels, look for him."

For its size, Stiles was fortunate to warrant an onsite forensic lab. What had started as a test project by the government to streamline expenses proved to be a success. Now they were blessed with full-time specialists in the areas of ballistics, DNA and fingerprint analysis, serology, and trace. Additionally, they were provided with the cutting-edge technology that enabled them to do the job.

Cynthia was standing by the fingerprint smoker when Madison opened the door. Her dark hair was tucked behind one ear, and her glasses were perched on the tip of her nose. *Maybe it's her cavalier approach to life that makes her attractive to men.*

Madison approached her.

Or maybe it's the way her perfume smells, sweet musk.

"I see you were able to ditch Terry," Cynthia said.

"Did you have any doubt?"

She smiled. "Not really."

"You've got something for me?"

"I don't, and that's the strange part. Not one print."

When Terry had stepped outside the crime scene to discipline the media, Madison convinced her friend the framed photo of Laura and the mystery man needed to be scrutinized. She knew if she stressed it in front of Terry, he would have given her a hard time about it. According to him, her thinking was too dependent on her feelings sometimes.

"Not one? How is that possible?" Madison asked.

"I smoked it, and there wasn't even a partial."

"Whoever placed it there would have touched it." Madison scanned Cynthia's eyes.

"I don't know what else to say."

"No prints? That's excluding Laura's?"

"Nope. None, period."

Madison took a few seconds to let that sink in. "Someone would have to be extremely careful not to leave prints. Who does that? Or maybe the photo was planted there." The theory was out before she could give it any thought.

"Why?"

She didn't have the answer. "Am I the only one who finds a single photo of the happy couple odd?"

"Maddy, we're friends, right?"

"Yes." What was she getting at? Was a speech coming about how Madison was losing her mind?

"I'm going to be honest with you. You've got to focus on the solid evidence first. The house was pretty tidy. Maybe she used a cloth when she put the frame down?"

"If I wanted a lecture on my gut feelings, I would be talking to Terry about this." She connected with Cynthia's gaze and didn't waver. "You don't even find it odd there are no fingerprints?"

"You think the man from the photo's involved?"

Madison hesitated to state it in those exact words, but when confronted with the direct question, she found it hard to keep quiet. "Don't you find it funny this man"—she pointed to the photo—"who appears to love Laura, hasn't come forward yet?"

"She was just found today."

"Her murder was on the news already, and you'd think they'd be in regular contact."

"Okay, if we assume the guy in the photo knows something, where does that get us?"

Madison thought her friend was trying to appease her until she saw the flash in her eyes. They had already checked the frame, but what about…

"The photo itself?" Both women had spoken at the same time.

Madison saw Terry was browsing the website for Southwest Welding Products. She sat across from him.

"You were gone long enough," he said, his eyes never leaving the screen.

"Did you find anything while I was gone?"

"There are two convention centers in the area. Both administration offices are closed, and their website doesn't advertise any events for Southwest." He looked over at her with narrowed eyes. "Did Cynthia tell you something about the case?"

"They're working on the evidence. She's got the entire team on it. What about the local hotels?"

"There are the main chains. You got your Holiday Inns, Ramadas, and so on, but there are probably about twenty mom-and-pops. We could be trying to chase down someone who's not in the city."

"But can we afford to trust the office manager's word that there's a conference?"

"I'm not sure why you wouldn't."

"She didn't give me a reason to."

Terry picked up the telephone. "Great. Now I'm going to be stuck here all night."

"It goes with the territory when you're on a case."

"It's just not a good time." His eyes were back on the monitor. He dialed.

"Are you going to talk to me about it?"

"Nope."

How could he expect her to open up about emotions she harbored about unsolved cases when he blocked her out? If Annabelle was cheating on him, it would explain his foul mood, but not his constant urge to be with his wife. Terry seemed to be avoiding eye contact, so she'd let it go for now.

She pulled up Layton's file to see if there were relatives in the area of the supposed business meeting. Maybe he was staying with them.

"Let's make a bet." Terry cupped the receiver.

"Excuse me?" So much for him not talking to her.

"A bet. I say we…" He paused, spoke into the phone. "I'll hold." Back to Madison, he said, "I wager that we don't find Layton."

They did this with most cases. Maybe it was childish, maybe it was inappropriate. She wasn't sure how she felt about it, but she kept doing it. "Sure, I'll take your money," she said.

Terry talked into the phone and hung up a few seconds later. "That's one down." He handed her a printout. "I'll start with mom-and-pop motels. You do the chains."

She looked at the list. Maybe they should wait until they could reach the head office and confirm there was a conference. The only downside was, if Layton was running, he could get farther away.

"Maybe we should wait until morning," she said. There was a glimmer in her partner's eyes. It seemed he thought she was calling it an early night. "Don't get excited. I'm just saying let's wait on calling all the hotels. There are other avenues to investigate. Officer Walsh noted we might want to talk to a Felix Hill. Says he'll only talk to the investigating detectives. Hill lives across the street from Laura's."

"You think the guy from the photo is involved," he said, his statement random.

"Why do you—"

"You're cooking something up with Cynthia. It was all over your face when you came back here." He narrowed his eyes again.

She wasn't in the mood to deny his allegation or in the mood to fight, so she said nothing. She wasn't fixated on Photo Guy, but she did want to know who the hell he was.

"Why do you do this every single time? Plain evidence can be in front of you, but you dig for something. The picture could have been taken at any time. Years ago, even. It's probably nothing," Terry said.

"Or it may be *something*. Why is it only me who thinks so?"

"If you think it's him, why are we here trying to confirm Layton's agenda?"

"I'm not denying the possibility of his involvement."

"Why, because he's the obvious suspect?" He shook his head. "I believe you think the answer's in a photo."

"Answer this, then. If they were truly close, like the picture indicates, where is he and why doesn't anyone recognize him?"

"Maybe Laura kept him a secret. It doesn't mean he killed her. What this case needs is Jeff Layton. We find him, and I guarantee you we'll get some answers."

She hoped he was right.

CHAPTER EIGHT

Madison waited for Terry on the sidewalk in front of Felix Hill's house. "How is it that I made it from the car to here so much ahead of you?"

"Is it my fault you have a nitro booster attached to your ass?" Terry scowled. "Or maybe it's up your—"

Madison held up a hand. "Don't even finish that sentence." She could tell by his tone, he wasn't joking. "If you're having problems at home, leave them there."

"Nice."

"Well, if I mention anything about it, you clam up and tell me it's none of my business."

"Not everything is for you to stick your little investigative nose into. And don't you dare give me your speech about how vital communication is between partners." He glared at her, seemingly daring her to do just that, yet she remained silent. He started up the walkway to the house but stopped and spun halfway there. "Are you coming?"

She flailed her arms in the air. "Yeah, I'm coming."

Hill was in the middle of the front lawn, leaning over a lawn mower. He pushed the mower over on its side and hunched down to look closer at the undercarriage. "Damn contraption."

Contraption? Madison raised her eyebrows and spoke to Terry under her breath. "This is going to be interesting." Then she called out, "Mr. Hill?"

He kept cursing under his breath.

She enlarged her eyes at her partner, who shrugged his shoulders. She repeated herself, louder this time, "Mr. Hill!"

The man fell back on his ass, and his hand snapped up to his heart. "Holy crap! You scared me. You can't sneak up on people. Holy—" His eyes caught Madison's, and his words fell short. He struggled to his feet. "Excuse me, Miss."

Hill was a tall, lanky man who appeared to be in his mid-thirties. A razor hadn't touched his face in days. Black grease marked his T-shirt, and every crevice in his hands was either black or dark green. He wiped his hands on the front of his jeans before holding one toward Madison.

She recoiled at the thought of coming into physical contact with him, but she forced a smile and extended her hand. She had hand sanitizer in the car. She made the introductions and then got to the point. "We understand you might have some information that could help us regarding the murder of Laura Saunders."

The man's shoulders sagged. He pulled up his shirt and wiped his forehead. Madison averted her gaze.

"Don't know nothin' about her murder. Other than it's a damn tragedy. She was a beautiful woman," he said.

"Officer Walsh came by earlier. He said you had something to share with us." Madison hoped to steer him on course.

"Yeah, that's what I told him." He rubbed one eye as if an eyelash or dirt was irritating it.

"Were you good friends with Laura?" Madison asked.

"I don't know if you'd say friends, although I liked to think of her that way." His voice turned gravelly. "She understood what it's like to make a livin', work hard for what you have. Some folks are handed everything these days. Laura worked as hard as anyone, yet she strived to make a difference even if it was a small one. She said people don't hold doors for others enough anymore."

"Hold doors?" Terry asked.

Hill faced him. "Yeah, doors. You know…what you go through to get in and out of a building." He made a walking movement with his fingers.

A twitch started in her partner's cheek, and due to their earlier disagreement, she took some satisfaction in his aggravation.

"She said people used to hold a door for a woman more before...*before* women-libbers. And I know what she was talking about." He smiled at Madison. "Although an old-fashioned guy like me would be honored to hold a door for you, Detective."

Her patience had run out. "You have something to tell us?"

Hill bobbed his head. "It's just this guy she used to see. He wouldn't take the hint and kept coming around. Last week—I believe it was Friday morning—he was at her house. She yelled at him from the front door to get lost."

"Was that the last time you saw him?"

"No. Saturday night. He was on the road out front of her house."

"What time Saturday?" She found herself leaning in closer to Hill.

"Man, I don't know. Late." He rubbed the stubble on his jaw. "I was brushin' my teeth and gettin' ready for bed. Would have been somewhere near midnight."

That put Laura's unwanted visitor at her house within the time-of-death window, which was close enough to the estimated time of death: the wee hours of Sunday morning.

Terry put a hand on his hip. "Why were you watching out your window at midnight?"

Hill's cheeks flushed red, and he tucked his chin in. "Why am I being interrogated? I'm trying to help."

She wasn't used to playing the role of good cop, but Terry had forced her hand. "You were looking out for Laura," she said softly.

His body relaxed, his shoulders lowered, and he nodded. "That guy was obsessed with her. He probably killed her."

She couldn't get anywhere with assumptions. She pressed forward. "You feared for her safety, then?"

A slow nod.

"You said he was someone Laura used to see," Madison started. "Do you know his name?"

"Nope, I don't. Drives some purple car, though. Freak."

Jeff Layton drives a purple Taurus…

Madison pulled up a photo of Layton on her phone and held it for Hill to see. "Do you recognize him?"

"Oh, yeah, that's the guy."

"Did you do anything when you saw him?" Madison asked.

"I ran out of the house, yellin' at him. Told him to get out of the neighborhood."

"And how did he react to that?" Terry asked.

Hill bristled at Terry's question. "He swore at me, told me to mind my own business. And that's all there was to it. No fist fight or anything. He drove off. I noticed that Laura must have had company, though."

Madison's ears perked up. "Company?"

"There was another car in her driveway. One that I never saw before."

She inhaled deeply and glanced at Terry. "Do you remember the make and model?"

Hill pressed his lips and shook his head. "Not too good with my cars. I think it was an import. Nothing fancy, an older model, nothing new. Don't ask me the exact year."

"It had rust? Dents?" she asked, but Hill was shaking his head again. "Do you remember the color of the car?"

"White." Hill paused and looked upward. "Or was it silver?"

Maybe a solid lead was too much to hope for, but Hill had at least provided them with something: one disgruntled ex-boyfriend and a mysterious party who were both at Laura's close to the TOD window. She wondered if one of them was the man from the photo. She handed him a printout of the picture. "Do you recognize him?"

Hill leaned in close and squinted to see the image, then pulled back a few seconds later. "I've never seen him before."

She thanked Hill for his time, and she and Terry left.

Once they were back in the department car, she said, "This mystery car, Laura's mystery visitor, it could be the guy from that photo." She glanced over at Terry, who was running a hand through his hair. "Terry?"

"It would be a huge assumption."

Anger was making her earlobes hot and her breathing labored. "Are you being difficult just to be difficult?"

Terry remained quiet, and she pulled away in the opposite direction from the station.

"Where are you going?" Terry asked.

She was too upset with him to look at him right then, but she'd answer him. "We've just started this investigation. You know how crucial the first twenty-four hours are."

"Any other time." His voice was brisk and tight.

"Listen, I can do this by myself, but we won't be talking." She gripped the steering wheel, turning her knuckles white. "Ever again. Tell me what's going on."

"I need some time with Annabelle."

So he was having problems at home, but that wasn't her fault. And it certainly wasn't Laura's fault. And while she felt for what he must be going through, it was obvious he wasn't in the mood to discuss the details. And at least one of them had to keep focused on this case. For Laura's sake. For justice's sake. "We'll take care of one thing first, then I'll get you back to the station."

CHAPTER NINE

The Weathered Rose was a pub with a dated interior that was a tribute to the seventies with its oak bar, gold-speckled mirror, and glass shelving that housed alcohol bottles. Two levels with nearly every table filled with patrons, lots of flat-screen TVs, and a couple of pool tables. A jukebox at the far end of the room was blaring out "Money for Nothing" by Dire Straits. The place smelled of beer and chicken wings and... She sniffed a little deeper. Cigarette smoke. Pretty soon smoking in public places would be banned, and Madison, for one, looked forward to that day.

The floor was tacky, and Madison would guess it hadn't seen the head of a mop in a while. As they walked toward the bar, they passed two men in their sixties playing pool, both intent on their game. One had a head of white hair, and the other had very little. But he made up for what he lacked in hair in a substantial paunch that spilled over his belt buckle when he leaned over to eye up his shot.

"Not hard to see where they got the name for place," Madison said. "Most of the clientele is older, and the place could use a remodel." She glanced over at Terry, but he didn't seem to be listening. "Anyway, it's an interesting name. Kind of like your dogs'—Todd and Bailey? Shouldn't dogs be named Spot or Blackie?"

Terry let out an exasperated sigh. "Maddy, why are you even bringing this up? I've told you many times that my dogs are family. Every one's different, and they have their own personalities. Some people give their dogs middle names."

She laughed. "You've got to be kidding me. On all counts. First of all, they've got four legs, they stink, they drink out of the toilet bowl. And you told me they eat their own shit."

"You can't hold that against them," he deadpanned.

"Oh, yes, I can." She scrunched up her face in disgust. "And speaking of unsavory, this place…"

"Yet you tell me that I state the obvious."

She punched his arm as inconspicuously as possible. He pulled back and rubbed it like she'd hurt him. "Always the smart ass," she said.

He steepled his hands and bent forward but stopped short of a full bow. "My master has taught me well."

She shot him a dirty look, and a man in a leather vest brushed past her headed for the door. She watched him walk by, and he watched her. People were starting to notice her and Terry and make them as cops. They reached the bar, and she briefly caught eyes with the bartender, who tried to act as if he hadn't seen her. He pulled down on a beer tap, and smiled at Terry, though.

Well, how about that? I think he's sweet on my partner. To each his own, I suppose.

She looked over at Terry; he might as well have had drool seeping from the corners of his mouth as he stared at the beer.

"Could I get you one?" the tender asked him.

"I'd love to—"

"But he can't," she cut in, displaying her badge. "We're detectives with the Stiles PD. I'm Madison Knight, and he's Terry Grant. We'd like to ask you a few questions about Laura Saunders."

"Be back in a sec." He walked off with the fresh beer and placed it in front of an older man who was seated a couple stools away from them. The tender seemed to be moving slower on his return trip.

"We told you who we are," Madison started. "It's your turn. First name will do for now."

"Justin." He grabbed a white towel from the counter and began wiping. A delay-and-detour tactic.

"Who was the man in a hurry to get out of here?"

Justin paused his cleaning and looked up at her. His eyes were deep pools and hard to read. His gaze wasn't shifty, but it wasn't settled either. "I'm going to need more than that," Justin began. "This place sees cops, and I'm surprised more haven't left."

"You know who I'm referring to… I saw you watching a few seconds ago. He was approximately six-three, a solid three hundred pounds, carried most of it out front. He had a beard, mustache, beady eyes."

Justin let go of the towel and motioned for them to follow him to the end of the bar. "'His name is Lou Mann."

"Is there anything more you can tell us about him?" Madison asked.

"Other than he's harmless? He comes in every night about this time, orders a double whiskey on the rocks. Jack Daniel's." The tender made a face, indicating his distaste for the beverage. "He sips it for an hour while staring into space." He snorted, making this horrible noise. He acted like he didn't notice.

Madison rested her eyes on her partner. She couldn't help but think how she got to where she was some days. She could have had a prestigious law career with her choice of clientele at this point, but instead she chose law enforcement where she didn't have a say about the people she ran into. Where the hell did some of them come from, anyway?

"He's not involved." Justin's eyes scanned the room.

"In what?" Madison eyed him. *Let him come out and say it.*

Justin rubbed one of his arms. "In Laura's murder."

Madison remained silent, so did Terry.

"You said you had questions about Laura, so I figured…"

It was harder to remain silent this time around, but it was working to get Justin to talk.

Justin continued. "Well, Lou couldn't have killed her because he stayed longer than usual on Saturday night. That was the night she was murdered, right? That's what they're saying on the news."

She, for the most part, hated the media. Sure, maybe they could prove useful *sometimes* but not enough to compensate for when they weren't.

"Was Laura here Saturday night?" she asked, taking a brief detour before she'd swing back to Lou.

"Yeah." He sounded sad at the admission.

Madison was pleased; Laura's last night was starting to fill in. The Weathered Rose could have been her final stop before going home. In fact, she could have picked up her killer in this bar. "When? And how long did she stay?"

"Around midnight."

That's the time Hill had mentioned seeing Jeff Layton in front of Laura's house. "What about Lou?" she asked. "How late was he here on Saturday night?"

"Until close at three Sunday morning." He looked down at the floor.

It was only a ten-minute drive from the bar to Laura's house. That still left time for Mann to get to Laura's and kill her. But there was something telling in the way Justin had diverted his gaze. "You're sure he was here until three?"

Justin's jaw tightened, and his mouth rested in a straight line.

"How late?" She didn't care if they operated an after-hours poker tournament or whatever. Her job was to solve Laura's murder.

"Six."

"Why lie to us the first time?" Madison drilled him.

Justin paled and swallowed roughly. "I can't tell you why, but I know he wouldn't have hurt her. Laura pretty much lived here. And even though I like men, I loved her." Tears welled up in his eyes as if on cue.

I cocked an eyebrow at my partner. "Wow, Terry, Laura must have had a special touch."

Justin's brow furrowed. "I'm telling you the truth. And if other people are telling you they loved her, it's because she was in love with life, and it was contagious. It drew people to her." He pinched his nose and shut his eyes.

"Another!" The older man slammed his empty mug down on to the bar top with enough force that Madison felt the vibration in the wood. She lifted her arms.

Justin held up a hand to the man and turned to Madison and Terry. "Listen, it's crazy in here…"

If he thought that meant he was off the hook, he was highly mistaken. "We'll wait," she said.

Terry turned to her and tapped her elbow with his hand. "Surprised you haven't shown him the photo yet." A corner of his mouth lifted in a smile.

"Surprised you brought it up. I thought it was meaningless?" She didn't return the smile.

As they stood there waiting for Justin, Madison's mind went to the fact that so many people seemed to care about Laura, yet the unspeakable had happened to her. It led to thoughts of her own mortality and whether anyone would even care if something happened to her. She shook the ridiculous notion aside. After all, there were people who would miss her.

Justin came back, and Madison held up a copy of the photograph. "Do you recognize him?" His eyes brightened slightly, indicating recognition. He said nothing, though. She slapped the picture down on the counter. "He could be her killer, Justin."

"He was here." He spoke with his eyes on the photo.

It felt like everything went quiet—all except for her own heartbeat in her ears. "When was he here?"

He lifted his head but let his gaze travel to some point behind them. "Saturday night."

Madison followed the direction of gaze. He was looking at the two older men playing pool. "What about those two?"

"They got into an argument with the guy in the picture. That one—" Justin nodded toward the one with no hair "—hit him hard enough that I thought he might have broken his nose. I handed the guy a towel, not that I felt sorry for him. I just didn't want my bar covered in blood."

"Was he ever in here before?" Madison wagged the photo. "Do you know his name?"

"No, but he just had an aura about him that he was looking for trouble."

Madison pointed toward the older men. "What's their stories?"

"They're regulars. Glen's the one who punched him. His friend is Clint."

Madison and Terry left Justin to talk to the two men, who continued to be absorbed in their game.

"Glen?" Madison called out.

The man straightened from having taken his shot. "Who wants to know?"

"Stiles PD." Madison flashed her badge and held out the photo of Laura with the man. "Recognize either of them?"

"I know her." Glen cast looks between them, rested his gaze on Terry. "Something wrong?"

"You could say that."

"She's dead. Killed in her home," Madison stated. "Tell me that you didn't hear it on the news."

"We've been here all night." The man's shoulders sagged, and he rubbed his bald head. "Thought it was strange she hadn't been in…" His words stalled, and he turned to his friend. "I told you something wasn't right about that guy." His gaze went to the photo. "Actually, it was *that* guy. Where did you get that picture?"

"That's not important right now," Madison said. "There's a witness who says you punched him." Both men looked toward the bar, but she didn't feel badly for exposing the tender's betrayal. "What was that about?"

"Tell her, Glen." Clint ran a hand through his white hair.

Glen took a deep breath. "Clint and I were talking to Laura when he walked up. He butted into our business, and when he didn't back off, yeah, I punched him." Glen was all matter-of-fact and fished a cigarette out from his pocket. He perched it in his lips and lit it, inhaling deeply before blowing out a white cloud of smoke.

Madison took the cigarette, dropped it to the floor, and extinguished it with a twist of her shoe. It seemed like he was about to protest. She silently dared him to.

His eyes went to the smashed nicotine dose she had taken away from him. A hand padded his pocket again, but he must have thought better of taking another one out. "Anyway, you can thank me. I've probably made it easier for you to spot the son of a bitch. I think I broke his nose."

Madison raised her brows, not interested in listening to the old man's boasts. "What did you do after you punched him?"

"Nothing. We just carried on." Glen paused. "Laura didn't seem to mind his attention, though. And now I see that photo…" He turned to Clint. "Maybe they were together."

It was possible that Laura and Photo Guy were secretly involved. The scene at the bar could have been role-playing. "What was your relationship with Laura? You're old enough to be her father. She was attractive, young."

Glen held up a hand. "As flattering as you are, woman, please stop there. You could say the three of us were friends. We were close with her father." He did the sign the cross. "May he rest in peace. He was always very proud of her, showing us pictures of her and bragging about her."

"She would have been how old when she lost him?" Madison pretended to be curious but was testing the man's claim.

"I think she was approaching her fifth birthday."

Madison nodded as his response coincided with fact. "So Laura seemed to like this man?"

"She left with him," Glen said grumpily. "I was planning to talk to her about it the next time I saw her." He sniffled and said, "I guess that won't be happening now."

Madison's chest felt heavy, and her stomach tightened.

"She really did know how to pick them, though." Clint's voice was thick with sarcasm. He sat on the edge of the pool table. "Just look at that ex of hers. You want to talk about a persistent man. He was a prime-A example right there. Pretty much a stalker. He wouldn't take no for an answer."

"What was his name?" Madison asked, silently petitioning the gods for a lead.

Glen shook his head, as did Clint. "She kept their names to herself. Never introduced us to her boyfriends," Clint said.

Madison and Terry shared a look. No one seemed to know much about Laura's relationships—whether she wanted to settle down, or the opposite. She showed them a photo of Jeff Layton, and both men confirmed that was the ex they were referring to.

"When was the last time you saw her ex?" Terry asked.

"Saturday night. He sat right there." Glen pointed to a table. "He was seething that this other guy, the one in the picture there, was trying to pick up Laura—and succeeding. He was staring a hole into their heads, but neither of them seemed to notice or care."

"So when Laura left with this man—the one you punched—how did her ex react?" Madison asked.

"He sat there for a few minutes," Clint said, "and finished off his beer. Then he got up and left."

"He followed them?" Madison remembered Hill's comment about Jeff being outside Laura's house at midnight.

"Well, that I can't say for sure. I could say it wouldn't shock me if he had. He was pretty mad. He got up and punched his fist against the table. No one else probably noticed, but I had my eye on him." He pointed his two fingers in a V toward his eyes.

Madison extended her card toward the men. Glen took it. "Call if you think of anything else."

"Will do."

Madison and Terry walked back toward Justin at the bar.

Madison said, "All right, there's one more thing you could do for us. We need to get our hands on that towel, the one with the blood. Do you know where it went? A disposal bin out back?"

"I kept it." Justin reached underneath the bar and pulled up a plastic bag. "Like I said, I had a feeling about the guy. I didn't like him."

She reached for the bag, partially in shock, partially suspicious of his claimed reason for holding on to it.

"Just catch the guy." Justin's gaze drifted to Terry, and he made a show of looking at his watch. "Nine forty-five. Surely you're off the clock now."

While her partner might have had his mind on a drink, all Madison could think about was getting the towel into a paper bag before the plastic would render any DNA useless—that's if it hadn't already.

Terry plopped onto a stool. "I'd love one."

"But he can't have one." She turned away from the bar and looked back at her partner. "Come on, let's go."

"Oh, Maddy," Terry groaned and tapped the counter, his longing for a cold one tangible. "You always have to be so serious?"

"One of us has to be," she tossed back, not comprehending how her partner could be considering a drink when there was work to do. After all, chain of evidence dictated they get the towel back to the lab immediately.

"I don't understand why another few minutes in the bag would hurt. We could always pretend we didn't get it until after a drink."

Despite her agitation, she shook her head and laughed.

CHAPTER TEN

Madison sat behind her desk at the station waiting for the clock to strike eight so she could call Southwest Welding Products the minute they opened. She'd used her time trying Layton repeatedly on his cell phone, but each time, she was greeted by his voice mail—just like last night.

Terry entered the bullpen with his phone to an ear. "I'm not sure…I'm at work." He met Madison's gaze. "I've got to go."

It had been too much to hope that Terry's personal problems would be behind him this morning. Then again, Madison would never let a relationship interfere with the job. It probably helped that, for better or worse, she was married to her career.

She watched as he sat at his desk and made a call on his desk telephone.

"Hello," he said into the receiver. "Yes…I'm trying to reach my brother, and I believe he's there attending a conference… Oh…He said it was for the week…Okay…Thank you." Terry hung up.

She cocked her head. "Where did you just call?"

"The head office for Southwest Welding."

Her eyes snapped to the clock. *7:45 AM.* Then it hit her. "They're an hour ahead," she said, feeling stupid for overlooking that fact.

"Uh-huh." He flashed a grin. "Yet you claim you'd manage fine without me."

"Oh, shut up." She narrowed her eyes wishing she had a better comeback, but had nothing. She blamed it on sleep deprivation.

Terry's face fell serious. "You're not going to believe what Southwest told me."

Madison and Terry walked into Winston's office without knocking, and he looked up from stacks of paperwork.

Madison brought him up to speed on the case and concluded with Terry's gem from his phone call. "There isn't a conference," she said. "Layton's on the run."

"I'll issue a BOLO. Anyone finds him or his purple Ford Taurus, we'll hear about it." He reached for his phone and excused them with the wave of a hand.

She hoped the be-on-the-lookout bulletin brought them closer to Layton, but she wasn't giving over to optimism just yet. Outside the sergeant's office, both Madison's and Terry's phones rang. She finished with her caller first and then listened in on Terry's conversations. His tone told her it was likely his wife on the other end.

"Terry," Madison prompted.

He glared at her, his eyes telling her to back off.

She waited for a few minutes, but her patience had a low threshold. Her call had been from Richards, and he had something for them to see. She tapped her foot on the floor, but it had no effect on hurrying her partner along. He was now avoiding eye contact with her.

"I'm heading to morgue," she snarled, hoping that would prompt him to end the call. She started down the hall.

"I've gotta go," he grumbled.

She looked at him over a shoulder, and he was scowling. She probably shouldn't pry, but her concern for him won out. She stopped walking and waited for Terry to catch up. "Are you guys okay?"

He brushed past her. "Stay out of it."

Okay, well that is a firm *no.*

Madison hated trips to the morgue for two reasons: one, she always felt as if she was invading a private moment, and second, she hated how it made her conscious of her mortality.

She and Terry found Cole Richards next to Laura Saunders, who was lying on a steel gurney in the middle of the room. Her face was relaxed, giving the impression she was at peace—something that was common with the dead.

Richards's eyes went to the clock on the wall, like they'd taken far too long to get there. "I'm about to start the autopsy and noticed this." Richards turned Laura's left arm slowly. "Look at her wrist, and both of them are like that." He reached over and held up the other one.

Her wrists were marked by bruises, and there was a cut on her left wrist.

Richards continued. "The contusions happened peri-mortem or just around the time of death. What they tell me is that the victim was bound by something hard and rigid. As you can see, she was also nicked. I believe by whatever bound her."

"I found a pair of metal handcuffs," Madison said.

"That could be what caused the contusions."

She remembered something just then. "The bed's headboard was scuffed. She was likely bound there, but she wasn't found with the cuffs on her wrists. They were in a drawer. Why leave the tie but hide the cuffs?" she asked rhetorically. They didn't even know for sure that the cuffs had been worn by Laura, but processing them would be one of Cynthia's priorities. Now it moved up on Madison's list, because they might even get usable prints from the killer.

Richards held Laura's fingers out before placing her arm gently back on the table. "And I have more for you. I scraped under her nails and found epithelial." He butted his head toward a nearby table where there was a sealed evidence envelope and a vial. "There was also evidence of rough sex, but my conclusion is it was consensual. There was no tearing. I swabbed the area," he added, and by doing so, it confirmed the contents of the vial. "I'll be finishing up here this morning, but to be thorough, I'll be requesting a toxicology report on her blood and stomach contents."

"How long will that take?" Madison asked.

"Guess it depends on how backed up they are in the lab. It's something Jennifer should be able to handle so we won't need to outsource it."

Jennifer Adams reported to Cynthia, and her specialty was serology and toxicology, which in layman's terms meant that she knew about bodily fluids and how to analyze them.

Madison's gaze drifted to Laura's body, and she felt for her. At least in life she'd known some love and affection, but was one of the men who had made this claim her killer? Madison would have to figure out who had the most to lose. She said, "If anything else shows up—"

"I'll call you. I always do." He smiled at her, flashing those sparkly teeth. "She can be a micromanager sometimes, can't she?" Richards said to Terry. "How do you handle it?"

"Shut up and take it, I guess." There was no lightheartedness in Terry's reply.

Richards disregarded Terry's attitude. "Well, that's all I've got for now," he said and reached for his scalpel from a nearby table.

Madison always had a hard time making herself stay for the autopsies, but one day, she'd make it all the way through them and do so each time. She just wasn't going to start today. "I can take those upstairs," she offered, referring to the envelope and the vial.

"Works for me." Richards handed her a clipboard to sign over custody of evidence. "You really do run short on patience." He smiled at her, black skin creasing and displaying those pearly whites again.

She returned his smile and scribbled her signature. "Nobody's perfect." Her phone rang, and caller ID told her it was Cynthia. She accepted the call. "Tell me you have news."

"Why don't I ever get a 'Hi, how are you doing, Cyn?' Nope, it's always a variation of 'get to the point.'" A few seconds passed. "Hello?"

"Yes?" Madison had let herself become distracted by Richards's deep chocolate eyes.

"Get up here," Cynthia requested. "I've got news for you."

"Okay, we'll be right up." Madison ended the call and said to Richards, "Thanks for your help."

"Anytime."

She really had to stop fantasizing about the man the way she did sometimes. For starters, he was a married. But in her defense, it wasn't like she daydreamed about him intentionally.

Madison hit the lab and entered with, "Okay, whatcha got?" to Cynthia.

Cynthia seemed to look through her. "Where's Terry?"

"You never answer a question directly, do you?"

"I've learned from association." Cynthia adjusted her glasses on her nose.

"Forget about being a comedian and stick to the lab work." Madison winked at her. "Terry's off. He had to go see the wife or something. I don't know. Maybe one of his dogs crapped on the floor." Both women shared a laugh. It brought to light two other aspects in which they were similar. Neither wanted to be married or have the responsibility of caring for a four-legged furry critter.

"What's that?" Cynthia pointed to the evidence Madison was holding.

"From Richards with love," Madison said, making a play on the name of an old Bond movie *From Russia with Love*. "Fingernail clippings and a vaginal swab."

"Well, my job's certainly not a glamourous one," Cynthia said taking the evidence and updating the chain of custody. She placed the envelope and vial on the table. "We'll get to it, but we're backed up so you'll have to bear with us. Anyway, like I said, I do have some news for you. Mark examined the tie."

"And…?" Madison pressed.

"The tie is a Gallo & Costa. G&C for short. It's Italian silk. I searched online, and the lowest-priced tie is over a hundred dollars. However, this specific design was discontinued back in 1999."

"That means our killer must have had it a while," Madison rushed out but then backpedaled. "Or he picked it up at a used-clothing store. Is there any way of tracking down a buyer?"

"For a tie?"

"I know you work miracles." She'd flash a cheesy grin if she were in the mood.

"That's pushing it. Besides even back in 1999, G&C sold their ties online. In addition, there are fifteen men's apparel stores that carry them in Stiles alone, never mind surrounding areas—that's not even considering your used-clothing-store theory."

"Okay, so we might not be able to find our killer that way, but what made him use it as a weapon?"

Cynthia shrugged. "It's possible he had it on the night he was with the vic—Laura," she corrected for Madison's sake, "and she did something that set him off."

Madison shook her head. "I think we're looking at premeditation."

Cynthia looked at Madison over her glasses. "What makes you so confident?"

"I don't think someone emotionally affected in the moment would have the mental faculty to pose her and remove the handcuffs. Of course, I'm assuming that she was bound with them. And speaking of…what's the status on the cuffs?"

"They're on the list, and I'll get to them as soon as I can."

Just the response Madison had expected.

She thought back to what Richards had shared with her and Terry. "Richards concluded Laura had consensual sex before she died, but then she was bound, and there's evidence of bruising and that would lead my mind to the fact that she may have tried to break free or fight back, something. Have you found anything that might indicate there was a struggle?"

"Not so far. In fact, none of her clothes that were strewn on the main level were torn, not even one broken clasp on her bra."

Madison's phone rang, and she picked it up. She stood in silence as she listened to her caller. Twenty seconds later, she hung up. "Cyn, I've gotta go."

CHAPTER ELEVEN

Layton's Taurus had been found at Ricky's Wrenches and Repair, a local body shop. Madison pulled into their parking lot and didn't see any sign of Layton or her AWOL partner. She'd tried to reach him numerous times on the way over and finally opted to leave a voice mail.

She got out of the car, and Officer Harding, who'd made the find, approached her. "Were you driving by?" Madison asked, somewhat skeptical as to what Harding was doing here at this time of day.

"My brother-in-law owns the joint. I'd clocked out for a break and was talking with Ricky when I heard the BOLO." Harding looked toward the building, and Madison noticed a man inside stood behind a counter and was watching them. Harding continued. "The description matched the vehicle that's up on the hoist, so I took a closer look and sure enough… What are the chances?"

"Any sign of the owner?"

"None. Ricky remembers a woman dropping off the car. A redhead. He's pulling up the service record now."

A redhead… They'd come across one of those in the investigation so far—Sandra Butler.

"He said she'd brought it in yesterday for an oil change, but his guys noticed it needed some brake work. They had to wait for the parts. She wasn't too happy about it. Said it wasn't her car, and she didn't want to get stuck with the bill, but she told him to go ahead."

The door chimed, and the man who'd been watching them came out holding a piece of paper. Madison assumed this was Ricky. He was clean-shaven with a neatly groomed mustache—the opposite persona one expected from a man in his line of work. He regarded her skeptically and handed what he had over to his brother-in-law. In turn, Harding passed it along to Madison.

Ricky squinted and placed a hand over his forehead to block out the sun. "Her name is—"

"Sandra Butler," Madison interjected and glanced at the sheet for confirmation.

"Yeah," Ricky said with surprise. "She left her number." Ricky leaned over and pointed it out on the page.

"All right," she said to Ricky, then turned to Harding. "You stay here in case she shows up, but send a car to back me up." She left him the address where she was headed. "In the meantime, if she shows up here, take her downtown immediately. Put her in holding and—"

A taxi pulled into the lot, performed a quick U-turn, and sped off down the street. Madison caught a look at the passenger in the back seat.

"It's her," she rushed out. "Follow me, Officer." She ran to the department car, got in, turned on the lights, and tailed the taxi to the parking lot of a shopping plaza.

The cabbie got out. "Please, lady. I no speed. No ticket. I lose my license."

Madison ignored the man, more interested in his fare. She opened the back door. "Hello, Sandra."

Madison stood in the observation room, looking in on interrogation room two where Sandra Butler was fidgeting in her chair as if she were sitting on an ant hill. Winston was next to Madison, his hands perched on his hips, an unflattering mannerism for a man who carried some weight out front.

"Where is Layton?" Winston asked.

For a man who was never satisfied, he didn't seem to notice that Terry was missing. She swallowed her temper and said, "We conducted a search of her house, but Layton wasn't there."

"We got him?" Terry asked from the doorway.

We? Madison's earlobes heated with rage, and she turned to watch her partner walk in as if he'd just taken a bathroom break, not walked out on the job.

Madison stared at Terry, but he refused to make eye contact. If she had less tact, she'd ask him where the hell he had been, but she felt she already knew the answer. He'd been with his wife. And there was something about sticking up for your brothers in blue that wouldn't allow Madison to bring up the matter in front of Winston. "We have his car," was all she said.

"His car?" Terry asked with surprise.

"Yeah, hang back and catch up." She brushed by him and flung the door to the interrogation room open. Terry was right behind her.

Before Madison could get one word in, Sandra said, "I don't see what the issue is." She pulled down on her shirt and tilted out her chin. "I'm allowed to have his car."

"The part that concerns us is why you lied to us," Madison stated matter-of-factly.

"I didn't lie to you."

So this is how it's going to be.

Madison leaned back in her chair. "You said he was at a business conference."

"He is."

Madison remained silent.

Sandra blinked quickly. "That's what he told me. I swear."

"You're certain that's what he told you?"

"Yes, why would I lie about it?"

"I was hoping you could tell us."

Silence.

"You knew there wasn't a conference," Madison accused and pulled out a crime-scene photo of Laura and slid it toward Sandra.

She shut her eyes and held up a hand. "Please, get that away from me."

Madison left the picture where it was. "Why are you protecting him?"

"I'm…" Her eyes lifted to meet Madison's. "From what?"

"From a murder charge," Madison tossed back with an air of indifference.

"I don't know anything."

Madison didn't buy it. "I'll ask you again: why are you protecting him?"

"I told you what I know."

Madison leaned forward, elbows on the table, her impatience getting the better of her. "Where is he, Sandra? Why do you have his car?"

"He asked me to take it in for him."

"Where is he?" Madison repeated.

"I'm not sure. Okay?" She bit on a fingernail.

"No, it's not okay." Madison got up and paced the room, keeping her eyes on Sandra. "May I remind you that he's a suspect in a murder investigation? If you know where he is and are hiding that from us, that makes you an accessory, punishable by law."

Silence.

"Why would he have you take his car in for service? Why not do it himself?" Madison kept the questions going.

More silence.

"Was he planning on selling it, making a real run for it? Kind of stupid to leave it in town, though, don't you think?"

"Jeff's not stupid."

"So, you *are* covering for him."

"No…No…It's not what it looks like."

Madison bent over, leaning on the table beside Sandra. "You better get talking or—" She stood up straight and snapped her fingers, and Terry approached Sandra.

"No. I'll tell you. Please, don't arrest me." Sandra tucked a strand of red hair behind an ear. "He's going to kill me."

"Why would he do that?"

Panic pieced Sandra's eyes, and she bit her bottom lip.

Madison wasn't sure if Sandra was a good actress and had blurted out those words as some sort of delay tactic or whether she really feared for her life. "Tell us everything you know."

Sandra cleared her throat. "Jeff rented a car, told me he was taking off on a mini holiday."

"But he didn't tell you to where?"

"No." She shook her head. "I told head office he was attending a local conference so he could still get a paycheck. His vacation was all used up, as were his sick days."

"Do you know where he rented a car?" Madison asked. If they had that info, it would be much easier to track him down.

"Sal's Rentals," Sandra said quietly. "They're here in town."

Guess we've got our next stop…

Madison sat across from Sandra again, hungry to flush out more from her. "Are you romantically involved with Jeff?"

"What does that have to do with—"

"Pretty much everything. You've already lied to protect him. What else would you do? If he killed someone, would you look the other way? Are you?"

"No…" Her voice was low, and her eyes averted Madison's.

"Ms. Butler?" Madison prompted.

Sandra looked straight at Madison. "No."

Madison felt there was a lot this woman wasn't telling them, but they weren't going to get any further with her. And the truth was, Sandra could prove more valuable outside of the station. Maybe Layton would seek her out—and if he did, they'd be waiting. She'd call into the station and get an officer to watch her place.

CHAPTER TWELVE

A small cowbell hung over the front door of Sal's Rentals and rang when Madison and Terry entered.

"Can I help you?" a man of about fifty called out from behind a long counter.

Terry spun a display of maps near the register.

"We're looking for information on someone you rented a vehicle to," Madison said.

His arms crossed, and he regarded her with suspicion. "What's this about?"

"We can't say."

"Then I can't help you."

Madison debated how to continue. "We're detectives with—"

"And I'm Santa Claus, lady. What's your point? Don't you need a warrant to demand my customer list?"

"How much for one of these?" Terry held up a map as if it was a piece of art.

"Five dollars. The sign says right there." He pointed to a piece of Bristol board wedged on an angle at the top of the display.

"That's a lot for some directions." Terry slowly found the slot where he took the map from and put it back.

"Four dollars. For officers of the law."

"Three-fifty," Terry countered.

"Three seventy-five."

Terry pressed his lips. "Deal." He picked the map up again and placed it on the counter. He took his time counting out the change.

"You know, maybe I can help you guys," the older man said.

Madison looked from him to her partner. What had just happened? Was this like a small diner? If you want to use the restroom, buy something? If you wanted information, buy a map?

Terry smiled. "I was hoping you'd see my side. I have friends, you know." He tapped the edge of the map on the counter. "Collectors."

The man didn't seem to catch Terry's sarcasm, but she had to fight off laughing.

"Who is it you're looking for?" The man moved toward a computer near the register and pulled out a keyboard tray.

"Last name Layton. First Jeff," Terry told him.

He pulled up a pair of glasses from a chain around his neck and put them on. His fingers grazed the keys. "Not seeing anyone by that name."

"Are you sure?" Madison asked.

The man took off his glasses and let them dangle from the chain. "Yes, I'm sure. No Layton."

Madison pulled out a black-and-white printout of Layton's driver's license photo and held it in front of the man. "Do you recognize him?"

The man took the photo from her hands and studied it. "Awful grainy picture, isn't it?" He pulled up his glasses and put them on again. "He looks familiar."

"Did he rent a car from you?" Madison asked.

The man stared at the picture for another twenty seconds, then passed it back to Madison. "Can't say."

Madison tried to read his eyes and finally concluded that he was telling the truth. Beyond a vague recognition, nothing else about Layton seemed to stand out to the man.

"Okay. Well, thanks for looking." Terry winked at the man and then pointed at the map display. "I'll be back."

Madison unlocked the car. "That was pretty good in there."

"Thanks. Is he looking?"

"No. I don't think so. Why?"

He tossed the map into a garbage can. "What the hell would I need a map of Stiles for?"

The corners of her lips lifted. "Nice to have you back."

"Uh-huh."

"So what do you make of what just happened in there?"

"The part about me being out three seventy-five or Layton not being on record?" He grinned.

"Layton."

"He could have used another name."

"Or Sandra's lying to us again—" Her phone rang, and she answered, "Knight...We don't have him...Yes...I know... Don't worry...We're following a lead." She palmed her phone. "Why can't the man leave us to do our jobs?"

"Because he thinks he's doing his by harassing us."

"Wish he'd go back to his paperwork and focus on that."

The patrol car was only a few doors down from Sandra Butler's house. So much for being discreet.

Madison tapped on the driver's window, ready to lay into the officer behind the wheel, but it was Higgins. He should have been running the department, but he had no interest in advancement. His argument was the Stiles PD needed someone with his smarts and experience out on the streets, not holed up behind a desk.

"What are you doing here?" she asked him.

"I picked the shortest straw," he teased.

She smiled at him. "Lucky you. But I'm going to need you to back off a bit. We wouldn't want to scare off Layton if he comes around."

"For you, Knight...anything."

She stepped back, and Higgins moved his cruiser to a nearby park where trees helped give him some cover.

"You have power over him," Terry said.

She shrugged. "He's a sweet man."

They headed for the front door, which opened when they reached the top step. Hot air spilled out from the house.

"He's not here." It was Sandra, and she wore a camisole and a pair of shorts, her arms crossed.

"You're sure about that, or is this another lie?"

"I never lied to you," Sandra argued and stepped outside.

"Well, Jeff never rented a car from Sal's Rentals," Madison spat, exposing the real reason for their dropping by.

Sandra tightened her folded arms, and her forehead wrinkled. "He told me…" There was a desperateness to her voice.

Maybe she was telling the truth, and if so, Madison had an idea, though it would be a stretch. It was possible that Layton had used another name to rent the vehicle, but that would require a fake ID. He would have had to surrender a license and insurance paperwork to Sal's Rentals for them to copy before leaving their lot. A fake ID would show forethought, which could mean Layton really was on the run. And how would they ever find him without knowing his identity? It was possible that he'd pick a name that meant something to him. It was a reach, but she'd try anyhow. "Is there any other name he might have used?" Madison asked.

Sandra shook her head and then rubbed her arms as if she were cold, but that would be impossible with the heatwave they were experiencing. Madison's question had made Sandra uncomfortable.

"Anyone he idolizes? Resents? Talks about constantly?" Madison pressed.

"Laura," Sandra said bitterly, "but I don't see why he'd use her name to rent a car." She snuffed out derision. "She's all he ever talks about. He doesn't understand why she doesn't— *didn't*—love him. I don't, either."

"You love him?"

"Damn right I do."

Pain and rejection emanated from Sandra.

"Listen, I've gotta go." Sandra retreated into her house and closed the door with enough force to confirm the conversation was indeed over.

Terry rubbed his neck. "We can't make her talk to us."

"She's already told us enough. She said all he talks about is Laura."

"Yeah…"

"Well, I have an idea. Get in the car."

"You're back for another map?" The older man's face lit up at Sal's Rentals.

"Not yet." Terry approached the counter. They agreed he would be the one to make the request. "We have another favor to ask."

"But you don't want another map?" He lifted the glasses from his chain, put them on, and looked in the direction of the display. "Not sure if I can—"

"I'll get one. And I'll pay the full five." Madison snatched a map and tossed it on the counter along with a five-dollar bill.

The man drew a pointed finger between her and Terry. "You guys are serious about this investigation."

"We have another name for you," she rushed out. So much for relinquishing the lead to Terry.

The man hesitated. "Okay."

"Anyone with the last name Saunders rent a car from you in the last week?"

"Saunders?" He took off his glasses and let them dangle on the chain. "That name sounds familiar…" His eyes widened. "The murdered girl?"

"Anything you can do to help us with our investigation would be—"

"So it is her." The man smiled, pleased with his skills of deduction. "Why would you care if she rented a car from me?"

"We need to know if a man by the last name of Saunders did," Terry clarified.

The man leaned on the counter. "He a murder suspect?"

Madison and Terry didn't reply.

"Wowie, the wife will never believe this." He lifted up his glasses again, pulled out the keyboard, and typed. "I'm helping the police find a killer." He paused and read the screen. "I show a Jeff Saunders."

Madison's breath caught. "Do you have a photocopy of his license and insurance?"

"Sure do." The man reached under the counter and pulled out a small box with alphabet separators. "Saunders," he muttered as he went to the letter S. "Here we go." He retrieved the stapled rental agreement and flipped to the back two pages and turned them around for Madison and Terry to see.

In front of them, plain as day, the license and the insurance paperwork read Jeff *Layton*.

Madison glanced at Terry, then at the man, but there was nothing to gain from pointing out that the name Jeff told the older man was different that his identification. He was feeling so proud that he was helping them, she didn't want to draw attention to his mess-up. "Thank you," she said.

"Uh-huh." He filed the paperwork back under S.

"When did he rent it?" Terry asked.

"This past Sunday."

Layton was spotted outside Laura's house, in his own car, in the wee hours of Sunday morning, and then rents a car later that day under her name. That must be more than a coincidence.

"How long did he rent it for?" Terry asked.

"The week. Does this help you?"

"We'll need to know the make, model, and license plate," Madison requested.

"Here, I'll just copy the front page of the rental agreement." The man went through the trouble of hauling out the box and the paperwork again. He made a copy and handed it over to Madison.

"Thanks, again," she said. "Do you know where he was going?"

He shook his head. "None of my business."

"Do you have GPS trackers in your cars?" Terry asked.

"Does it look like I'm large enough for that fancy technical stuff? I don't have those thingies in my car. I use maps."

Of course he did.

CHAPTER THIRTEEN

After leaving Sal's Rentals, Madison called Winston to issue another BOLO, this time for the rental Chevrolet Malibu, and Winston told her to return to the station.

"It's come to my attention that you had surveillance on the Butler house," Winston said.

Madison and Terry were seated across from Winston in his office; the pile of papers on the desk were higher than ever. But that's what happened when the sergeant was too preoccupied being a busybody in her and Terry's case—he neglected his other responsibilities.

"Yeah, for good reason," Madison replied. "Butler and Layton have a connection. He could—"

"We can't have man hours tied up watching for something that *could* happen. Maybe I made a rash decision issuing the second BOLO."

"You have to be kidding," she snapped. "He was involved with the victim. He disappeared the day of the murder."

Winston shrugged. "Could be coincidental."

Madison couldn't believe what she was hearing, but then again, considering the source, it shouldn't surprise her. "He had every reason to want Laura dead—"

"Because she wanted to end the relationship?"

"People have killed for less. Please listen to what I'm saying."

Winston leaned back and crossed his arms.

"Why would an innocent man rent a car under an assumed name that links back to the victim? A victim he has connections to, no less?" Madison said.

Winston took a deep breath. "It's possible the coincidences add up and mean something."

Well, thanks, for giving me that much!

"I do want to make myself clear about something," Winston said, eyeballing first Terry, who hadn't said a word, then Madison. "If we don't find Layton within the week, surveillance on the Butler house is finished, and so is the BOLO."

Her phone rang, putting a literal spin on "saved by the bell." Otherwise, she likely would have responded to her boss with some smartass comment. She answered the phone, listened to her caller, and was smiling smugly when she hung up. "We now have a forensic connection between Laura Saunders and Jeff Layton," she said. "Her blood was on the handcuffs…and so were his prints."

"Cyn, your timing was perfect." Madison walked into the lab with Terry. "You said you have even more for us?" She was feeling like she won the forensic lottery already.

"I do. Mark was able to find epithelial on the tie. That's the good news. The bad news is Jennifer analyzed it, and there isn't a match in the system."

"Okay, well it could still be Layton's," Madison said, not ready to give up hope just yet. "They wouldn't have collected his DNA back when the charges were laid for his DUI."

Cynthia nodded. "Mark also pulled hairs from the vic's comforter, and a few of them had skin tags. Excluding Laura's DNA, the other samples were male."

"*Samples*, as in plural?" Madison asked.

"That's right. DNA from two males. What I didn't tell you on the phone—you hung up so fast—was that there was another set of prints on the cuffs besides Laura's and Layton's.

I don't know who the third set of prints belong to. No hit in the system. But it was also pulled from the wineglass left in Laura's living room."

"Great," Madison said sarcastically. A day ago, this news would have excited her and lent more possibility to Photo Guy's involvement, but Layton was a face they had a name for, and he looked guilty as hell. Cynthia's update only muddied the waters.

"I thought you'd be happy."

Madison shrugged her shoulders. "So did I."

"Well, go get the guy," Cynthia said.

"Don't you think we've been trying?" Madison shot back. "How's all the evidence processing coming along? Done yet?"

Cynthia narrowed her eyes. "You bitch."

Both women started laughing.

Terry shook his head. "I'll never understand women."

CHAPTER FOURTEEN

Days went by, and there was nothing new to go on. Layton still hadn't shown up, and Madison was starting to think they'd never find him. She tried to get his picture put in the papers, but Winston wasn't agreeable. He knew the evidence supported more than one man in Laura's bedroom. He didn't want to be responsible for destroying a potentially innocent man's life, and it had Madison starting to question if they were wasting time hunting Layton. What if he was innocent? What if the man they needed to find was the one in a photograph? But if Winston wouldn't put Layton's picture in the photo, there was no way he'd have Photo Guy's sent to the media.

"What do you think you're doing?"

Cynthia's voice made her jump. "Holy crap, Cyn. You trying to kill me?" The startle transformed to aggravation. It was ten o'clock on a Friday night, and she'd thought she'd have the lab to herself. Terry had long since called it a day and staff was running at the bare minimum.

Cynthia walked over to the table where Madison hunched over the picture of Photo Guy and tapped the photograph. "Should have known," Cynthia said.

"I just wanted some peace and quiet to—"

"Obsess," Cynthia finished.

"You know me too well."

"I thought you had Layton in mind for the murder."

"You say you know me? Come on, Cyn. There's evidence of two DNA profiles—one of which could belong to Layton, though we have no way of knowing that yet. But who does the other profile belong to and is it the same person who left the unidentified third set of prints on the cuffs? And is that person the guy in the photo? Did you get the towel from the bar analyzed?"

Cynthia went rigid.

"What is it?" Madison asked with a sense of foreboding.

"Okay, I was going to tell you, I promise."

"What?"

"The genetic analyzer is down, the machine that processes DNA."

"What? You've got to be kidding."

"Trust me, I wish I was."

"When should I have results?"

Cynthia held up her hand. "Before you gain momentum on this tangent of yours, I sent the towel over to a third-party lab. We've used them before when we gotten overloaded. Their work is admired in the scientific field."

"Why can't anything come together with this case?" Madison threw her hands in the air then let them flop against her sides. "When did you send it over to them?"

"Today, and I asked that it be rushed."

"You've had the towel since Monday. That was days ago."

"I've told you this before, but you're not the only person needing lab work."

Aha! It was in Cynthia's eyes. "You're working on something for Sovereign." Spoken from her lips as if he were the enemy, but in a way he was. Toby Sovereign was another detective in Major Crimes, but Madison and he shared a history. They'd been engaged until she found him in bed with another woman. That had been several years ago, but he'd made her lose her faith in men and love.

"Not just him."

"You're kidding—"

"Sorry, but I'm not. The sarge said to prioritize."

"Prioritize mine."

"Can't do that. His case involves a home invasion, assault. It just happened yesterday. There's a lot of evidence to wade through. The entire team's busy with—"

"Save it."

"Why do you always get like this?"

"Like what?"

"Like your case is the only one out there?"

"You know what? Forget—" Madison stopped talking, her eyes on the photograph again. "There's something about it that seems familiar."

"It should be *very* familiar. You've done enough staring at it."

Madison cocked her head to the side. "Please give me more credit than that." She flipped open the folder she'd brought to the lab with her that contained a listing of the case's evidence. "Tell me we have a picture of it."

"Of what, Maddy? Are you okay?"

Madison paused her rummaging for a second and looked at her friend. "The people at The Weathered Rose said he tried to pick her up the night of her murder. But if they met there, where did the photo come from?" She was just starting to brainstorm out loud and continued her hunt for the framed picture of Laura with the Saunderses, but came up empty. "There was a picture of Laura on her bookshelf with her aunt and uncle. Did you bring it in as evidence?"

Cynthia shook her head. "Didn't think it factored in."

"I think it might."

"What are you thinking?"

"Well, it's going to sound out there, but I swear Laura looks the same in the picture from her nightstand as she did in the one with her aunt and uncle. But without seeing it again..."

"So you're thinking someone doctored the photo in her bedroom? They took Laura's image out of the framed photo on the bookshelf and added the mystery man?"

"Yeah."

"Okay, the question would be: why?"

"That I don't know yet," Madison said, "but if I'm right, they put obvious time and effort into it. The picture was printed on actual photo paper."

"An obsessed stalker," Cynthia concluded.

"Could be. The fantasy of being with Laura got out of hand, and when reality didn't line up with his perceptions, he killed her."

"I don't see why a killer would leave his face at the scene."

"People have done stranger things."

"I don't know if I'm taking the leap just yet, but I'd say the guy in this photo is sick. He would have had to break in, scan Laura's photo, and place it back."

"If he is the killer, that shows premeditation." Madison's heart was racing, and she took a deep breath. "We've got to find out who Photo Guy is."

"And whether he's behind Laura's murder," Cynthia added. "Did he work alone or with Layton?"

Madison met Cynthia's eyes.

Cynthia went on. "Layton would have easily gotten into Laura's house. Who knows? Maybe he worked in conjunction with Photo Guy? As you said, stranger things."

After receiving the news from Cynthia, Madison went back to her desk and allowed her obsessive compulsion to take over. She kept leafing through the evidence in Laura's case, despite the late hour. She didn't have anywhere else to be, or anyone to be with, for that matter.

She didn't have a man in her life right now, which was fine. Boyfriends were overrated. Her last date was at least six months ago, maybe even as far back as a year ago. And if that man was any indication of what was out there, she wasn't missing out on anything—unless a sleazy drunk was a prized possession these days.

Speaking of sleazy, her thoughts went to Toby Sovereign. He'd possessed the ability to piss her off with minimal effort from the first day of officer training. He took his name to literally mean he was God's gift to women, and it continued to surprise her that he'd wormed his way into her bed and into her heart. She couldn't believe that she ever saw herself settling down with him. And as far as she was concerned, he owed her for breaking her heart. Maybe she'd work the past to her advantage, have him call the lab and lower the importance on the evidence from his case.

She picked up her cell phone and hated that his home number was still in her contacts list. She told herself she hadn't had an opportunity to delete it and ignored the fact they'd broken up fourteen years ago. She depressed the number two, waited for the connection. He picked up after two rings.

"Hello, Vixen."

She took a deep breath. He must have had her on caller display, which meant her number could still be in his phone. Oh, his voice made her sick…and his cocky attitude…and *Vixen*? She'd hated it when he called her that when they were dating. Did a strong enough word exist to describe how she felt about it now? "Why don't you and I meet up at the firing range?" she said. "You know, like the old days?"

The line fell silent. Likely, he was stumped by her proposal. "Serious?"

"Sure, but on one condition."

"Should have known."

"Just one."

"What?"

"You're the target." Her temper flared. "You went over my head. You placed your evidence ahead of mine."

"What are you talking about? The home invasion?" He sounded irritated. "One of the victims was a sixteen-year-old girl, Maddy. She was raped."

Cynthia had not mentioned the ages of the victims. A tsunami of guilt threatened to drown her.

He broke the few seconds of silence. "You have to think outside of your box."

"Wouldn't you know all about that?" With her twist on the interpretation of his statement, the memories flooded back with more clarity.

"Why is everything about that?"

Madison wanted to lash out, but it would be pointless and not worth her energy. Instead, she wouldn't give him the satisfaction of an answer.

He lowered his voice when he continued. "You know I'm—"

"Don't even say it." He'd apologized so many times that all meaning—if it ever existed—was long gone.

"Fine, I won't," he spat. "But you do need to realize your case isn't the only one out there."

She said nothing.

"I know the cop you are, and that will never change. You're good at what you do, but—"

"What is this now? A pep rally?" she snapped.

He exhaled loudly.

Good, she thought, *but we're nowhere close to even.*

"Maddy?"

She heard him say her name as she clicked off. Let him deal with it. The way he talked to her—condescending while at the same time trying to flatter her—made her realize he was playing the same old mind games. It was time that he moved on. She would never get back with him. Ever.

Her gaze fell to a page in the case file. A lead she'd never followed up on: Lou Mann. He was the man from The Weathered Rose who was in a hurry to leave when she showed up. She brought up his background, but there was nothing noteworthy.

Her phone rang. "What do you want?" she answered without looking at caller ID, assuming it was Sovereign.

"Sorry, wrong number." It was a man's voice, but it wasn't Toby, and then the man was gone.

She pulled up her call history. The number was local, and it was familiar to her. She called it back, but it rang repeatedly and never went through to voice mail.

Strange.

She flipped through some pages in the file, confirmed the caller's identity, and then dialed Terry.

"You know what time it is right?" Terry sounded like he'd been asleep.

"It doesn't matter."

"It does," he hissed. "Annabelle's asleep."

"Layton just called my cell."

CHAPTER FIFTEEN

Madison's landline rang, rousing her from a dead sleep, and notifying her someone was in her apartment's lobby calling up.

"Knew it was too good to be true," she mumbled to her empty apartment. She hadn't slept that soundly in a while and could have gone on much longer in Dreamland. She answered, "Hello."

"Maddy, I've been trying to reach you," Terry said. "Your cell kept ringing to voice mail."

"Oh." She recalled she'd actually turned her cell off last night after returning from Laura's funeral. She'd gone hoping that Layton or Photo Guy would show up, but no luck. She also hadn't been able to reach Layton since he'd called her. "Now, I guess you know what it's like," she dished out to Terry.

"Sure, be smart if you need to be, but get down here. We've got Layton."

On the way to the station, Terry explained that Higgins had nabbed Layton when he showed up at Sandra's house. Layton was set up in an interrogation room wearing a suit and tie and looking thoroughly unamused. His license photo didn't do him fairness. She didn't consider him an attractive man, but he was above average. He wore glasses, unlike in the photo, and they suited him.

Madison pointed at Layton through the one-way mirror. "Why's he in a suit?"

"He says he came from Laura's gravesite. Said he left a card and flowers if we wanted to prove it."

"Send someone out there."

"Already have."

Madison kept her attention on Layton. "He's mine. Let's go."

When they walked into the interrogation room, Layton was leaning back in his chair, his legs crossed. Casual, but impatient. Madison caught a glimpse of his shoes. Large. Size twelve, maybe. Just like the muddy print impression in Laura's house.

"Why were you hiding from us?" Madison asked, getting right to the point.

"I wasn't hiding from you."

"Your ex-girlfriend was murdered. You know anything about that?"

Silence.

"Where were you last Saturday night?"

Layton's eyes drifted past her and off into the distance, and his face paled. A noticeable change from the grimace he'd been wearing. Her question hung in the air for a few moments, and then he spoke, his tone softer. "I came to you willingly. I didn't have to."

"Not what I heard." She slapped a crime-scene photo of Laura on the table.

He averted his eyes from it.

"Why did you do it?" she asked.

"I didn't."

"Answer the question, then: where were you last Saturday night?"

He visibly swallowed. "It's not going to look good for me."

"Try us," Terry said.

"Guess it would depend on what time."

Madison stood abruptly. "We don't have time for bullshit. Why don't you give us a complete recap from, say, six in

the evening 'til…heck, let's say three Sunday morning."
She sensed Terry's eyes on her. Maybe she was being a bit
aggressive. Maybe she would silence him into requesting a
lawyer, but all she could see was Laura's dead body and her
right to justice.

"I know my rights. I don't have to speak to you."

"If you know something about her murder, you do."
Madison shrugged. "Otherwise we'll lock you up as an
accessory. Minimum."

"I was at The Weathered Rose. It's a bar."

"How long were you there?"

"Okay, this is where it gets tougher. Until about midnight
or so."

"Is it midnight…or 'so'?"

"Specifically, I left about eleven forty-five."

"Then where did you go?"

He let out a deep breath and dropped his head. "Laura's."

Madison took a seat again and leaned forward, her eyes
sharp on the man before her. "Why were you there?"

His fingers tapped the table, fast at first, then slower. It
was almost like he was pacing himself. He finally lifted his
gaze to look at Madison, a blank expression on his face.

"It's an easy question," she pressed. "Why were you at
Laura's?"

"Maybe I should get a lawyer." Spoken as a threat, but
lacking conviction.

"You are within your rights." Madison sat back as if
suddenly uninterested.

"Damn right I am." He paused, and for a moment, she
questioned whether he would continue. A few seconds later,
he said, "I'll keep talking. I have nothing to hide."

"Then, please." She gestured with a hand, asked her
question again, "Why were you there?"

"I should have known that little freak from across the
street would have said something."

Madison bit back her impatience. "Are you referring to
Mr. Hill, her neighbor?"

Layton contorted his face. "Don't know his name. Tall, skinny guy. Typical redneck imagery. I can picture him missing both front teeth, wearing overalls, and playing a banjo." He sat back, crossing his arms in front of his chest. The attitude was definitely back. "I was there that night 'cause I loved her, Detective. He's a no-good SOB—just didn't like him."

"Who? Mr. Hill?" She detected a crossover in his thoughts. Could he be referring to the unnamed man—Photo Guy?

Layton shook his head. "No, the guy from the bar."

Bingo.

He raised an eyebrow at Madison. "I can tell you know who I'm referring to. The old guy nearly broke his nose. Quite impressive actually."

"So, you watched but didn't step in?"

"To what means?" His eyes darted downward. "She made it clear our relationship was over."

"That made you angry?"

"No…Yes…I guess so—but it's not what you think. You've probably heard a couple versions of it. We were involved."

"Yeah, well, that's quite different from what we've heard," she admitted.

"We ended the relationship, but Laura would get lonely. I was actually at her place on Thursday…" He rolled his hand to indicate the Thursday before the murder.

"Did you have sex with Laura that night?" She could care less about their exploits except for the bearing they might have on the case—specifically Layton's prints on the handcuffs. Were they from Thursday or the night of the murder?

He nodded. "Yes."

"Did you have any sort of sexual fantasies you'd play out?" Madison asked, tiptoeing around the cuffs without mentioning them.

"Strange question, but I'll answer anyway. Laura liked to be bound." He cleared his throat, and Madison detected the subject made Layton uncomfortable. "She liked handcuffs."

If he was telling the truth, he'd provided good reason for the existence of his prints on the cuffs. Her eyes went to Layton's necktie—silk, expensive-looking. "You ever use anything else to tie her up?" She pointed at his tie.

"This?" Layton ran a hand down his tie, his thumb to the backside as he held it out. "Never. Are you kidding me? This tie is a G&C. Far too expensive to use on…" He stopped talking.

Madison fought the urge to look at Terry and kept her eyes riveted on Layton. The killer's MO, including weapon of choice, was kept from the media.

"G&C?" Terry pushed, acting as if he were ignorant about the brand name.

"Gallo & Costa," Layton clarified. "The only kind worth buying."

Terry looked at Madison, and addressing her more than Layton, he said, "You know I'm just an ordinary guy. Plain as they come. Up until this past week, I didn't know what G&C stood for."

Layton's eyes narrowed, his brow pinching in confusion. "I've been wearing them for years. What does that have to do with anything?"

For years… "Since before 1999?" She threw out the year the necktie had been discontinued. She wanted to gauge his reaction, but nothing came of it.

"Lady, I don't know what year. That's a stupid question, isn't it?"

She rose to her feet. "This guy is a waste of time. Put him in holding. Come on, Terry."

"Wait."

They both turned to look at him.

"I'll talk to you more, but first I need a lawyer."

CHAPTER SIXTEEN

"So we got the son of a bitch, I see," Winston said, walking toward Madison and Terry.

They were at their desks, catching up on paperwork and waiting for Layton's lawyer to show up.

"That we did." Terry grinned at the sergeant.

"Would have been nice to have received a heads-up." Winston glared at Madison.

She would have loved to point out that Terry had actually been the one who was around when Layton was brought in, but she kept silent.

"We're just waiting on Layton's lawyer to arrive," Terry offered. "He should be here soon."

Winston nodded, and Madison's phone rang.

She answered, "Knight…All right…Thanks." After she'd hung up, she noticed that both men were looking at her. "Well, that was Officer Higgins. Layton's story checks out: he went to the gravesite."

"So he told the truth for once? Big deal. It doesn't mean he's innocent in all this. He's been on the run." The sergeant crossed his arms and straightened out his back, popping out his gut and straining the buttons on his shirt.

"Apparently, he left flowers and a card," she continued as if Winston hadn't even spoken. "You're not going to believe what he wrote, though." Her phone chimed notification of a message as if on cue. She held the screen so Terry could see what Higgins had forwarded to her. Madison read it aloud: "I'm sorry. Love you forever. Will never forget you. Love, Jeff."

Terry said, "He's sorry? For what? Killing her? It doesn't look too good for this guy."

"He could be sorry for any number of things," she countered.

Winston scowled. "So you've sunk a bunch of resources into finding this guy, and now that we have him, you're doubting his guilt?"

"I never said he did it," she defended herself.

"You sure acted like you believed it."

Madison wished Winston would leave and take care of some of his paperwork. She addressed her partner. "What do we have besides circumstantial evidence?"

"We have the card."

"Those words could be twisted to mean different things. The district attorney will see that." She lifted her coffee mug, swallowed a large mouthful, and licked her lips. What she craved was a Hershey's bar. "We have his prints on cuffs, but he's explained that."

"He had the motive. He loved her. She wanted to end their relationship," Terry laid out.

"So other people say. They would still get together to—"

"I'll leave you to it," Winston said, "but call the minute you get your shit together." He made his exit.

When he was out of earshot, Madison muttered, "Yes, sir, I know you want to know everything, at every second." She caught eyes with her smiling partner. She had one way of wiping that grin off his face. "When he calls—and you know he will—I'm handing the phone to you."

"Good luck pulling that off. Going back to Layton and his relationship with Laura. It was written all over his face that their breakup wasn't a mutual decision. He didn't want to see her with anyone else. He was watching her in a bar."

Madison had to admit that was stalker-like, but she wasn't hanging Layton just yet. "I'd like to find out more about that guy in the photo."

"We're back to that—or should I say you're still *stuck* on that?"

"Why are you being so stubborn about it?"

"Why would a killer leave a photo of himself behind? Stupid, don't you think?"

"I'm not saying he's necessarily the killer, but I think he has something to offer the investigation. Why are you so set on Layton being Laura's killer?"

"Do you ever look at the evidence that stares you right in the face—at all? If you did, you'd see it as clearly as it is: Layton did it."

She let out a rush of air. Her mind was so jumbled with thoughts, she couldn't latch on to one with any clear focus.

"He did it, Maddy."

"Just listen, all right? I mean, if Laura was involved with Photo Guy as the photo suggests, why wouldn't he come forward? And since when is the obvious answer the right one?"

"Photo Guy? Is that what we're officially calling him now?"

"Sure. Why not? Or we could just call him Fred." Madison let out a small laugh and recalled their earlier bet on whether they'd find Layton. "Actually, you owe me twenty."

Terry slipped his hands into his pockets. "Sorry, Knight. I have nothing. My wife took all my money."

"Seriously?"

"Sorry, I'll have to owe you." His eyes lit up like he had a revelation. "Or," he drew out the word, "you could be a sweetheart and give me a chance to make my money back. Ah, but look who I'm talking to."

"If you're trying to manipulate me, you should be more flattering. Besides how can you make it back when it never left your pocket?" She raised her brows. "Fine, what do you have in mind?"

"Layton's guilty."

She let that sink in but didn't need time to mull it over. What did she have to lose? "Okay. And I'll be in favor of Fred the Photo Guy. But if you lose again, you also owe me dinner."

"Why?"

"Call it interest for being patient."

"You, patient? That'd be a first. Guinness, grab your record book, Madison Knight—" His voice rose with each word, drawing the attention of other officers.

"Quiet," she hissed.

He continued quieter. "Right. There's a cost involved. Guess we should hold off on the record book for now."

She balled up a fist and cuffed him with all the strength in her right arm. He seemed genuinely hurt, and for a brief moment, she regretted putting force behind it.

He bent forward, his one hand over where she punched him. She moved closer to him and put a hand on his back, which was heaving. Her feelings of remorse came to an abrupt end as he straightened up, laughing heartily.

"Why, I oughtta kick your—"

"Layton's lawyer's here," Officer Ranson said as she walked over to them. Her hair was such a fierce red. A dye job that had gone awry—hopefully.

Madison looked in the direction of the reception desk, which was within sight of their desks. A heavyset man with sweat-stained armpits stood there looking like he was struggling for breath.

"Okay, let him back," Madison said, surprised Ranson had left her post.

Ranson waved the lawyer in and took off in the direction of the restrooms.

Before the lawyer got to them, Madison said, "It makes you wonder why Layton wanted a lawyer, I'll give you that. It's not like we've charged him with a crime. Heck, we haven't really worked him over yet."

"Possibly a guilty conscience." A glint fired in Terry's eyes.

The lawyer stopped short of Madison and Terry. "What have you got him for?"

"Mr. Layton has not been charged with anything, Mister…" Madison raised her eyebrows hoping to coax him into saying his name.

"Then why are you holding him?"

"We believe he might know something about Laura Saunders's murder." Madison assumed Layton would have at least filled him in.

"Murder?" He drew an arm across his forehead, wiping off his wet brow.

Madison was going to go on hunch here. "You're not a criminal attorney, are you?"

"Heck no," he rushed out. "Divorce attorney, but I won't disclose my relationship with Layton."

Madison was surprised the man had passed the bar: he didn't seem too bright. She led him to the interrogation room, where his client waited once again, and gestured for him to go inside. She hung back for a few seconds with Terry. "Some days, I seriously wonder if there's a hidden camera somewhere."

By the time she and Terry joined the lawyer and Layton, Layton appeared more relaxed than he'd been during the first round of questioning. Was he relieved to have a lawyer present? What comfort could this sweaty man possibly offer? He wasn't even a defense attorney.

"As you can see, your lawyer is here, but you do realize that his area of expertise is not criminal?" Madison felt obligated to point that out.

"Yes, I realize that. He helped me through my divorce, but he's the only lawyer I know."

"Well then, let's get started. You said you went to Laura's gravesite," Madison started.

"I did."

"And we have since verified that."

"Then I'm free to go?"

"Not quite. We found the flowers and the card you left." Madison slid across the photo of the flowers and the card from the site. "Is this what you left?"

"Yes."

"Then you can understand why we have concerns."

He remained quiet.

"You apologized. What were you sorry for?" Madison asked.

Prolonged silence.

"Are you sorry for killing her?"

"I went there to say goodbye." Tears pooled in the corners of his eyes.

Madison glimpsed at the nameless lawyer, who wasn't putting up any protests to her questions or accusations. She kept pressing. "You were sorry for something you did."

His face flushed, and a mild twitch pulsed in his cheek.

"Why are you sorry?" she snarled.

His jaw clenched, and a few tears slid down his cheeks.

"I lost someone I loved." His gaze went blank briefly before meeting with her eyes. "Maybe you should try it."

His statement cut her. "What the—" She struggled for control. "What would you know about my losses?" Her grandmother's death was so fresh in her mind, as was her struggle, the chemo, the fighting for her life. She'd lost when the violent brain tumor refused to retreat. Inoperable—at least that was the prognosis. It took years for Madison to stop blaming the health-care practitioners. All the money, all the funding, all the scientific advances, and still no cure for cancer? That was hard to believe. She worked to force the vivid recollections to the background.

Her eyes steadied on Layton. "Let's get back to why we're here. You never answered the question. Why were you sorry?"

He leaned forward, placed an elbow on the table, and rested his chin in his hand. "I was sorry that I did nothing to prevent this from happening to her, that I wasn't brave enough to stop this."

Madison straightened. "You talk like you could have prevented it."

His eyes snapped to hers, then settled on the table.

What is he holding back and why?

The intensity in his eyes begged her to see the truth of his statement. Her thoughts diverted back to the photograph and the nameless man. She pulled the picture out of a folder and slid it across the table. "Do you recognize him?" she asked as a test.

Layton remained silent. His jaw clenched. The silence didn't seem to originate from pain or regret, but from anger. Layton held the unknown man responsible, but in what capacity? Had the man pushed Layton to kill Laura in a jealous rage, or was it because he felt the man in the photo had?

"Mr. Layton?" Madison asked.

"Yes, that's him." His eyes remained fixed on the photo.

"Him…" Madison glanced at the lawyer who had yet to speak.

As if reading her mind, he turned to Layton and said, "Maybe you need another kind of lawyer. I know some terrific defense attorneys."

Layton stayed fixated on the picture for seconds before lifting his head to look at the lawyer. "I'm not being charged, Harvey. I need you for legal advice, is all. You're making a buck off it." He paused long enough for emphasis before continuing, "I trust the money should be enough reason for you to sit there and let me know when to keep my mouth shut." His tone of voice was ominous and carried an underlying threat. His anger was so close to the surface, it was like lava under a paper-thin crust of earth.

The lawyer nodded and waved his hand as if approving for them to proceed.

Madison didn't care for this side of Layton, intimidating. "Is there anything you can tell us about this man?"

"He's the guy from The Weathered Rose who went home with Laura." His eyes diverted when he realized he had involuntarily made a confession. Layton was, for certain now, the ex that the two older men had said was watching Laura.

"I followed them back to her place," Layton offered.

"You got jealous?"

"That's not the point."

"That's exactly the point," Madison said firmly. "You admit to following her home Saturday night. You admit to having sex with her on Thursday night."

"Yes."

"Things didn't work out between you, and then there's another man, although there was no DNA evidence to prove she'd had sexual intercourse before her death." Cynthia had processed the results prior to their DNA analyzer breaking down. There was no useful DNA from Laura's vaginal swab. So either the man she had sex with had no semen or had used a condom. There wasn't one at the scene, but it could have been flushed. She wanted to see if she could stir up rage.

Instead, Layton's face softened. "She didn't have sex with him?"

"I didn't exactly say that."

His face contorted in disgust. "I was right to think she had."

"And that changes things? You got jealous, you—"

"Stop there," the lawyer interjected. "I don't like the direction of this interrogation and request that you desist from badgering my client." He jutted out his chin.

Madison remained quiet for a few seconds and then decided to stab at things from another angle. "When you had sex with Laura, did you use condoms?"

"Why? There'd be no need," Layton replied. "I'm surprised you don't know from my file that I've had a vasectomy." Pain darkened his eyes.

"We've had no reason to subpoena your medical records," she said, "but people use condoms for reasons other than birth control. Is the real reason you broke up because you couldn't give Laura children?"

He cleared his throat. "Part of the reason."

"So, Laura did want to be with you, but since you couldn't have her, no one else could," Madison suggested.

"No…" His voice trailed off, lending little credence to his words.

Despite Madison's pull to Photo Guy, the one in front of her seemed more culpable with every syllable uttered. But did he have what it took to murder Laura, watch the spirit fade in her eyes? Someone he professed to love so deeply? On the other hand, jealousy could be such a forceful motivator.

She continued to press. "Did you murder Laura?"

"No." He adjusted the glasses on his nose before crossing his arms in front of his chest.

"Any jury could understand, sympathize with you. You loved her, she broke your heart, slept with other men."

"How many—" He snapped his mouth shut.

She smirked. "You were jealous. Jealousy makes us do things we wouldn't normally do."

"I didn't."

"Like you stated for the record, you had a vasectomy. It appears that so did Laura's killer." Again, she was exaggerating the findings to suit her purpose. All they knew was there was no usable DNA from Laura's last sexual encounter.

He ran his palms down his face before turning to look at his lawyer. "I would like new representation."

CHAPTER SEVENTEEN

Madison barely possessed enough patience to wait in line at Starbucks, and now she was stuck waiting for another lawyer.

Winston called out her name.

If she didn't turn around, maybe he'd go away. She took a bite of her Hershey's bar. *Milky, chocolatey heaven.*

"What happened to Layton's lawyer?"

Wishful thinking.

She faced Winston. "We're waiting for another one." She refused to look directly at her partner because she could see in her peripheral that his mouth was twitching like he was fending off laughter.

Winston stood by her desk. "Next time, keep me more in the loop. Why do I have to remind you of this all the time?" He folded his hands together in front him and relaxed his posture, one leg slightly forward of the other. "Seriously, if you were any less of a detective…"

"I know. You'd have my badge." Madison resisted the urge to point out the reason she was good at her job was because she took action and didn't stand around rehashing everything.

"Don't mock me, Knight."

She stuffed the last of her Hershey's bar in her mouth and tossed the wrapper in the garbage. "You're welcome to sit in for the next round of questioning."

"No thank you. I've got bigger things to take care of." With that, Winston walked off.

Bigger things to take care of? Had me fooled.

"Layton's looking pretty guilty," Terry said, angling to win their bet.

"I'm not admitting any defeat yet, but I'm starting to focus more on Layton again."

"Why's that?"

"The guy has a motive as old as time itself." The words came out, and she cursed her mother for inflicting her with clichés at a vulnerable age. Madison figured Terry would make a comment, but the phone on his desk rang.

He picked up the call, and she watched his face, trying to get a read on who the caller might be. He hung up before she could even guess a name.

"That was Officer Ranson," he said. "It seems Layton's new lawyer won't be able to get here until tomorrow."

She felt the smirk spread across her lips.

"Maddy? That face scares me."

"I think it will do him some good. It will definitely shake him up if he's guilty."

"Oh, he's guilty. I feel it."

"Yet you tell me that I rely too much on my hunches. We don't have DNA proof he was in that room."

"Yet. We do have prints on the cuffs."

"Which he admitted to using with her. He even admitted to being in her bedroom."

"Where they pulled two male DNA profiles—one from hair and one from the tie. So depending on how this matches up, that could be enough to toss him behind bars for good." Terry stood to his feet. "Then again, you never know. Maybe Layton and the guy in the photo are both involved."

She stared at him, her heart thumping, as his words brought back the fact she'd briefly entertained that very thought with Cynthia.

"Don't tell me you never thought of it," Terry said. "Two men both known to be enamored with the victim, both outside her home the night of the murder."

Madison held up her hand. "Stop it. You're giving me a headache." She didn't want to dwell on it or get carried away with that possibility. At least not right now. She stood. "Let's go tell Layton the good news. He'll be a guest of the city tonight."

Madison rapped on the door before entering. Layton sat there looking half asleep.

"Where's my lawyer?"

"Here's the thing," Madison began.

"Oh shit, he can't make it. You're keeping me overnight, aren't you?"

Technically, given that he was a suspect in a murder case, she could hold him for ninety-six hours without pressing charges. "You're a suspect in Laura's murd—"

"I didn't do it."

"And if that's the truth, it will come out in time. We have more questions." She motioned for him to stand. "And one more thing, while you're so cooperative." Her tone was full of sarcasm.

His eyes fired with rage. "Whatever I can do to help, Detective."

"We'd like to get a DNA sample."

A fast pulse swelled in his cheek. "Go to hell."

His comment took her aback. This man could transform from placid to monster in fractions of time. He really could have pulled off the murder.

CHAPTER EIGHTEEN

Madison hung up from Ranson at reception and spoke to Terry, who was seated at his desk. "You're not going to believe who Layton's lawyer is," she said, her eyes darting to the front.

He started to turn toward the reception desk.

"Don't look," she hissed.

"Really? Come on, who is it?"

"Blake Golden."

"*The* Blake Golden?"

"Yep."

This lawyer was one worth having. He was the "Golden" in Golden, Broderick and Maine, a prestigious defense firm that founded itself upon its media publicity and high-profile cases.

"Maybe he does charity work?" Terry suggested.

"You mean pro bono," Madison corrected.

"Sure. Whatever."

In the interrogation room, Madison laid out a photo of the necktie that had been used to strangle Laura. "Does this tie look familiar to you?"

Layton consulted with Golden, who Madison thought resembled a character belonging to a past time—say, a 1930s Italian Mafia boss. His black hair reached about an inch over the ridge of his shirt collar and was slicked back, shining with gel. The way he carried himself conveyed arrogance and entitlement.

Golden nodded for Layton to proceed.

"Well, it's a Gallo & Costa, style B581," Layton rattled off. *Whoa.*

"You certainly know your ties, Mr. Layton." She sensed Golden looking at her and felt he was ready to pounce. She continued. "Do you own a tie like this one?"

"You don't have to answer that," Golden cautioned his client.

Layton proceeded anyhow. "I never cleared enough back then to consider G&C."

Madison let the matter of the tie go for a moment and focused on Layton's big feet. "What size shoe do you wear?"

"Twelve. What does it matter?" His pitch rose.

"Relevance, Detective," Golden said calmly.

"A muddy shoeprint was lifted from the scene. Size twelve. And this tie—" she tapped the photo "—the one your client just recognized so perfectly was the one used to strangle Laura Saunders."

"Detective, that's hardly enough to view my client as guilty. I wear size twelves. Do you think I'm the killer?"

She jutted out her chin but said nothing. She held no respect for those who played their part in freeing criminals and chastised herself for ever considering—no matter how briefly—a career in law.

Golden continued. "And the fact my client recognizes the tie is proof that he strangled a woman? Hardly."

"His fingerprints were found on handcuffs used to subdue Laura Saunders."

"And I believe he offered an explanation for that." Golden glanced at Layton, who nodded.

She wasn't gaining any ground. She'd approach it from another angle. "The killer left behind DNA evidence at the scene. We'll need a sample from your client."

"I don't think you have enough to warrant that, Detective."

"We have more than enough circumstantial evidence. We have—"

"Circumstantial only," he cut in.

"Should it also be deemed *circumstantial* that Layton fled town after Laura was murdered?"

Golden glanced at Layton, then back to Madison. A light smile grazed his lips. "Who says he *fled town*?" He used finger quotes on those last words. "He never *left* town."

Madison clenched her jaw. *Where* Layton had been was inconsequential; he had avoided them. "He rented a car under an assumed name."

"And this makes him guilty of murder?"

"Why use the deceased's last name to rent a car?" she fired back.

Layton leaned in toward his lawyer, spoke in his ear. Golden sat back, gestured for his client to speak.

"I'll give you my DNA," Layton said, "but it won't give you anything."

She had to wonder why now and not yesterday, and she bobbed her head. "We'll see."

Layton adjusted his glasses, sat back in the chair, and crossed his arms.

Golden straightened his tie. "Let the record note that my client has already disclosed the fact he was in the victim's—"

"Laura's," Layton corrected him. "Just say her damned name. Laura!"

Golden gave it a few seconds before speaking again. "*Laura's* bedroom. Therefore, it's presumed you may find DNA that ties back to my client. This in no way implicates him as her killer."

Madison connected eyes with Golden. "Correction." She paused for dramatic emphasis. "If his DNA comes back a match, I assure you, this will implicate your client." She stood to leave, and Terry followed.

"What happened to your thinking he was innocent?" Terry asked once they were out of the room.

She didn't answer her partner, because she didn't know if Layton was guilty or not. What she did know was Golden got under her skin.

"We need the results rushed, Cyn," Madison told her over the phone. She was talking about processing the DNA they'd collected from Layton.

"I appreciate you're in a bind, but I can't do anything. The analyzer's still down. I can request a rush from the lab like I did with the towel."

"I see how that rush worked," she said sardonically. "We'll have to release him until the results come back."

"Sor—"

Madison hung up before she heard the full apology. Apologies meant nothing. They could have Laura's killer in their custody, but they didn't have enough to keep holding him. And another thing aggravating her was Terry, who took off trying to reconcile with his wife every time she turned to look the other way.

Madison watched the sergeant approach. *This day just keeps getting better and better.*

"Have you laid the charges?" Winston asked.

"There's not enough there."

"We conducted a search for the man. You wanted his face in the papers, from what I recall. And we're letting him go?"

"No option at this point." She angled her head and put her hands on her hips.

"Find a reason to arrest him so we can hold him."

She and Winston rarely saw eye to eye, and he was more about arrests than getting the right person behind bars. "What am I supposed to do?"

"You need the DNA results?"

"Yes."

"Leave it with me."

Finally, her boss was actually going to do something that would help the progress of the case.

CHAPTER NINETEEN

"You've held my client for thirty-seven hours." Golden leaned forward and folded his hands on the table in front of him. "I trust you haven't found anything significant with his DNA, or charges would have been laid already."

"You know we have the right to hold him longer."

"Sure, and risk a lawsuit."

"Is that a threat, Mr. Golden?" She looked him square in the eye.

"Are you willing to risk your career on a possibility?" he served back.

Someone rapped on the door. Terry rose to answer it and then turned back to look at her, a file in his hand. He gestured for her to join him in the hall.

Once out there, Terry stood over Madison as she read the results. "DNA is a match to one profile pulled from hairs off the comforter..." She scanned down the page. "Negative match to the epithelial found on the tie. Shit."

"No, that's great news."

"How is that?"

"We can put him in that room."

"He's already admitted to being in her room," Madison said, failing to see why her partner was excited.

"That's only his word. We have enough to establish a case based upon motive, character, and relationship with the deceased."

"Certainly not based on his background record. There are no prior assaults in his file."

Terry moved toward the interrogation room door, then paused with his hand resting on the knob. "Maddy, listen to me. This is our guy."

"Don't tell me I go by gut feelings."

"This isn't the same thing. He had a reason. Years ago, prior to fingerprinting and DNA, he'd have been charged."

She hated being forced to do something she didn't feel was right. The scientific advances in forensics were invaluable to holding the guilty liable and keeping the innocent out of prison. Why could they manage to rush through a DNA for Layton while the towel sat waiting its turn? Winston obviously put no more credence in her Photo Guy theory than her partner. Terry had already convicted Layton.

Madison felt Layton's eyes on her every move as she reentered the interrogation room. She sat across from him and slapped the new file on the table. She addressed Golden. "The results are in from the lab."

Golden pulled down on his suit jacket. "And what were the findings?"

"We did find your client's DNA—"

"You said they wouldn't find anything!" Layton jolted to his feet and scowled at his lawyer.

"Actually, *you* said that," Golden tossed back matter-of-factly.

"I trusted you."

"Maybe it's about time you learned the lesson that you can't trust everyone," Madison said. "Especially lawyers." Golden's jaw tightened, and she continued. "Your DNA was found in Laura's bedroom."

"I told you I was there." Layton paced the room.

"Please sit down." Madison motioned with her arms, but Layton refused to sit.

Golden leaned forward, and he clasped his hands. "This won't stick. My client and the deceased were in a relationship. He doesn't deny that."

Madison felt like she was being tugged on. If her partner and sergeant had their way, Layton would be charged, but she couldn't take that path just because it was the easy route. Golden was right: they didn't have Layton to the wall. The forensic evidence could be worked, and there was no eyewitness that could put Layton in Laura's house around the time of death. She also couldn't ignore the other set of prints on the cuffs that were unaccounted for.

Madison cleared her throat, pulled out a picture of Photo Guy, and put it in front of Layton.

"You recognized him earlier," Madison said.

"I told you—he was there that night at the bar, and he went home with Laura."

"You also said you had a bad feeling about him. Why?"

Silence.

"What are you hiding from us? Who is he?"

Silence.

She knew Terry wasn't going to be happy with the direction this was about to take, but she had to go with her gut feeling and what the evidence was telling her. "We know you didn't kill Laura."

Terry gasped.

Golden snorted. "We will be leaving now." He went to get up.

"But you know something," Madison said, hoping to appeal to Layton's conscience.

"It doesn't matter. She's dead," he said, pain piercing his eyes.

"We can leave. Let's go." Golden put a hand on Layton's shoulder, but it was quickly shrugged off.

"I'm not going anywhere."

"You're a free man. She just said—"

"You leave, then," Layton seethed. "I'm staying." His eyes filled with tears.

"I'm your attorney and—"

"Now, you're not. You're fired."

Golden's jaw clenched. He nodded and left the room.

CHAPTER TWENTY

Layton cupped his face and sobbed, sucking in air as if it would be his dying breath.

"Do you know who did this to Laura?" Madison asked.

He dropped his hands and shook his head.

"Do you think he did this?" She pointed to the image of Photo Guy still on the table.

He took a cleansing breath and then said one word. "No."

Madison felt disappointed by his answer. "The woman you loved was murdered. If you do know who did it…"

"I don't know. Not for certain. What the hell good is it going to do? She's already dead." His eyes communicated more than his words.

"Don't you want her to get justice?" she snapped.

"Yes, but—"

"You're afraid of someone," Madison concluded, thinking back to Sandra who mentioned fearing for her life. "You speak to us, and we'll get you into protective custody."

"Yeah, *protective custody*. I've heard all about that. People still get murdered. There are dirty cops."

"Why did you take off from work?" Madison asked, slipping back to how he'd up and left.

"I needed to get away for a bit."

"If you're not going to be completely honest, this is a waste of time." She gathered up the photo, put it in the folder, and closed it.

"I have debts to pay."

"I'm not following you."

"Gambling debts."

"I couldn't care less," Madison said. "My job is to solve Laura's murder."

Layton shut his eyes a moment and then took off his glasses, lifted them toward the light and wiped them. "I owe someone a lot of money."

She wanted to scream, *What does that have to do with Laura's murder,* but played along. "A bookie?"

"Yeah, that's right."

"That's why you took off?"

"Damn right. I owe this guy twenty-five grand. Do you have any idea how much money that is?" His face paled. "I took time off to try and gather money. He told me if I didn't have the money to him by last Friday, I'd be a dead man."

That would explain why Layton would rent a car and live under the radar. "Today is Tuesday. Why not speak up about this sooner?"

"Would you have believed me? But I came to realize I might be safer in jail."

Madison was trying to piece together what Layton was telling her. "You think he killed Laura because of your debt?" she asked, feeling it was a reach.

"Dang straight. My place was broken into. My television was smashed and—"

"Did you report this?"

"What was I supposed to say? I owe a bookie for gambling illegally, and I think he trashed my place?"

"If you had filed a report—"

"Like I'm trying to tell you: it wouldn't have done any good or changed anything. I knew who did it, and I know why."

"How do you know for sure it was your bookie behind the break-in?"

"He left a note."

Madison shook her head. Some people were stark crazy. "Do you still have it?"

He reached into a pocket and pulled out a piece of lined paper folded into eighths and handed it to Madison.

She read it out loud: "You have 'til Friday or you die." She looked at Terry. "Sounds kind of hokey, if you ask me."

"Maybe you wouldn't think so if you heard some of the stories going around about this guy. He's cut people's fingers off. Who knows all that he's capable of? That's why when I heard about Laura, I panicked. I couldn't come to you. I was stuck in a corner. If I came to you, I figured I was as good as dead, too. My best chance was to come up with the money."

"What's your bookie's name?"

"Oh no, I'm not saying."

"We can't protect you from someone we don't know. Where do you meet him?"

"It doesn't matter. He'll have his money. Late, but he'll have it. I've already got fifteen grand in cash. I'm also selling my car and have some investments to draw from, but all that takes time to turn into cash. That's why I was crashing at Sandra's. He wouldn't know about her."

She had to take a pause and step back from the conversation. Analyze. She pulled out the picture of Photo Guy again. "Do you know if Laura was involved with him?"

Rage darkened his features.

"Witnesses say he picked her up that night. You even said they went back to Laura's together."

Layton smiled, his eyes glazed over as if he were caught in a memory. "She had this way about her…" He rubbed his chin and let out a small laugh. "She liked the game. It could have been a setup. She probably spent most of the night kissing his nose after the old guy hit him." He raised his hands. "Laura could have been seeing him. Hell, if I know."

. . .

Madison felt for Layton's predicament, but they had no further cause to hold him at this point. They released him, and she got twenty-four-hour protection approved until his bookie was found. Though that would be easier if Layton was more forthcoming with his bookie's name.

"I can't believe you let him off. We had everything lined up," Terry sulked.

"Yeah, I don't think so."

"We'll be seeing him again. He did it. As far as I'm concerned, case closed. And if he's so concerned about his bookie, why not give him up?"

"You mean besides fear?" Her eyes widened. "And *case closed*? It wasn't Layton's DNA on the tie. Getting a little ahead of yourself, don't you think?"

"Well, maybe Layton didn't choke her, but I'd bet he was an accessory. He wanted to be there when she took her last breath."

"That's speculation."

"Now who sounds like a lawyer?"

Winston's booming voice interrupted their argument as he approached their desks. "I must say, Knight, I'm disappointed."

"Disappointed?" she tossed back.

"We had him. You let him go."

"The evidence wouldn't have been enough to hold up to the district attorney."

"You let me worry about that. I know you like everything in order and want everything to perfectly line up, but real life isn't always like that."

Now he's trying to impart a life lesson?

"Knight, you did your job, what needed to be done. But you've got to stop relying on your gut so much," Winston preached. He turned to Terry and added, "Or women's intuition, as you call it."

Anger rose within her like hot lava. "Let me assure you it's my gut feelings and intuition that makes me who I am, that makes for a good cop. I'll even go so far as to go on record right now and tell you Layton didn't do it."

Winston's face hardened. "Doesn't mean he wasn't involved. We just haven't found the forensic evidence to nail him to the wall. Otherwise, the guy's got motive and opportunity."

"Please don't talk to me like I'm an idiot."

"Knight, I demand respect."

Then earn it!

"As much fun as this conversation is, I've got to go." Madison shoved past Winston and, despite protest from him and Terry, kept walking. She needed a drink, and she rarely needed one. She thought of the perfect place to go.

CHAPTER TWENTY-ONE

The Weathered Rose seemed like it had aged since she was here days ago. Maybe it had something to do with the number of gray-haired patrons tonight. Regardless, they were a rowdy bunch and spoke loudly, trying to talk over the jukebox that blared Blondie's "One Way or Another."

One way or another—that's how she felt about catching the killer. Too bad not everyone at the Stiles PD was playing on the same team with her.

She plopped onto a barstool and flagged down the bartender.

"I answered your questions last time." Justin's eyes scanned the room. They were hard to read, as before, but his body language wasn't: he feared losing his customers due to a cop.

"I'll have Daniels on the rocks," she requested.

"Oh. Rough day?" Justin poured her drink and placed it in front of her. "Must've been one hell of a day. Where's the Beer Man?"

"Actually, on second thought, maybe add a little club soda." She pinched her index finger and thumb to within an inch of each other.

He took the glass back and added the soda. "On the house. Enjoy."

She wasn't in the mood to discuss her partner or offer an explanation, no matter how brief, as to his whereabouts. How could a good cop—a *respectable* cop—shut his eyes to the fact Layton didn't match the epithelial left on the necktie? There was more at stake than closing a case. It was called getting justice.

She took a long draw on her whiskey, and the liquid burned going down her throat. Thoughts of Terry and their different approaches and motivations paraded in her mind as she did some people-watching. One man was working his way around the bar, hitting on women, and blatantly getting shot down. One woman yelled at him, though Madison couldn't make out what it was.

Laura hadn't fought off Photo Guy's attempts. Had her cavalier attitude toward a stranger killed her? Of course, that didn't support a forged photo. Madison juggled two other potential suspects: Layton and his bookie. She really didn't think Layton killed Laura himself, but maybe her rejection had led to him hiring someone to do the deed? And would a bookie go so far as murdering the girlfriend of someone who owed him money? Unlikely.

Madison took another sip, this time welcoming the burn. A waitress went by with an order of chicken wings, and Madison's stomach growled at the smell of them.

"I'll have one of what you're drinkin'." Desperate Romeo sat on the stool next to her.

Maybe if she ignored him, he'd take the hint and get lost.

"I said I'll have one of what you're drinkin'." He bumped her elbow with his.

I'm not in the mood, buddy. She leaned away from him, hoping he could at least read body language.

"All right, that's how it's going to be," he said, rubbing his hands. "I'll have to use my psychic powers. Narrow in on what you've got—" He held a hand over her glass.

She turned to look at him, and he was smiling. Being nice wasn't going to get her point across. "Can you just fuck off?"

His eyes enlarged, and he held up his hands. "Someone takes herself a little too seriously." He slipped off the stool in search of someone else to harass.

Thank God.

She took another sip and felt the booze go straight to her head.

Justin came over. "Everything good? Want another?"

She held her glass at an angle, studied the small amount she had left, debated whether to have any more. "I'd love another. And an order of wings. Mild BBQ."

"You got it." Justin smiled at her, wiped the counter, and walked away.

No doubt he smiled because he recognized her weakness—or maybe her conscience was making her think so. Once she reached a certain point, she could continue drinking until she was cross-eyed. She started to regret having her car outside. Otherwise, she could sit here and drink all night while thinking about the life Laura had lived. She seemed to have so many people who cared about her, including her share of men. Madison had no one. She was all work, no play. She drained the rest of her drink and glanced at the jukebox, actually considering putting some money in and selecting a song.

It was then that two men tucked in a back corner caught her attention. One of them looked like Lou Mann, the man who was in a hurry to leave when she and Terry had come to The Weathered Rose the last time—but she'd need to get closer to be sure. What she could tell was the two men were exchanging something under the table. The dim lighting made it hard to make out what.

She got to her feet, and her head rushed from the alcohol. She took a few deep breaths and set out across the room. She couldn't believe she was this tipsy from one drink.

She stopped next to the jukebox, using it as a cover while she watched the men. It was definitely Mann, and he was with a corporate type who wore a suit, his tie loosened. Both men were now looking up at a baseball game playing on a wall-mounted television. Jeering calls went out in the stadium, signaling the Yankees had lost. Mr. Corporate turned to Mann and said something.

"Your wings are ready," Justin said, walking past and stealing her gaze. "I left them on the bar."

By the time she turned back to look at Mann and Mr. Corporate, they were both gone.

Damn.

She headed back to her stool, cursing herself for missing the opportunity to talk to Mann. Then again, she really wasn't in any shape to conduct an interview, no matter how casual. Maybe tonight she'd actually take some time away from the case. After all, she was entitled to enjoy a taste of frivolity. Still, she wondered what she'd just witnessed and if it had meant anything.

She traced her fingertips up and down the glass and watched the world slow down around her.

CHAPTER TWENTY-TWO

Madison woke up the next morning with an epiphany about what Mann had been doing with Mr. Corporate, and she decided that it could have a bearing on the case. She tried to reach Terry, but his phone kept going to voice mail, so she'd go about her next stop solo—again.

She pulled the department car in front of Sandra's house and waved to Higgins.

"Hey, beautiful." He was such a charmer and ever so innocent.

"So you're stuck here again?"

"Again? Try *still*." He smiled. He didn't care. He loved his job. Even shitty details like this, as he'd put it before.

Madison's phone chimed notification of a new message. She pulled it out—a text from Jennifer, who specialized in serology.

No poison. Laura's BAC came back at 53 mg.

BAC stood for blood alcohol concentration, but she didn't know if 53 mg meant Laura was intoxicated or not.

She'd call Cynthia for clarification later, but she needed to do something else first. She took a step in the direction of Sandra's house, and her phone rang. Caller ID showed it was Cynthia.

She answered, "Knight."

Cynthia started, "Okay, I have some news for—"

"I hope so, or you're wasting my time."

The line fell silent for a moment. "Maddy, you're the only one I'd put up with all this shit from, you know that?" There was slight amusement in Cynthia's voice. "The trace from the Laura's fingernails showed the normal things such as food residue, hair products, but there was also a trace of epithelial not belonging to the victim."

"Does it match to anything else from the crime scene—Oh, right, the stupid machine is down."

"I'll be sending it over to the lab this morning."

"Speaking of the lab, any update on the towel?"

Cynthia went quiet.

"What aren't you telling me?"

"For one, I'm happy this conversation is taking place over the phone."

"Cyn," Madison prompted.

"The third-party lab lost the towel."

"What?" Madison spat.

"They assure me they have everyone looking for it."

"A line of bullshit to cover up 'it's gone for good.'"

"Don't know what else to say."

"Guess there isn't much. Shit…" Madison would have to figure out another way to identify the man in the photo. Their conversation had paused for a few seconds before Madison continued. "I just got a message from Jennifer about Laura's blood alcohol being 53 milligrams. What does that mean exactly?"

"It means she would have been feeling pretty good."

"So she was drunk," Madison concluded, not sure what to make of this knowledge. "All right, well, I've gotta go." She hung up and felt paralyzed. How the hell had the lab lost the towel?

"I'm guessing that wasn't good news," Higgins called out to her.

"You could say that."

"Something to do with your absent partner?"

"My partner is—" Her phone rang again, and she answered without looking at caller ID.

"I left a voice mail," Winston said. "A few minutes ago now."

Wow, a whole few *minutes?*

"I was on the phone," she said, endeavoring to keep her tone even.

"Where are you?" Winston asked.

She bit her tongue.

"Is Terry with you?"

She considered faking static and a bad connection, but partners had each other's backs. "Yes," she replied, not knowing if he'd buy it. She wasn't a good actress.

"All right. You get something. Update me."

"Always do."

"We both know that isn't true."

"I just find more value in *doing* than talking."

"I don't want any snide remarks, Knight. I want answers."

"Well, I…" She paused and corrected herself to keep up her earlier lie. "*We've* got a new lead. I'll let you know how it plays out." She hung up, not caring if he considered the conversation over.

"You must want to ditch your cell some days." Higgins had an arm hanging out the window and tapped the door panel.

"You have no idea."

Layton cracked the door open just far enough to peek through. His eyes widened in recognition at the sight of her, and he opened the door all the way. "Detective?"

"Can I come in?"

"Sure." He stepped back, making room for her to enter.

A blast of heat rushed out of the house, like it had when she'd been here talking to Sandra before, but it also carried the smell of bacon and fried potatoes. Her bagel with cream cheese was long gone, and the aroma made her stomach growl.

He led her to a living room with a tweed couch, where he sat, and he directed her to a leather swivel chair with an ottoman.

She declined the invitation. "I'm not going to be long."

"Suit yourself."

She'd get out of the house as fast as she possibly could. Two oscillating fans whirled in the corner of the room, but they weren't making a difference. Either Sandra didn't have central air, or it was on the fritz. She inhaled deeply, trying to derive a satisfying breath.

"Ah, you're hot. You get used to it." He studied her face. "What can I do for you, Detective?"

"Lou Mann," she put out as bait.

"Who?" His brow wrinkled as if he was confused, but she wasn't buying it.

"Your bookie," Madison concluded. The exchange under the table at The Weathered Rose, combined with the men's interest in the baseball game on TV, had allowed her to put two and two together.

"I don't know that name. Lou Mann."

"You meet your bookie at The Weathered Rose. Am I right? He has a thing for leather vests and has a paunch. He's an older guy."

"Yeah, I know that guy, but it's not Lou."

"You know him by another name?"

Silence.

"But he is your bookie?"

More silence.

"He could have killed Laura," she said, hoping to prompt some humanity in him.

Layton chewed on his bottom lip.

Her cell rang, and she tore her eyes from Layton to glance at the caller ID. She rejected the call and addressed Layton. "One way I can find out is I'll bring Mr. Mann downtown for questioning, tell him you led us to—"

"Fine, yes, that guy's my bookie, but I don't know him as Lou. I know him as Mick. But, please, don't drag him in."

She was never good at doing what she was told to do…

. . .

Terry walked into the observation room and glanced at Lou Mann in the neighboring interrogation room. His gaze drifted over Winston but fixed on Madison. "Can we talk?"

"Sure." She barely made it to the hallway before Terry spoke.

"You act on your own now?" he hissed. His face was red, and a twitch kept a constant beat in his cheek.

Madison felt her earlobes heat with anger. "I tried to reach you."

"I know, and I called you back. You shuffled my call to voice mail."

She hadn't been in the mood to speak with him when his name popped up on caller ID. So what? "You do realize that I put my ass on the line for yours? I told the sarge…" She paused and worked to compose herself. She continued in a lower voice. "I told him you were with me this morning when I spoke with Layton and, later, when I picked up Lou Mann."

"You should have left a message for me."

"You call me back *once*, but you do have a call log? You should have a slew of missed calls from me. Maybe you should just answer your damned phone."

Terry held up a hand. "You have no idea what's going on with me right now."

"Your choice," she barked. "Whatever your issue is, it's carried on long enough. You're running off and taking umpteen personal calls—and that's when you're here. Leave your personal problems at home like everyone else."

Terry's didn't say anything, and though hostility flickered in his eyes, there was also sadness.

She felt regret at her harsh words and sighed. "You do know you can talk to me."

His gaze hardened to stone. "Just mind your own business, Maddy."

Oh, you're infuriating!

"When it affects a case, it is my business." She paused, considering her next words. "And you don't *talk* to me anymore; you accuse me." His eyes remained fixed on hers. She could hardly believe the self-restraint she was able to muster and the peaceable approach she felt inclined to extend. She told herself it wasn't her character weakening. It was because it was Terry. "What's going on?" she dared to ask again.

The question hung in the air for a solid forty seconds.

He sighed and rubbed his temple. "Can I claim PMS? I mean, it works for you women." A partial smile tugged at the edges of his lips.

"Shut up, Terry." She considered punching him but decided against it. "Such a sexist thing to say—and by the way, that excuse never works."

After another thirty seconds or so of silence, he said, "It's Annabelle. Maybe you made the right choice not to get married."

She'd had suspicions there was trouble in paradise but hearing him essentially confirming that made her speechless.

"I open up to you and…silence?" He threw his arms in the air. "I mean, what could you possibly say anyhow?"

He had crossed a line, his offhanded comment implying that she couldn't possibly understand relationship issues. "You don't think I have anything to say because I'm single? Wow."

"Forget I said anything."

"I don't know what to say," she admitted. Sure, marriage sounded suffocating to her, but that was beside the point. Terry seemed to need the age-old institution to feel fulfilled. "I thought you guys were each other's best friends." She hoped he'd open up to her and not walk away.

"Don't patronize me. You must have had a clue," he said bitterly, his defense back up.

She didn't respond, and eventually, his face softened as his eyes filled with tears. Madison's chest sank.

"Up until recently, we were…" Terry's voice cracked.

So what had caused the rift? Had Annabelle cheated on him? She wasn't about to pry that far, but Annabelle didn't strike her as a cheater—although things change, people change. All Madison knew was it had to be something pretty huge to be tearing them apart like this. Terry walked toward the interrogation room before she could ask more questions. She shrugged to herself and followed. After all, they had a job to do.

Madison sat down at the table and opened a file folder in front of her, and Terry went to the back of the room, where he leaned against the wall and jangled change in his pocket.

"For the record, your legal name is Lou Mann?" Madison said.

"What is this about? The gambling? You can't prove anything." Mann took off a baseball cap, scratched his head, and put it back in place.

Some criminals just aren't that bright…

"You go by the name Mick," she said, giving him the name Layton had provided. It yielded no reaction. "Let's get to the point: last week, a young woman was murdered, and you're a suspect."

He laughed. "That's insane." He looked around. "Where's the hidden camera? Am I being punked? It's got to be here somewhere."

"Where were you last Saturday night through to Sunday morning?"

"At the track."

"That's your alibi?"

"It's not illegal to place bets for yourself, last time I checked."

"Sure, but that's not all you do." Madison crossed her arms on the table and leaned forward. "You take other people's money and place bets."

"You can't prove a thing."

"You brought up the gambling right away," she said, amused. "And we have someone who will testify to your taking money on their behalf." She intentionally left it gender neutral.

Mann's gaze met Madison's. There was anger in his eyes, but did that mean he was a murderer? If only the eyes really were the window to the soul, her job would be a lot easier. Still, according to what she knew so far, he was one nasty bastard.

"This person claims you broke into his house and left a note," she said.

Silence.

Madison sat back. "Now you're not going to talk?"

"I didn't do anything to no one."

"We've heard you have a temper, cut off people's fingers when they don't pay their debts to you."

Mann laughed hard enough that tears pooled in the corners of his eyes. "Cut…fingers…" His words interspersed with his laughter.

"I don't see how that's funny, Mr. Mann."

"I hate blood." He was snorting, trying to stifle laughter.

His confession brought a graphic image to her mind of severed fingers—of blood. Madison swallowed. If he felt anywhere close to how she did about blood, he couldn't have severed the fingers. Still, she had to focus. "You said you were at the race track," she said, focusing on his alibi. "You were there from what times?"

"From about ten Saturday until eight Sunday morning. They also have a small-slot casino."

Madison tapped the file on the table, and then got up and left. She found Winston in the observation room.

"Are you letting him go?" Winston asked.

She shook her head. "Not until his alibi checks out, but I think he's telling the truth."

"How do you know from that brief meeting?"

"Just a feeling," she dished out, not giving a crap how that would fly. No one could know about her distaste for blood.

CHAPTER TWENTY-THREE

Mann's alibi checked out, and with no way to prove his involvement, Madison cut him loose. She worked hard to convince herself that Laura's case wouldn't become like her cold case: the defense attorney shot down in his own driveway—one bullet to his chest, the other to his forehead, execution style. The hardest part about that investigation was knowing the Russian Mafia was involved but having no way of proving it. She promised one day she'd find that man justice, but until then, she had to live with the guilt of failure.

In Laura's case, though, maybe if Terry were actually around and not continually running off, they'd have caught the killer by now.

Her desk phone rang, and she answered.

"Please tell me you've got her killer," the female caller said.

It took a few seconds for Madison pin the voice, but it was Mrs. Saunders.

The woman continued. "The paper says someone was brought in for questioning. Is it that Jeff guy? Why didn't you call us?"

Madison briefly pinched her eyes shut. The damned media. "Please know I'm doing all I can to have the right man held responsible." She noticed how she hadn't included Terry in her summation but wasn't about to correct herself. She felt like she was working this case alone.

"You don't think he did it." Mrs. Saunders started to sob, and there was a garbled voice coming through behind her.

"What is this nonsense my wife's saying?" Mr. Saunders took over the call.

Madison softened her tone. "All I can say is Laura's murderer will be held accountable." She massaged her temple with her free hand. "You have my word on that." And there it was—the solemn oath that drove any respectable cop—spoken aloud. She liked to think no matter how many times she made that promise it still carried meaning. "I'll call you, Mr. Saunders, once there's anything new to share. You have my—"

"I know. I have your word." He hung up.

The tone of a dead line delivered mixed emotions. She poured her heart and soul into this job and sacrificed a social life for the sake of justice—and this unappreciative attitude was her reward? She felt like she'd been slapped in the face. Maybe it was time to take a breather.

She pulled out her cell phone and picked Cynthia from her contacts. She answered on the second ring.

"Tell me you can get together tonight and just hang," Madison said.

"Sure. Say seven?"

"Sounds good," Madison said, but she wished tonight had worked out. She added, "My place, food delivery, chick flicks…"

"Sure."

"And wine," Madison tagged on.

"Now you *really* have me."

They both laughed, but it was broken by Winston calling out Madison's name. "I've got to go," she groaned. She hung up and turned to face both Winston and her partner. Seeing them together made her question Terry's loyalties.

"Layton is threatening a lawsuit for harassment," Winston said.

"Really?" Madison was shocked, given how he'd been so friendly to her when she'd shown up at Sandra's house. Maybe this was payback for bringing in Mann, assuming he somehow found out.

"Really," Winston stamped home.

"Well, good luck to him." She'd recovered from her shock and was angry.

"Maybe you shouldn't have kept him so long."

She grinded her teeth. "The only reason we held him so long, *Sergeant*, is because of the two of you." Madison butted her head toward Terry. "I would have let him go sooner, but Terry wanted to hold off releasing him. It was you and Terry pushing me on Layton so we could just close the case."

"There's no need to take that tone," Winston snarled. "Maybe you should take a few days off and relax."

"In the middle of an investigation?" she gasped.

"There's always going to be one—"

"Fine. Then you know what? I will take you up on that." She shrugged her shoulders. "Was kind of thinking of taking a break anyway." She stomped off.

Maybe she was overreacting, maybe she was taking things too personally, but that's what made her who she was. She wasn't some embodiment of an unfeeling individual. Her work was her lifeblood. It coursed through her and made her great at what she did. If they couldn't respect that aspect about her, then they missed the full picture.

CHAPTER TWENTY-FOUR

"You actually took time off?" Cynthia was tucked into the corner of Madison's couch with her legs tucked beneath her.

"And that's hard to believe?" Madison took a sip of her wine. She hadn't exactly told Cynthia how she'd ended up with some free time.

"Coming from you, yes, it is."

"Maybe it's time to change who I am," she said with a shrug.

Cynthia pressed her lips together. "Now it sounds like you're pouting."

"Fine, I was backed into a corner," she confessed. "But I am a little burned-out lately."

"But that's the state you thrive in."

Madison knew she should just tell her friend the real reason she'd ended up with time off—pride. But she was too…proud.

Before she could say another word, she saw a smirk tugging at the corners of Cynthia's mouth.

"Oh, I know what it is. I get it. You're taking time off to prove a point," Cynthia said.

"'Prove a point?'" She waved a hand of dismissal, not willing to admit how close her friend was to the truth.

"Yeah." Cynthia pressed her lips and nodded. "The Madison I know always has to prove a point, be the one to have the last—"

"You think you know me so well." Madison narrowed her eyes, though she had to admit Cynthia might know her better than she knew herself.

Cynthia smiled at her and circled a finger around Madison's face. "It's your eyes that give you away. You were proving a point." She drained the rest of her wine and set her glass on the coffee table. "But there are some things I don't know."

Madison didn't like the mischievous look in her friend's eyes. "I don't want to ask."

"Well, there is one thing I'm dying to know, and every time I bring it up, you clam right up or find a way of changing the subject." Madison started to speak, but Cynthia held up her hand. "What is the deal with you and Toby Sovereign?"

Madison lifted her wineglass, a *fish bowl*, that was nearly empty from its second refill. She downed the remainder and said, "Still haven't had enough."

"Come on."

"Begging doesn't suit you, Cyn." She smiled at her friend, her eyes drifting to the television where *An Affair to Remember* played at a low volume. Both women had been talking so much, the show had mostly served as background noise. Madison pointed to the screen as if she wanted to catch the scene, but she was really just avoiding the question.

Nickie Ferrante was desperately appealing to Terry McKay, working his charm and trying to make her forget her fiancé in a moment of weakness. The whole idea of a playboy using his charisma to manipulate a woman—how was it that some women could be so gullible? Maybe it was the alcohol, but her heart skipped a beat. She glanced over at Cynthia, who was watching her. "Look." Madison pointed again at Cary Grant. "Can you believe Terry was named after him? A Casanova?" She laughed...and sighed with relief when Cynthia did, too.

"That's really where he got his name from?"

"Yep. His mom was a fan of Cary Grant, but his dad refused to let his son be called Cary. Said people would confuse it with a girl's name. Not that Terry is that much better." Madison chuckled.

"That's hilarious. The Stiles PD has their very own Casanova. You should start calling him that."

"I think he'd kill me."

"You're probably right. But I guess Terry must have had the Casanova effect on his wife."

"At least at one time," Madison blurted out and instantly wished she could reel the words back. "Refill?" She got up with her glass, grabbed Cynthia's, and went to the kitchen, which was a stone's throw from the living room.

Cynthia didn't answer her.

"What about a cigarette?" Madison never typically encouraged Cynthia's smoking habit, but she didn't want to get into Terry's marriage problems, either.

"They're having problems?" Cynthia turned and looked at Madison over the back of the couch.

As her mom would say: *out of the frying pan, into the fire.*

"Forget I said anything." Madison poured wine into their glasses.

"You're kidding, right? I'm just supposed to forget?"

"Yes." Madison plastered on a toothy grin.

"Oh man, shut that mouth."

"What?"

"Your teeth are purple." Cynthia pointed at the red wine. "Been drinking a little, missy?"

"Hey, no more than you. And speaking of teeth…" She needed to stop drinking.

Cynthia's eyes widened. "Oh, yes, Mr. Bright White."

"Shut up." Of course, Cynthia picked up on her reference— the beautiful ME, Cole Richards, and his bright white teeth. They had to be fake.

"Yep, it's love."

Madison tossed an empty takeout container toward her, and Cynthia raised her arms to fend off the projectile.

"Please, I'll have you know he's a happily married man," Madison said.

"So he is, but Terry isn't?"

"How are we back to that?" Madison made a show of looking around her kitchen. "I don't have any more small containers over here. Next time, it will be something heavy."

"It's not like it's hard to read between the lines here. Besides my detective skills are well honed, thanks to you."

"Don't blame me for your shoddy ability."

Cynthia hurried toward her, and Madison moved.

"Now, would I ever hit you..." Cynthia's voice dripped with sarcasm.

Madison enlarged her eyes and went to step back. But Cynthia caught her and jabbed her right shoulder. "At least your detective skills are in better condition than your reaction time."

With another mention of Madison's job title, the lightheartedness from the wine transformed into serious reflection and her heart sank.

"And you've gone back to work."

Madison handed Cynthia a topped-off glass.

"You need to let work go when you're not on shift," Cynthia said.

"This isn't a job I can turn on and off. It stays with me—haunts me, if you want to call it that—twenty-four seven, three sixty-five. It's like oxygen to me." She inhaled deeply as if to emphasize her point. She just wanted to find Laura's killer and get her hands on the man in that photo—whether he was their killer or not. "My job is, sad to say, my life."

Cynthia opened her mouth, closed it, opened it, closed it.

"See. Even *you* have nothing to say."

A sinister grin encompassed Cynthia's face. "You need to get laid."

Madison choked on her wine; burgundy mist spewed into the air before she reached the sink to spit out the rest of her mouthful. She thought about the man who had done his best to hit on her earlier in the week at the bar. Yeah, she'd keep that to herself. "I tell you I have no life, and your first response is I need sex?"

Cynthia nodded.

Madison laughed, shook her head, and looked up at the ceiling. "Where do I meet these people?"

"People, Maddy, or *men*? Anywhere. In a bar, grocery shopping, online—"

Madison reciprocated the punch her friend had given her earlier. "By people, I really meant you. What kind of person tells someone else that they need sex?"

"A good friend. Here I am thinking of your best interests, and this is the thanks I get." Cynthia did a poor job of acting slighted when her performance was cut off by a purple, toothy grin of her own. She went back to the couch and proceeded to lie on her side and snuggle her head into a throw pillow. "I'm sleeping over."

"Oh, you think so, huh?"

No response.

"Cyn?" When Madison got no reply, she walked around the front of the couch to see her friend had already fallen asleep.

"Guess we're getting too old for this," Madison whispered, turning off the electronics in the room and hitting the lights. She took her wineglass to her bedroom.

She had a few more sips and got under the sheets. As she lay there, she was more wired than tired. Her eyes were wide open, searching the dark corners of her room. A chill ran through her, and she lifted the covers and burrowed all but the top of her head beneath them.

Nighttime was the enemy. With it came all the distorted, twisted people bent on violence and destruction. Goose bumps rose over her body. Laura would have seen her death coming. She would have faced it. And Photo Guy…

Her thought stopped short of conclusion. All she knew was she had to find him.

His feelings of anger against the world, the awkwardness of his first murder, were subsiding. They were being replaced with an intense amount of grief, remorse, and possible regret. But for once in his life, he had to prove himself. He couldn't allow himself to stop now, weaken. The time had come.

He had performed a favor, making for one less thankless person in the world. One less person to cause pain and suffering to another. One more person closer to his next target, his true target, the one who was to blame for everything. The one who had caused all of this. The one who had created him and made him who he was becoming.

He sat on the edge of his bed, fanning fingers through his hair. Sunlight was starting to spill around the curtains, but the room appeared hazy. But he knew it was just his hangover playing with his eyes. He'd tried to drown his memories of taking a life, of her begging for mercy, of the feel of her spirit leaving her body, in the hopes of catching some sleep. Flashbacks hit him even during the day now. It exhausted him. But he had no choice: he had to follow through with his plan. For sanity's sake, but more importantly, for justice's sake. He couldn't be the loser this time. The thought of that was simply unacceptable.

Instead, he needed to focus on the rush and liberation that came with killing. How in the moment of the act, he loved being the one with the control, the one with the power, the one playing God, as the expression goes.

Who has the right to decide life or death? I do.

Who has made the world a better place? I did.

He'd chant those words to keep himself moving forward. He had to. Today demanded that he take care of the next one on his list, another beautiful woman. Yet one deserving to have the breath squeezed from her body.

CHAPTER TWENTY-FIVE

"Someone better be dead." Madison reached for her phone on the nightstand. Was one day to sleep in too much to ask for?

She couldn't get a grip on the phone—like her hand didn't want to work—and it fell to the floor. Still ringing.

She caught the time on her alarm clock as she leaned over the bed to snatch the phone. *9:03 AM.*

"Knight," she said breathlessly, and her greeting met with nothing. The call must have been shuffled to voice mail.

She was mid-yawn when the phone started ringing again. She dropped back her head back onto her pillow and answered, "Knight."

"It's Terry."

Hearing his voice brought Friday back and how he'd seemed aligned with the sergeant. "I'm taking time off, remember?" she said bitterly. She was about to hang up when he spoke.

"A woman's body was found on Bradshaw Trail."

Bradshaw Trail ran through the city from east to west. "What part specifically?"

"Where it winds through Mitchell Park. You know where the woods are to the north side of it?"

"I'll meet you there—"

"The vic's only in her mid-thirties."

"Stop there. I'll gather the rest at the scene. You know how I like to work." She preferred to keep an open mind before arriving on scene so as not to speculate too much beforehand.

"Wait," he rushed out, "there's something you will want to know."

She sighed loudly. "What, Terry?"

"The victim has a Gallo & Costa tie around her neck."

Madison couldn't maneuver her way through the mass of lazy Sunday drivers fast enough. And, unfortunately, the slow-moving traffic caused her to do exactly what she didn't want to: speculate. The fact the murder involved another G&C necktie was too much to ignore—and it meant her thoughts that Laura's murder had been an isolated incident was incorrect. And with no mention of G&C ties in the media, it ruled out a copycat. Were they looking at a repeat murderer, possibly the start of a serial killer?

Both victims were women. The killer—running with the assumption they had all along, that it was a man—could have easily overpowered them, but what was his motive? Was he wronged by a woman at some point in his life? Was it these women in particular that drew him for some reason? Regardless, his choice to strangle these women spoke to an incredibly personal wound. He was getting revenge of some sort, and with the tightening of the tie, he'd feel a sense of power, control. It was certainly an intimate killing method. He would feel their last breath on his arms. The thought sent chills through her.

And with a second body on their hands, it would seem the killer was escalating and becoming less inhibited. Tag onto that, he'd risked exposure by coming out from the seclusion of a house and into a public place.

Terry had told her the body was where the trail went through Mitchell Park. She headed to the lot for the park. Gravel crunched under the tires, spewing dust into the air, and she caught a glimpse in the rearview mirror. Terry was pulling in behind her.

She couldn't see the body, but a couple of uniformed officers stood at the north edge of the parking lot, speaking with two young girls sitting on a bench. From their body language, she knew they must have found the body. One of them was gesturing animatedly while the other was leaned forward with her face cradled in her hands, rocking back and forth.

"Hey, Maddy." Terry performed a light jog to catch up to her, but she kept walking.

"I didn't pick sides," he said.

"Sure seems like you did," she tossed back.

He just shook his head and walked past her.

Before they got to the bench, a third officer came toward them. He barely looked twenty. "Her name is Heather Olivia Nguyen, age thirty-five, married. She lives at 86 Springbrook Crescent. No children. She holds a job as general manager at Wow FX. They're a special-effects company for the entertainment industry. Fog machines, snow machines, stuff like that. Anyway, I'm FOS."

"FOS?" Madison asked.

"Yeah, first officer on scene," he said as if it was self-explanatory.

Damn acronyms. The world was becoming obsessed with them. Before people knew it, laughing would be replaced by saying "LOL."

"Those two found the vic?" She nodded toward the girls on the bench.

"Yes, about forty minutes ago. The body's over there." He pointed to where the trail rounded a bend and dipped down.

"Anything else to tell us?" Madison asked.

"The girls both claim they've never seen her before, and by the way they're shaking, I'd say they weren't involved."

"Yes, that would seem obvious." The words came off so clipped she felt like a bitch for saying them. She needed more sleep, to be able to crawl back into bed, and get back to that good dream she was having. Too late for that, though. "We'll have to speak to them. I assume you called Crime Scene and the ME?"

The officer nodded. "Same time as you."

She stepped in the direction of the body, when the officer spoke again. "By the way, it's Officer Tendum."

Madison nodded. His name didn't matter to her as she'd probably forget it in five minutes. So many uniforms, and she preferred to keep her mind free for her investigations.

She rounded the bend in the walkway and could hear one of the girls crying loudly. It stabbed at Madison's heart, but she had to filter out the noise and focus.

She took a few deep breaths. Another victim, about the same age as herself. Thoughts of her own mortality struck, as they always seemed to do during these moments. But this woman's life had been stolen from her, and that alone made Madison hungry for justice.

The victim was lying supine in the middle of the paved trail. A row of bushes about seven feet tall stood to the right of her and blocked view of her from the parking lot. The soles of her feet were facing away from Madison. Her arms were not posed in front of her torso, like Laura's had been, but lay at her sides.

Is the killer out of remorse?

A Mace sprayer was on the ground beside the body. She'd had some time to react to her attacker, but it had done her no good. He'd come at her with intent and purpose.

Like most murder scenes, an eerie silence encompassed the surrounding area, despite the amount of activity taking place. There was a thick quality to the air that impacted the severity of what had transpired. Some believed it was the ghost of the deceased, but Madison gave no consideration to that. It was simply the heavy reminder that we are all mortal. The body that had once housed a breathing soul, personality, life force, would never be heard again…silenced for all time.

As Madison rounded the victim, she focused on her face. She was Asian, unlike Laura who was Caucasian. But like Laura, her eyes were open, and petechial hemorrhaging dotted them. They weren't as milky as Laura's had been, and her body appeared somewhat flexible. Rigor hadn't set in yet.

The woman appeared underweight. Her running outfit looked expensive, indicating regularity and an investment in her health.

Madison had to wonder why he'd chosen this woman. She was in the same age range as Laura, but at first impression, there was nothing else that overtly connected the women.

Her gaze fell to the tie, which was striped like the one used to strangle Laura, but in shades of green not blue. Such a beautiful piece of fabric to be used as an instrument of death…

Terry stood beside her. "At least this victim—"

"Heather," she corrected. Saying the names, thinking of the victims as people delivered more urgency. That was not something she'd picked up from police training, which instilled the importance of detachment and keeping a distance. Chalk it up to a problem with authority and direction, but to her, a name versus a label made the difference of the dead being a body, or the dead having been a *person*—someone's child, someone's lover or best friend. The latter was what gave her purpose and strength to continue. Otherwise, she could become so weighed down with the specifics of a case the severity of what happened would be blurred.

"Well, at least Heather hasn't been here too long," Terry said, cutting into her thoughts. "That should put us closer to the killer."

"We'll see." She was terrified of being too hopeful.

They made their way toward the two girls, who looked to be teenagers. Their faces were both blotchy, eyes bloodshot. One of them wore braces and had a spread of acne on her forehead; the other was easily fifty pounds overweight (which might as well have been two hundred at her age) and had a small gap between her two front teeth.

"Hi, girls. I'm Detective Madison Knight, and this is Detective Terry Grant. What are your names?"

"Tiffany Allen," the heavier girl said, then looked at her friend.

The second girl wet her lips and fought for a voice. "Julie Duncan."

"We understand that you were the ones to find the woman?"

Julie started sobbing, and Tiffany nodded.

"What time?"

"Maybe a half hour ago now," Tiffany said. "We never jog but thought we'd start today." She reached for her friend's hand.

"When you found her, what did you do?"

Julie sniffled. "Screamed. Pitched a fit. I was saying over and over again, 'OMG, OMG.'"

Not omigod; the actual letters...

"Did you touch her, move her?" Madison cocked her head.

Both girls scrunched up their faces and answered in unison. "No way."

"See anyone else in the park this morning or along the trail?"

"There was someone," Tiffany said.

Madison perked up and was about to say something when the crunching of gravel announced the arrival of more vehicles. She glanced at the lot. It was Crime Scene, Richards, the sergeant—and the chief.

Crap! Chief McAlexandar made Winston look like a walk in the park.

Madison turned back to Tiffany. "You said you saw someone?"

She nodded. "Don't you remember, Julie?" She nudged her friend's elbow.

Julie was focused on the ground and quaking. "Kind of." Her voice was barely audible.

"Tiffany, I cannot stress how important it is that you tell me who you saw," Madison said, applying some pressure.

"He was handsome." Tiffany faced Julie. "You don't remember?"

Julie's eyes rested on the ground. "Like I said, a little."

"When we got here, he was pulling out of a spot right there." Tiffany pointed to a parking spot near the trail. "He stopped moving and rolled down his passenger window and winked at me." She blushed.

"Describe him."

"Besides handsome?" She attempted a smile, but it faltered. "Brown hair, short. Think he had brown eyes, and he appeared to have a nice build. I mean from what I could tell through the window."

Madison reached into her pocket and pulled out a picture of Photo Guy. Terry shook his head.

"That's him!" Tiffany exclaimed. Her excitement faded, and she raised a hand to cover her mouth, then dropped it. "You think maybe he…he killed that lady?"

The answer was an emphatic *yes*. Madison felt Terry's eyes on her, but she kept hers trained on Tiffany. The adrenaline rush that came with narrowing in on this bastard nearly stole her breath. But she had to hold it together. "What kind of car?" she asked matter-of-factly.

"It was older. A Honda Accord, I think. Gray, silver." Tiffany's eyes went up and to the right, which told Madison she was telling the truth.

"What year do you figure the car was?"

"I'm a girl and not into cars. Thought I was doing good knowing the make and model."

Madison bit her tongue. Gender had nothing to do with her lack of vehicle knowledge. "Did you see the license plate?"

"I did," Julie said, "but I can only remember part of it. A…V…L." Each letter came out slowly and with hesitation.

"AVL?" Madison prompted.

"Yeah, I think so. There were numbers in there, too, but I can't remember them."

"It's really important, Julie, if you can remember any more."

Julie sighed. "Sorry."

"No, it's okay. This is helpful," Madison said, trying a softer approach, feeling for her. "You said he was just leaving when you got here, and that wasn't long before you found the woman, right?"

"That's right," Tiffany said.

Madison put a hand on Terry's shoulder, moved off to the side with him. "We need to get a BOLO issued."

He nodded.

They were potentially an hour or a little more behind Photo Guy, but he could easily be a hundred miles away at this point.

CHAPTER TWENTY-SIX

He pounded the steering wheel with his hands. Was every elderly person out for a leisurely drive today? He lit up a smoke at the fifth red light. His hands were unsteady when he lifted it to take a drag. Murder two, complete. The thought brought with it liberation and conviction to stay the course. The second kill was easier, but part of him feared it had been a mistake to wink at the overweight girl. He'd replayed it repeatedly in his mind in the last hour. He should have just left and gotten out of Dodge.

But his attention surely would have made the heavier girl's day—both of those girls, for that matter. They were obvious outcasts. He had done them a kindness by making them feel good about themselves. After all, he knew what it was like to be judged unworthy, unlovable.

It had been careless, though. He'd made himself memorable.

He rubbed the stubble on his face, brooding over his error in judgment and then releasing himself from its shackles. His emotions were all over the place, ranging from fear to euphoria.

If he was going to keep going, he had to focus on the good that would come out of the murders and keep his mind on his primary target. She was the reason he was doing all this practice, and the killing would only stop on his time schedule, on his terms. He was the one with the control. And when he did kill his final mark, the satisfaction that would come with it would exceed the others. He was almost too excited to wait any longer.

"Knight," Chief McAlexandar called out to her. She turned to see him coming toward her, his long strides quickly eating up ground and his height dwarfing Winston, who was walking next to him.

"Chief," she said, a wave of hopelessness setting in. McAlexandar had been her sergeant before he became police chief, and it was starting to feel like this man would always be her superior. Him taking an early retirement was apparently too much to wish for.

"Another body," he said in an accusing tone and came to a stop in front of her. He looked down at her, and while his six-foot-four frame would intimidate most, it didn't her. "What are we looking at now? I understand the MO lines up with the Saunders murder. You concluded that was an isolated incident. So much for that damned theory. Make sure we find this guy before there's a third victim and this graduates to a serial."

As if it's my fault some lunatic is out there killing women!

"Suspects," McAlexandar punched out, and she wasn't sure if it was a statement or a question. He had a tendency to leave her guessing most of the time. He cocked his head and raised his brows.

So, it was a question…

"Yes, we do, Chief," she replied.

He braced his hands on his hips, and his blue eyes hardened, focused on her. She felt a moment of sympathy for Winston—just the briefest of seconds. Maybe Winston was simply guilty of flinging shit down the ladder. McAlexandar was in Winston's face; Winston was in hers.

Madison handed him the image of Photo Guy. "We don't have a name for him yet, but his face keeps showing up at the crime scenes. That's a copy of a framed picture that was on Laura Saunders's nightstand, and now—" she gestured toward the teenage girls "—they've identified him as leaving from this parking lot just as they'd arrived. It seems it would be around the time of the murder, but we'll need to wait on Richards to know for sure. The girls also provided us with a make and model of car and a partial plate. We need to—"

"Have a BOLO issued," McAlexandar interrupted.

"Yeah," she said bitterly, as if she didn't know how the hell to do her job. "Terry was just about to—"

"What are you waiting for?" McAlexandar cut in and turned to Terry, glanced at Winston. Both men didn't move. "Well…" the chief prompted.

Winston and Terry stepped away to discuss the particulars and get the bulletin issued.

"You've had this picture all along?" The chief waved the photo as if he were trying to flag down a car.

It was too late to put the cat back in the bag; she'd already told him it had been on Saunders's nightstand. "Yes, but—"

"She had no reason to think the Saunders case was anything more than an isolated incident," Terry interjected, coming to her defense, and walking back to her and the chief. "I admit I didn't see any merit in the photo, but it's a good thing she did."

She didn't know whether to be appreciative of Terry's stepping in or angry with him. She could handle the chief herself.

McAlexandar watched the two of them for a few seconds, then said, "We need to get on this."

"I realize that, Chief, but we can't go running all over the city in a panic to apprehend a suspect, either." The words tumbled out of her; she been thrown by Terry's jumping to her defense.

"I am not suggesting we cause *a panic*," he countered, the last two words full of derision. He pointed a finger at her. "However, I do suggest you get answers and quick. I want to know where this case rests by the end of the day." The chief walked away with the photo still in his hand.

Terry turned to Winston and fed him the details for the BOLO, and Winston left.

"You didn't need to do that," she said after the sergeant was well out of earshot.

"I know I didn't *need* to." Terry shrugged. "But maybe you were right to be suspicious of Photo Guy."

"Time will tell." She walked away, needing to put some space between her and her partner and the interaction she'd had with McAlexandar. She headed for Richards and was pleased Terry didn't follow. If he had, she couldn't be held accountable for what she might do. The chief had frayed her last nerve, and she wanted to punch something—or *someone*—and that would be a surefire CLM, a career-limiting move.

Richards stood back from the body, waiting for Mark and Jennifer to gather evidence. There was no sign of Cynthia. Maybe she was still tucked in on Madison's couch. When Madison had tried to wake her, she hadn't even groaned, but her chest was rising and falling, so Madison knew she was alive. When her friend woke up, she'd be in pain. Madison was fortunate she had some tolerance when it came to alcohol. "At least we have a fresher body this time," Madison said to Richards.

He played along. "Yes, she looks pretty *fresh*."

"You're here fast," she said, her heartrate slowing down; the ME had a soothing presence.

"Honestly—" He snapped his mouth shut. "Oh, you're going to hate me. It will sound so selfish."

"What?"

"Well, Sunday is my golfing day…"

She nodded slowly, hoping he wouldn't see through her and realize she already knew that.

He went on. "I'd like to get things wrapped up sooner than later. You know what I mean."

"Oh, I know what you mean," was what she said—even if she didn't know. "The chief wants answers today."

"Of course he does."

The conversation stalled for a few seconds, but Madison knew he was likely thinking the same thing as she was: the chief would leave the crime scene, return to his home unaffected, and settle into his leather chair, likely with a brandy snifter in hand.

"Ah, maybe we'll be lucky. He'll go home, have a few drinks, forget all about this," Richards said as if reading her mind.

"Yeah, we're not that lucky." Madison laughed and, with the sound of it echoing back to her ears, realized how flirtatious she sounded. Of all the men on the planet, why a married man? He just made her so comfortable, but maybe part of his appeal was the fact there was no risk of a relationship with him. He was a fantasy and nothing more.

"Mark?" she said.

He was on his haunches, his ponytail tied at the base of his neck. He looked up at her.

"You already got the Mace sprayer?" she asked, though the fact it was no longer on the ground really answered her question.

"Yep." He smiled at her and gestured toward his kit. He must have already had the Mace sprayer sealed in an evidence bag.

"Do you know if she was able to spray her attacker, would-be killer?"

Mark lifted up the bag and seemed to be assessing its weight. "My guess would be no. It seems quite full, but Cynthia can answer it for you once she's looked at it closer back at the lab."

Madison nodded.

"Oh, here they come." Terry came over and looked over a shoulder. "Like hounds on a scent."

Madison stepped back to look around the tall bushes and saw officers working to block access to the parking lot. It was doing little to persuade local television news crews, whose vans were parking on the road at the entrance to the lot. Forget hounds, they were more like vultures, striving to make something of themselves on the back of tragedy. And speaking of making a name…

The police chief was walking right up to them, one long-legged female reporter in particular.

"What the hell does he think he's doing?" Madison rushed over, Terry at her heels.

There had to be at least half a dozen reporters hammering out questions.

"Is this the work of a serial?"

"Who is the victim?"

"Two victims in two weeks. Were they killed by the same person?"

"Is the safety of our city at risk?"

Chief McAlexandar held up a hand. "A woman was found—"

He was cut off by more questions.

"So it was another woman? How old?"

"Was she killed in the same way?"

"Strangled?"

Madison smirked at how quickly the chief was losing control of the situation—not that he'd view it that way. He worked the media crowd like a politician: dodging questions he didn't want to answer by ignoring them or countering with another question.

"Only comment at this time is the Stiles PD is investigating a suspicious death," the chief said.

"I'm Ms. Wade with *Stiles One*." It was the leggy blonde, her voice sugar sweet. She pursed her lips, looking McAlexandar straight in the eye. She took working her femininity one step further and moved closer to the chief, practically brushing her substantive cleavage against his arm. "What makes police suspect foul play?"

Unbelievable. This reporter wielded her sex appeal expertly, and Madison had no respect for the approach.

The reporter tossed her long hair over a shoulder and smiled at McAlexandar. He smiled back, which he rarely did, and resembled a creepy reptile.

He leaned in to the reporter and said something Madison couldn't hear, but it resulted in the woman laughing a high-pitched laugh.

The crowd started talking among themselves, but Madison fixated on the chief. He pulled back from the reporter.

"Ms. Wade," he started, but Madison's attention went to a man who was walking at a brisk rate through the reporters and past the police barricade.

"Heather?" the man called out. "Was it Heather?" His voice cracked.

Madison rushed to him and held up her hands to stop him, but he darted toward the crime scene. She ran after him but was too late.

"Oh my God, it is her," he wailed, and his legs buckled. Madison helped steady him.

"I'm sorry for your loss," she told him. "I'm Detective Madison Knight."

Tears were streaming down his face, and he sniffled. "I knew it…I knew it. I had a bad feeling when I saw all the vehicles drive by the house. The cops, the TV vans." He put a hand to the top of his bald head. "I can't believe this is happening."

"Why don't we step over here?" Madison directed him farther down the trail, away from the body, but he was still concealed from the media by the bushes.

"How was she—" He gulped and ran a hand along his nose. "I told her that jogging by herself could get her into trouble."

"Are you related to Heather?" Madison asked.

He nodded, his eyelashes soaked with tears. "I'm her—" he balled a fist in his mouth, dropped his hand "—*was* her husband. Kevin Hampton. I can't believe it. Who would do this?"

"We plan on finding out."

"You have to, Detective. She was my…" He sobbed. "My everything."

"Your wife's last name, it was—"

"She didn't take mine for professional reasons," he spat as if it was self-explanatory.

Madison nodded. "Mr. Hampton, do you know of anyone who would do this?"

"No." His gaze went past Madison in the direction of Heather's body.

"I assure you we will do all we can to find who did this." She meant the words each time she spoke them, even if they came off by rote.

The reporters were getting louder and calling out to Hampton. They wanted to know who he was and his connection to the victim.

"Get them out of here!" Madison yelled at a nearby officer. Still shots and videos were rolling. Men stood behind cameras almost as large as their torsos. They gave the impression of a futuristic android as they rotated at the waists and scanned the area. Their accompanying reporters all clamoring to be heard above all others. .

"What is her name?"

"Who are you?"

"What happened to her?"

Officers rushed to strengthen the perimeter and hold them back.

"Mister, please—" One of the reporters stopped talking when Hampton stomped toward them.

"Mr. Hampton, stop!" Madison rushed after the grieving widower. Terry noticed her efforts and joined her. She put a hand on one of Hampton's shoulders, and Terry gripped the other.

"He must pay for what he did," Hampton hissed and struggled to free himself from their hold.

A reporter yelled, "He knows the victim!"

Madison spoke in Hampton's ear. "I don't suggest you speak with them."

Hampton responded to the reporter, "I'm her husband."

"What's your name?"

"What's her name?"

"Who killed—"

Hampton held up a hand, rendering the reporters silent. He was handling the media better than the chief. "I want the person who did this to know that when I find you, I will kill you myself." His threat was spoken clearly and without hesitation.

Madison let out a deep breath that swelled her cheeks and looked at her partner. Hampton's bravado wasn't an act. Given the chance, he would follow through on his words.

CHAPTER TWENTY-SEVEN

"What the hell was that?" the chief spat. "You'd think we were running a damned circus down here."

"We tried to stop him," Terry said.

"Well, apparently there's quite a difference between trying and succeeding." His beady eyes grazed over Terry and fixed on Madison. He wagged a finger at her. "Make sure, with this case, it's a matter of succeeding. Here." He pushed the picture of Photo Guy toward Madison and walked away.

She tightened her fist, crumpling the printout into a ball. She could cut that man's finger off and not feel any remorse.

"What the hell was that?" Winston demanded.

He was a little slow to the show, but as hopped up as ever. It felt like déjà vu with another ass-ripping session about to commence.

Madison held up her hand. "It's all right. We've got things under control."

"Based on what I just saw, I'd disagree." His nostrils flared as he eyeballed her.

"Listen, we tried—"

"*Do.* Don't try." He glanced at his watch and walked off, waving a hand over his shoulder. "I've got something to take care of."

No doubt a glass or two of his favorite drink and a spot on his sofa in front of his large TV watching NASCAR. He and McAlexandar were equally predictable.

Madison and Terry were huddled behind the bushes near the crime scene, though the media was now gone. Hampton had been taken home by a couple of officers.

Richards was braced over the body, his lips moving in silent calculation as he factored in all the elements to gauge an estimated time of death. If he failed to accurately pinpoint it, the killer could get off on an alibi that might not have been in place otherwise.

When he felt Madison watching him, Richards rose.

"Based on the temperature of her body, factoring in the air temperature and current humidity, as well as the slight evidence of rigor mortis…" He lifted one of her arms with a gloved hand. "You see? It was starting to set into her hands. Now, it takes longer for rigor to start in warmer temperatures."

She nodded.

Richards continued. "I'd estimate TOD between five and eight this morning. And before you ask, I would definitely conclude COD is asphyxiation due to strangulation, as evidenced by the petechial hemorrhaging and the necktie bound tightly around her neck."

Five and eight? If Photo Guy was the killer, what had he still been doing at the park when the teenage girls arrived around eight thirty?

"Was she restrained at all?"

Richards looked around the immediate area. "There's no evidence of that."

"Detectives." Officer Tendum was hurrying toward them. "I've seen that man before."

"Excuse me?" Madison said, his words striking her out of the blue.

"The guy in the photo," Tendum clarified. "I saw it with the BOLO."

The sergeant must have included the man's image along with the BOLO on the car.

Tendum continued. "He was rougher looking, though. At least a day's facial growth."

"Where did you see him?" Madison felt excitement rush through her.

"Parked on the street down from Laura Saunders's house… when I was told to clear the streets." Tendum winced.

"You saw him the morning we showed up to investigate her murder? And you did nothing?" she huffed.

Tendum held up his hands. "I didn't know—"

"Did you even question why he was in the neighborhood?" If this uniform had been doing his job, he would have. It's not like the guy was parked in a driveway; he was at the curb, keeping a distance.

"No…I…" Tendum's eyes went to the trail.

"You let him get away," she snapped. "Did it not even occur to you to ask for his ID? It's not unheard of for killers to watch what they've set in motion. He was in the vicinity of a recent homicide. Due diligence, Officer. It's your fault we've got another vic—"

"Maddy," Terry beseeched her to find mercy.

She clenched her jaw and kept her gaze on Tendum. "How can you not know? How could you not think to ask why he was there?"

"He was smoking a cigarette." Tendum glanced at Terry and winced again.

"So you really have no clue what his purpose was for being in that neighborhood, at that time?"

Tendum shook his head, and Madison's temper flared even more.

"I'll tell you what he was doing there," she went on. "You ready? He was there to watch the Stiles PD make a complete joke of themselves." She couldn't look at Tendum anymore. "Terry, we've gotta go."

Terry gave Tendum a consoling look, and it rose her temperature.

"Don't coddle him. He screwed up, and now we have—"

"Maybe you can talk to a rookie like that, but not to me, Knight." He pulled out her last name. He was angry, too, but at her.

"He could have stopped this murder!"

"That's bull crap, and you know it."

"You think what you want. You always do." She headed to her car, Terry following.

The officers who had taken Kevin Hampton home stood sentinel outside his front door. When Madison and Terry approached, they stepped aside.

Madison knocked on the door.

"Ever occur to you he might want some time alone to digest what happened?" Terry asked.

"You're suggesting that we don't speak to him?" She raised her brows.

"I'm just saying he's probably in shock."

"He probably is. Regardless, we need to talk with him."

The door cracked open then, but no one stood in the opening. Rather, Hampton's back was to them, and he was walking down a hallway toward the back of the house.

"Mr. Hampton," she said, following him. "We want to make sure you're okay. Do you want us to wait with you until family arrives? Is there someone you want us to call?"

He stopped walking and spun. "Fam…ily?" His voice fractured. "Heather was my family."

The way he'd said it hurt Madison's heart, but she had a job to do. Eyewitness testimony might be able to place Photo Guy at the scene of the crime, but spouses were always suspect in murder cases. "Mr. Hampton—"

"You can just call me Kevin."

Madison bobbed her head. "Where were you this morning between five and eight?"

"What?" His eyes widened. "You're kidding, right? You think I…? I would *never* do anything to hurt her!"

"It's a question we need to ask," she countered, not being swayed by the dramatics.

"I went grocery shopping. Around six. I like to go early in the morning before it gets busy."

"Do you have a receipt you could give us?"

Hampton stared at her for a few seconds. "I told them to keep it."

"How did you pay for it?" If he'd used a credit or debit card, there'd be an electronic trail.

"Cash."

Now they'd be hoping someone at the store could recognize Hampton. She'd leave the line of inquiry—for now—unless they had more reason to suspect Hampton.

"Do you know anyone who didn't get along with her?" These were always the unpleasant questions that needed to be asked. No one liked to think of their loved one as being hated so badly someone would be motivated to kill them.

"There's quite a stretch between not getting along with someone and killing them."

"So there *were* people who didn't get along with her?"

"I'm sure. She was a manager, had people who reported to her at work. I'm sure some had issue with her," Hampton said, "but I don't think any of them would have killed her. Now, if you would please leave." He sniffled as he turned toward the front door and gestured for them to leave.

"One more thing before we go…" Madison took out the picture of Photo Guy and showed it to Hampton. "Do you recognize this person?"

Hampton studied the image closely and eventually shook his head. Madison put the photo away.

"Do you think he killed my Heather?"

"It's far too soon to know." Madison pulled out her card and set it on a hall table. "Anything comes to mind, call me."

He closed the door heavily behind them.

"I don't believe he's involved, but I think he knows something."

Terry nodded.

CHAPTER TWENTY-EIGHT

Madison and Terry were at the station searching the Department of Motor Vehicles for a Honda Accord with the letters "AVL" in its plate registered in Stiles.

Zero results.

"What the hell," Madison griped.

"The girls could have remembered the plate wrong or the car," Terry suggested.

Winston already had an active BOLO based on the information they'd obtained from the girls. She didn't want to imagine his reaction if she had to change any of the details. "Please, don't go there."

"Where is *there* exactly?"

"All negative."

"Negative? I'll tell you what's negative. The direction my Sunday took."

"At least it didn't take the turn Heather's did," she countered with heat. She keyed in another search, this time expanding it to the state, then she got up. "I'm running a statewide search, and I'll check back on it later." While looking within a city yielded fairly fast results, a wider net took longer.

"Something I said?"

"Terry, it's always something you say."

"Where are we going?"

"*We?* I know *I'm* going to Laura's."

"Laura's?"

"You sound like a parrot, Terry."

He cocked his head to the side. "What about the chief and the Nguyen case?"

"This is about the case. The chief wants answers, and that's what we're working on getting him. What more can the guy want?"

"I don't know…"

"Fine, suit yourself. Sit here, keep tweaking the search. Hope you strike pay dirt."

"I'm coming," he huffed. "What do you honestly expect to find at Laura's?"

If she told him she wanted to collect that one photo of Laura with her aunt and uncle, and then compare it to the one of Laura with Photo Guy, they'd be arguing. Sure, he'd sided with her at the Nguyen crime scene—even essentially said that Photo Guy had been bumped up to a legitimate suspect—but she could see him changing his mind, saying something like the girls had jumped on the photo or they had been farther away from him than they let on.

"Let's put it this way," she said, "I'm sure we missed gathering a crucial piece of evidence."

Was it too much to hope they'd get lucky and find prints on the photo or frame, something that could lead to identifying Photo Guy?

"How are we getting in?" Terry asked at Laura's front door.

"A key." She snickered as she pulled it from her pocket, slipped it into the lock, and broke the Crime Scene's seal.

Walking through the front door, images from the first visit flooded her mind and were helped along by the lingering stench of decomposition.

She walked to the bookcase, where the photo she sought was displayed in a wooden frame. She put on a pair of gloves before lifting it and peered in Laura's eyes—and she knew. "It's definitely the same photo of her." Her legs turned to rubber, and the hairs rose on her arms. She pulled out an evidence bag and sealed the framed photo inside.

"Same photo as…" Terry prompted.

She caught him up to speed.

"So you think the killer, a.k.a. Photo Guy, photoshopped Laura's image onto the picture of the two of them, the one we found in her bedroom?"

"Exactly what I think."

"Huh." His phone rang, and he turned his back on her when he answered. She still caught snippets of the conversation. "Yes...I'm with Madison...I'll be home soon." He ended his call, and when he did, his cheeks were flushed.

"Everything all right?"

Terry dismissed her with a wave of his hand, and before she could push anymore, her phone rang.

"Knight," she answered.

"You have any answers yet?" It was the chief.

Do you think I'm the magical detective who can solve murder in a few hours?

"I'm working on getting some," she said defiantly.

"Good to hear. And that man from the crime scene, the husband, he's obviously been given proper notification?"

Madison rolled her eyes. He'd been there when the poor man saw his dead wife lying on the trail. Not necessarily a *proper* notification, but it counted as a notification, nonetheless. "Yes."

"Good." The chief hung up without another word.

Madison was disgusted as she imagined him running off to give the scoop to the bombshell reporter.

"The chief?" Terry watched her as he ran a hand along a bookshelf.

"What gave it away? My tone or apparent urge to want to punch something?"

"Both. Winston can press your buttons, but McAlexandar does it much more efficiently."

"He's had years of practice." She stood there clenching her phone in one hand, the bagged frame in the other. "Guess that reporter's going to get rich off someone's death."

"Happens all the time. You don't have to like it, Maddy."

"Good, 'cause I don't. Not one bit, actually. But this—" she held up the bagged frame "—this I like."

CHAPTER TWENTY-NINE

Madison flicked her pen and tapped it on the edge of the desk as she stared at the DMV results from the statewide search she'd run. "How can there be no matches?"

"Like I said before, the girls could have remembered things wrong," Terry said. When she didn't respond, he added, "Are you filtering the search by including an approximate year range for the Honda Accord or simply leaving it to all years of the make and model?"

"An approximate year range and the partial plate," she replied. She considered what Terry had said about the vehicle, though, and broadened the search by removing the year range. She told him what she did and said, "Now we'll have to wait on that."

Terry nodded and asked, "Richards go home?"

Madison nodded. "As far as I know." She recalled Richards's yearning to get out on the golf course, but he had texted her an update. "He'll be doing the full autopsy tomorrow morning, but he did a brief preliminary, and collected what trace he could from Heather, and sent it to the lab."

"I assume Mark will be starting on the evidence he got from Richards and what he collected from the crime scene?"

"Kidding, right? Without Cynthia's supervision? We can't jeopardize nailing this son of a bitch on a wet-behind-the-ears college grad. Besides, she's the best, and we need the best on this."

"Whoa, excuse me for mentioning it. Speaking of which, how did our Queen of the Lab manage to escape being pulled in?"

"That I don't know, but I'm thinking you and I could pick up some pointers." She wasn't about to tell Terry she thought Cynthia might be hungover. "It would be nice if being thoroughly exhausted worked as an excuse for not coming in, but there's not much more we can do today. Why don't you head out, and we'll catch up in the morning? Maybe have better luck searching the DMV database with a fresh start."

"What about the chief? He wanted everything stitched up today."

"Let me handle him." She yawned. "You know what? I'm calling it a day, too." The words came out, and she could hardly believe she'd said them. If the chief really wanted answers, he knew how to reach her.

"All right, well, you don't have to tell me again." Terry rose to leave.

"Oh, one thing."

"Yeah?" He turned to face her, his expression serious.

"Seems to me I won our bet." She held out an opened hand. "Layton was innocent, so it would seem someone owes me forty and a dinner."

He dug into his pockets, and his face scrunched up. "Sorry, I've got nothing." He broke into a run.

Madison yelled out behind him, "I know where you work!"

Madison must have been crazy to think she could bail at the start of a murder case. She could never be one of those people who left their work at work. As she was sitting in her apartment, she was feeling guiltier by the moment. She felt exhausted but couldn't even dream of sleeping. After all, how could she when those affected by murderers cried out for answers? She was simply destined to put the victims and their families first. It was probably a fantasy to entertain that one day she'd actually put herself first. If hadn't happened yet, it likely never would—but that was okay. It's not like she set out to be a type of social martyr, one who sacrificed a personal life for the job, but things had turned out that way. Maybe her life in law enforcement had started out due to her grandmother's encouragement, but it had taken on a life of its own. Madison realized she could shed light in a dark world and bring comfort to those seeking answers. With this job, she made a difference.

She dropped onto her sofa, promising herself she'd just relax for a little while. She lifted her legs and put her feet on the coffee table that ran the length of the couch. Her grandmother had left it to her, and besides the money, it was one of the few tangibles Madison had of her. When she let herself dwell on it, the loss tortured her.

As she sat there resting her eyes, she felt good that she'd at least accomplished something. She and Terry had dropped off the framed photo to the lab for processing when they'd first returned to the station.

Her phone rang, and Madison jumped. "Hello," she answered.

"Hey, sis." It was her sister, Chelsea, who was three years younger than Madison. Not only was she their parents "baby," she was the favorite and the one who made the parents proud. Chelsea had gone the traditional route with her life: she was married and had three kids. That pleased their parents, but especially their mother, who frowned on Madison's choice to enter law enforcement and remain single. Though, Madison didn't think that was all that caused a rift between them. Their mother would deny it, but Madison felt it had to do with her grandmother leaving money to her and not to her own daughter.

"What's up?" Madison smiled into the receiver. Despite a little underlying sibling rivalry, Chelsea was a friend as much as she was related by blood.

"I heard about the serial killer on the news."

Madison clenched her jaw, disgusted with the liberty the media took. "There's not enough to conclude there's a serial killer in Stiles."

"He killed two—"

"Who says the same killer is behind both murders?" How would the media know they suspected one man for two murders, anyhow? She had her answer the moment she thought of the question: McAlexandar had said as much to the bombshell reporter. Madison didn't even feel the need to point out that to technically qualify as a serial killer, he'd have to have killed three people.

Madison's nieces screamed in the background, and her sister's rings clicked against the phone as she must have been cupping the receiver. "Be quiet," Chelsea yelled at the girls, and Madison could tell she'd turn her head, but Madison's ears were still ringing. She shook her head.

Chelsea went on. "I wanted you to know that I worry about you, Maddy. Maybe you should get away for a while, take a holiday. To be around such negativity all the time can't be good for you."

"You're starting to sound a bit like mom."

"Thank you."

Only Chelsea would take that as a compliment…

Madison took another approach. "How is it you're the baby sister, yet you're always looking after me? I'm fine. A little tired—all right, *a lot* tired—but fine, nonetheless."

"Why don't I believe you?"

"Because you're a skeptic."

Her sister laughed. "Maybe…sometimes."

"No maybe, sis. You are. But trust me, I'm fine."

"Just be careful, okay? I don't want this psycho getting fixated on you."

Fixated. It was a good word that could turn dark in so many ways. Really, her sister had summed up the killer quite well. He had to have become *fixated* on his victims to know when to strike.

"I'm always careful. Once this case is over, how about we get together? Do a girls' night out on the town? That is, if I can break you away from your Hunky Monkey long enough."

Chelsea chuckled. "Nah, Jim can handle the girls for a night. They wouldn't have enough time to kill him and hide the body. I don't think so anyway…"

"Well, if they did, I could always turn the other way, discredit any clues. You know, for my nieces' welfare. But I likely wouldn't be assigned the case. Conflict of interest or some such nonsense," she said, followed by a giggle.

"All right, Mad—" Her sister stopped short and yelled something to the girls again. "I've got to go. Sorry. Love you."

"No need to be sorry. You're forever apologizing. You sound like a Canadian. Love you too, sis, and say hi to the girls for me."

Her sister clicked off, and Madison was left with overwhelming sadness and loneliness. Her sister had a seemingly perfect life, including a man who loved her. Madison had no one special, but she had no time for that person right now anyway: she had a killer to catch.

He was amused by Heather's husband calling out threats on the evening news. The cops didn't even know what they were dealing with, so what made Baldy think he could not only catch him but scare him?

What wasn't funny on the newscast, though, was that the police were interested in an older model, silver/gray Honda Accord. It was probably time to ditch the car, but for now, it was tucked safely away in the garage.

Eventually, he'd have to get rid of it, find another car. He couldn't stay housebound and carry out his mission.

His primary target still had to pay—and soon. He could smell his retribution, taste it, breathe it. He let himself become drunk with the euphoria it would bring. If he did just one more thing, Mother would die. After that, he didn't care if the cops tossed him in jail and threw away the key.

CHAPTER THIRTY

At ten the next morning, Madison headed straight for the lab. She wanted answers, and she wanted them now.

"I'm telling you: she won't have anything for us yet." Terry trailed her like a puppy trying to keep up.

"I know Cyn," Madison said. "She'll have at least started. Heck, she's probably been in for hours." Part of what made Madison good at her job was her ability to read people. Guilt over not being at the crime scene yesterday would have propelled her friend in early today.

They entered the lab and found Cynthia hunched over a table, examining evidence that was spread out there. She looked up at them, dark crescents lining her eyes.

"Still feeling our night, I see," Madison said.

"You guys spent the night together?" Terry grinned like a pervert. "Do tell."

Both women punched him in the arm.

"Hey, now." He scowled and backed away from them.

"We don't swing that way. Sorry to disappoint, Casanova." Cynthia smirked.

"*Casanova*?" Terry spat. "Where is that coming from?" He looked at Madison, and she shrugged.

Cynthia took her glasses off and pinched the bridge of her nose. "I've been here since three this morning. I'm soooo tired."

"Still? After *all* that sleep? Get over it, lady. Results?" Madison bobbed her brows, taunting her friend.

Cynthia glared at her and put her glasses back on.

"Come on, you're the Queen of the Lab. In fact, I would be shocked if you didn't have anything to tell us." She flashed a toothy grin. Flattery typically worked.

Cynthia pointed at Madison's open mouth. "At least they're not purple today," she said, referring to Madison's teeth.

"You want to go back down that road?"

Cynthia smiled and shook her head. "Okay, I'll start with the bad news. Jennifer didn't find any epithelial on the tie bound around Heather's—"

"We could never get that lucky twice," Madison commented snidely.

Cynthia grimaced. "As I said, *bad news.* Since the body was found outside, any DNA evidence could have been blown away. Moving on, I think Mark told you the Mace sprayer was never fired?"

Madison seesawed her head right and left. "He didn't think it was but didn't know for sure."

"I can tell you it was completely full and only the vic's prints were on it." Madison opened her mouth to speak, but Cynthia held up a finger to silence her. "Now, here's the good news. The vic was wearing a silver chain with a heart-shaped pendant, and there's an unidentified fingerprint on it. It may belong to the killer."

"I don't remember a necklace," Madison said.

"You wouldn't have seen it due to the other neck adornment," Cynthia countered.

The crime scene, Heather's pale face, the necktie bound tightly around her neck flashed to the front of Madison's thoughts, and she nodded solemnly. The rest of what Cynthia had said started to sink in. "You said a partial was left behind. Does it match anything pulled from Laura's crime—" Madison stopped talking when she noticed Cynthia's eyes darken. "Go ahead, I'll shut up."

"Why, thank you," Cynthia said. "As a matter of fact, the print from the pendant matched the third as of yet unidentified prints that were on the handcuffs and the one wineglass." Cynthia paused and locked her gaze with Madison's.

"Well, the prints tie our victims together," Terry said. Both women moaned at his choice of words. "Well…"

Madison asked, "Have you heard any more about the lost towel?"

Cynthia's mouth formed a smile. "I got a call from the lab this morning. They found it and confirmed the evidence bag is original and hasn't been tampered with. I stressed the importance of rushing it through and told them the investigation's been waiting long enough."

Madison grabbed her close and hugged her.

In life, sometimes Madison found her faith in others nearly nonexistent. Whether it was due to her line of work or being heartbroken at twenty, she wasn't sure. Maybe it was simply a protective mechanism: if you didn't expect anything from anyone, they couldn't hurt you. But moments like this restored her confidence in others.

"All right, all right. It's no problem." Cynthia giggled, pulling away from Madison's embrace. .

"Should I leave you two alone?" Terry bobbed his eyebrows.

"Oh, Lord." Madison rolled her eyes. "Getting back on topic," she said, "I assume you saw what we left for you yesterday."

"Yes," Cynthia said through clenched teeth. "And I'm doing everything I can, Maddy. As fast as I can."

"Oh, catfight." Terry rubbed his hands together. "Where do I place my bet?

"You can't make good on our wager. How do you intend to pay this one off?" Madison asked.

A fire lit in his eyes. "Well, I wouldn't be betting in favor of you winning."

"Yep, it's confirmed," Madison said, "you definitely need to stop betting. You're not good at it." She smiled at Cynthia.

"Hey, I take offense to that," Cynthia jested.

Madison waved a hand at her, smiled at Terry, and then said to him, "Why are you in such a good mood today?"

"I'm only a man, and the thought of you two spending the—"

"Well, may I be the first to suggest that you get over it?" A smile lurked on Cynthia's lips. "Now if you two would please excuse me. I have work to do."

Terry gestured toward Cynthia. "She talks to us like we have nothing to do—"

"Well, you two are the ones hanging out in my lab right now. Go do something. Investigate." She waved them off with a brush of her hand.

"We don't have to take this, Terry," Madison said jokingly. "Let's go do some real work."

"I'll pretend I didn't hear that," Cynthia called out.

"Yeah, yeah, you love me," Madison said over a shoulder.

"It's a good thing I do. Actually, before you go…"

Madison and Terry had already made it to the doorway but turned to face her.

Cynthia continued. "The pendant from Heather's necklace said, 'The past is never forgotten but embraced in dreams' on the inside and—" she handed Madison a photo of the jewelry "—on the outside, it was embossed with scrollwork, the acronym HOH."

"HOH," Madison repeated. "It's not her initials. Her last name is Nguyen."

"But her husband's surname is Hampton," Terry offered.

"And her middle name is Olivia," Madison recalled.

Cynthia held up her hands. "Then it's probably her initials using her husband's surname."

Madison pressed her lips. "Not sure about that. She didn't take her husband's last name in life so why have it embossed on a pendant?"

"People are crazy." Cynthia shrugged. "Who knows? But I'm sure you'll figure out what HOH stands for. I don't think I mentioned the partial print was found inside, did I?"

"You missed that part." Madison certainly would have remembered. "So the killer—assuming it was him—opened it before killing her?"

"Seems so."

"Heather wouldn't have just stayed still for him to read it. He must have subdued her somehow," she reasoned. "He used cuffs on Laura." Her mind mulled over the implications. It was one thing to kill in the privacy of a house and take some time; it was another to take time in a public place. That pendant must have meant something to him if he slowed down and risked being caught to read it. It might make sense given the timeline, though. Richards had said Heather was killed between five and eight, and the teenage girls saw him around eight thirty. He hadn't been in a hurry to leave. She looked at Terry. "We've got to question Kevin Hampton about the pendant. Maybe he'll be able to shed some light on its meaning and whether it could possibly mean something to anyone else."

Kevin Hampton wasn't home, and they couldn't reach him on the phone. Madison drove her and Terry to Wow FX, Heather's place of employment. Maybe they'd find someone there who could send light on the pendant or Heather's personal life in general. It seemed no matter how hard people tried to keep their personal lives from their coworkers, it always tended to wash over into the workplace.

The business was located on the opposite end of town from the Hamptons' house, and with traffic, stoplights, and summer construction, the drive took forty minutes. Any other time, she could have gotten there in fifteen, twenty minutes tops.

The two-story building had a large footprint, and its size surprised Madison, though maybe it shouldn't have. According to the company's website, their clients included big-name movie producers and theme-park industries.

Certainly what had started out as a family venture had grown into a successful corporation with a man named Roger Stanton, acting as chairman, at the helm.

"Let me do the talking in there," Madison said as they made their way to the front door.

"Sure, we know you're good at it."

"You just couldn't let it go, could you?"

The front doors entered into an atrium that housed a fine assortment of greenery. In the middle of the space, a flight of stairs led to a second floor, but she and Terry went to a glass door stenciled with the company's name and the word *Reception*.

Terry held the door open for her, and she gave him a funny look. He usually let her fend for herself.

"Mr. Hill," he said. "Don't you remember?"

She smirked. "Thanks." Good ol' Mr. Hill, who believed in the standards of old, but the man did have a point. No matter how advanced society had become or how feminist women became, they appreciated life's smaller courtesies, such as having a door held open for them.

No one was at the front desk, and cubicle partitions the height of six feet blocked out the rest of the office.

"Guess no one's home." Madison searched for a bell.

"Just show a little patience," Terry said. "She might have stepped away to grab a coffee or use the restroom."

"*She*? Why assume the person who sits here is a *she*?" Her eyes scanned the desk and caught a coffee mug tucked behind the monitor, the words *World's Greatest Mom*, on it, but Terry wouldn't be able to see it from where he was standing.

"Well, statistically this position is held by women."

"You might want to stop talking." She glared at him.

He held up his hands. "I'm just saying, is all."

Madison tapped her fingers on the front counter. "This is ridiculous. Surely the person who sits here—"

"Can I help you?" a man called out.

"Why, yes, you can." She reveled in the fact the post was held by a guy—not that it explained the mug—and smiled at her partner.

The man sat at the desk, grouped some papers and shuffled them to the side, while keeping one eye on her. The other eye was masked behind long bangs.

Madison gave a formal introduction and added, "We'd like to speak with Roger Stanton."

"This is about Heather?" His voice hinted at sadness but fell short of genuine grief.

"It is. What's your name?"

"Joel." He clicked on his keyboard. "Mr. Stanton is in on a conference call at the moment."

Madison made a dramatic show of lengthening her arm, bending it and looking at her watch. "Well, here's the thing, *Joel*, we're investigating the murder of your colleague, Heather Nguyen." Maybe hearing her name again would convey urgency and move him emotionally. "To do this, we need to speak with Mr. Stanton as soon as possible. A priority. Anything short of you getting him down here right away tells me you're not being cooperative." She paused for effect. "And you don't want us thinking that."

"Listen, Detective Knight, is it?" Joel's tone challenged her. "Mr. Stanton will have my job if I interrupt him right now."

"Think of it this way. You don't help us, we could take you in for obstruction. You'd likely lose your job anyway."

It seemed like it took minutes for her statement to sink in. Either the guy was good at hiding how he felt, or he truly didn't care.

"Fine," Joel mumbled, barely audible.

"I didn't hear you." Madison turned to Terry. "Did you?" Terry shook his head. She knew she was being pissy, but this guy was pushing all the right buttons.

"I said *fine*." He raised his voice. "I'll get Mr. Stanton for you." He was watching her like he was waiting for a *thank you*. He'd be waiting forever; one wasn't coming.

Joel eventually pressed a button on the desk phone and put on a headset. "Mr. Stanton, I—"

Stanton's voice could have been heard all the way to the atrium lobby. For some reason, knowing that Joel was getting his ass chewed gave her some satisfaction. Cruel, she knew, but she was only human…

Joel's cheeks flushed bright red. "Yes…It's urgent… It's about Heather…" The receptionist swallowed. "Two detectives are here to speak with you…Yes…Uh-huh… Okay, Mr. Stanton."

Joel pressed another button on the phone and took off his headset. The cord was caught up in his fingers. He worked to free himself. The minute he did, the phone rang again. His facial reaction was strong enough that he may as well have verbalized the swear word he was thinking.

"It's all right. We'll wait while you get that." Madison couldn't resist.

Joel kept his eyes on hers as he picked up the receiver directly without bothering with the headset. "Wow FX. One moment please." He depressed some keys, likely transferring the call. He looked up at her and jutted out his chin, seeming to garner some of his original composure. "Mr. Stanton told me to convey his sincerest apologies, but he's in the middle of a conference call. As I told you. But he did tell me to book you in for an appointment this afternoon. It will put the rest of his agenda behind…" He let his words stop there as he typed into a calendar. "Two fifteen would be the earliest we could squeeze you in."

"Two fifteen," she spat. This was a murder investigation, a damned inconvenience to all involved. It's not like Heather had a chance—or a *choice*—to book an appointment to be murdered. What would make this man think he deserved special consideration? "That's unacceptable."

Joel looked at her blankly. "Pardon?"

"I believe you heard what I said, but I will repeat it—nice and slow." She felt Terry tense beside her. She went on. Un… accept…ta…ble."

Joel's jaw slackened, and he tried to speak, but nothing coherent came out.

"How long will his meeting be?" Madison pressed.

"About an hour. Maybe a little longer."

"Okay, now let's talk compromise. Tell your boss once he's finished with his call, we'll be down here waiting for him."

Joel clenched his teeth and looked away.

Call it a gut feeling, but his attitude combined with the specialty mug… "Where is the person who usually manages the front desk?" she asked.

"Excuse me?" He blew air out of his mouth, causing his long bangs to rise upward.

"You don't normally sit here." She pointed at the mug and glanced at Terry with a smirk on her face.

"What does it matter if I work at this desk or not?"

Madison hitched her shoulders. "I'm curious where the regular receptionist might be."

"Her name's Rachel Clayton, and she took a personal day. She claims she's devastated over Heather's death."

"*Claims* she's devastated?'" Madison asked.

"Yeah," Joel said, offering nothing more. "Rach reported to Heather, like I do. Three others besides me and Rach reported to her, too, but we're all here."

"What's your position with the company?" Terry asked.

"I work in the media department."

"Since you reported to Heather and we have some time," Madison began, "do you know of anyone who had it out for her? Didn't get along with her?"

"Wow. I can't say we had it out for her per se, but the woman was…uh, how do you say it?"

"A real bitch?" Madison jumped in, taking a gamble, and ignored Terry's eyes on her.

"Yeah, I shouldn't say that about her now that she's dead, but she could be."

His words said one thing, but Madison didn't feel any guilt coming from him for speaking ill of the dead. His screaming living superior had far more impact on him.

Joel continued. "But you know the saying, 'Hindsight is 20/20.' I wish she was still here 'cause..." He looked up at the ceiling, and Madison gathered what he'd left unsaid was that it was far worse reporting to Stanton than it had been reporting to Heather. "I'm being completely honest when I say no one here would hurt her," he added. "Maybe some of us secretly thought of it and discussed how good it would be if something happened to her. But we would never have actually done anything to her ourselves. Why would we? She wasn't worth going to jail over."

Terry winced. "Ouch, that sounds pretty cold."

"Hey, I'm just being honest here. But maybe she was the way she was because she had to report to..." He pointed a finger toward the ceiling. "I've probably said too much, but you should definitely speak to Rachel. She served as Heather's right-hand girl. Still don't think she would have killed Heather, but she certainly wasn't appreciated. More like dumped on."

Madison nodded. "You said that you and some of the others around here would talk about how good it would be if Heather was out of the picture. In what way exactly?"

"You ever have a shitty boss?"

Don't get me started...

"Ah, I see it on your face. Anyway, you get a guy in charge, or woman in this case, and they run the place like a dictatorship without room for movement. *The micromanagers*," he said adding finger quotes. "The office was just a nicer place when she wasn't around. When she'd go on business trips or holidays, whatever, we'd joke about her plane crashing." He met her gaze and added, "I guess it wasn't that funny."

"Not really," Madison agreed.

Joel's eyes shot downward.

"We'd like to speak to the other three who reported to her," Madison said, figuring since they were waiting on Stanton anyway, they might as well put the time to good use. "Is there a boardroom we could use?"

"Yeah, I'll get everyone to come see you."

"Just one at a time," Madison specified.

"Sure."

It took Madison and Terry a solid hour to work their way through the other three employees who reported to Heather, and by the time they were finished, it was evident there was one common consensus: Heather was not an easy person to work for. Descriptions varied but mostly included "tyrant" and "whack job." One employee showed more sympathy toward Heather's fate but still expressed contempt for Heather as her boss. Another suggestion that always arose, too, was that Rachel would be good to speak with because she served as more than a professional assistant; she also helped Heather with some personal errands. None of them knew anything about the pendant.

When they finished speaking with the employees, they returned to the front desk and found Joel still sitting there. Madison opened her mouth to ask about Mr. Stanton when a door opened behind them. A stocky man of about five-foot-five, wearing a tailored Armani, entered the reception area.

He walked over to them. "I'm Roger Stanton. I assume you're the detectives here to see me." His deep baritone didn't seem to go with his image.

"I assume now would be a good time for you," Madison said, a little smug.

"Please forgive me for conducting business when you arrived," Stanton deadpanned. "Next time, if you would kindly call ahead, I could accommodate you more quickly. Now, if you would come with me." He led them up a set of back stairs to his office.

What was it with this guy? Did he have short-man syndrome or had his position given him a large ego? As he led them to his office, Madison noted how his office was isolated from everyone else. Paired with his demeanor, he viewed himself as separate from his employees, elevated. It might be a challenge to get this man to open up to them, but Madison loved a challenge.

Stanton's office was easily twenty-by-twenty feet and came with the smell of new carpet and a renovated feel. A large window at the back of the room overlooked a wooded area and let in a flood of natural light. A seating area off to the right of the room with a couch, a couple of chairs, and a long coffee table gave it a hotel-lobby feel, as did the bar credenza tucked into one corner.

Stanton sat at his desk and gestured toward two chairs that faced him. "Please, have a seat."

Madison and Terry complied.

"What a terrible tragedy, I tell you," Stanton said, shaking his head. "Absolutely terrible."

The sound of a flushing toilet broke Madison's focus on Stanton, and she looked around. A door opened—she had thought it was a closet—and man came out.

"This is my lawyer, Shawn Gregg," Stanton said.

Madison wondered why Stanton's lawyer was there. Had Stanton snuck him in the back door while she and Terry were in the conference room? Or was he already there for other unrelated business?

Stanton added, "He's just here in case I need any advice."

"Should you need any?" Madison asked matter-of-factly.

Stanton glanced at Gregg but addressed her. "Miss Knight—"

"*Detective* Knight," she corrected.

"Please know that in my position it is necessary to have representation in a situation like this."

"So you've been in a position *like this* before?"

"No, I... I believe we've gotten off to a poor start. Shawn, if you would please sit over there." He gestured toward the couch. "Just listen in."

"Will do." Gregg followed Stanton's directive.

To Madison and Terry, Stanton said, "There's something I need to tell you. Before Heather's..." He cleared his throat. "Before Heather's death, we were actually going to let her go."

Madison's eyes enlarged. "Why is that? I thought she'd worked for you several years. What, seven or eight?" She and Terry had found that out during their conversations with Heather's subordinates.

"Yes, yes, something like that." He waved a hand of dismissal. "But that isn't the point. The point is she was starting to lose her mind. She wasn't focused on her work anymore. She was jittery, didn't have reports done on time. Her employees didn't respect her."

If that's a factor, maybe you should let yourself go...

"When did she change?" Terry asked.

"I'm not sure. I suppose it's been two, maybe three months."

If Heather had a stalker and an inkling to that effect, it could be enough to make her act oddly. In doing so, she might appear crazy to those around her. Madison angled her head. "Did you ever confront her and ask why she was acting differently?"

Stanton leaned back in his chair, clasped his hands on his lap, and swiveled. "I did. She accused me of looking for a reason to get rid of her and save her salary. She was one of the highest paid around here, except for me and other members of the board," he added. "But Heather became jumpy, and she never used to be. Her desk faced the door, like mine, but when I'd come in, she'd gasp as if I'd scared the living daylights out of her. Her reaction to me made me jump sometimes, too, honestly."

"We think it's possible that Heather's killer was stalking her," Madison offered, just to see what sort of reaction she'd get. Stanton paled and wet his lips. "Did she mention anything to you about feeling like she was being followed?"

"Not in so many words and not directly." Stanton's eyes drifted to his lawyer.

"Mr. Stanton, if you know something that could help, you need to tell us," Madison told him.

"Like I said, not directly. But the rumor mill is alive and well around here, and one did get back to me about Heather." He paused, his face softening. It was as if saying her name again was driving home the reality of the situation. "I can't believe she's dead," he said, confirming Madison's suspicions.

"This rumor…" she pressed. "What was it?"

"Probably all it was, really. A rumor. Certainly nothing that could be backed up. People were saying she was losing her mind because she thought someone was watching her."

Tingles ran over Madison's shoulders. "Did anyone see this person?"

He shook his head. "Nope. That's why it seemed like she was going crazy. You don't think…" He met her gaze, and she nodded.

"Yes, Mr. Stanton, I do. I think Heather had a stalker, and he was the one who killed her." Madison reached into a pocket for a picture of Photo Guy and showed it to Stanton. "Do you recognize him?"

Stanton studied the picture, then said, "Sorry, I don't."

It had been a long shot, but she had to try.

CHAPTER THIRTY-ONE

Madison drove with purpose toward Rachel Clayton's apartment. "We've got to get Photo Guy's picture in the paper, Terry. We don't need to say he's a suspected murderer, just that he's a person of interest to police."

"Doesn't that practically say the same thing?"

"We'll we've got to do something. He could be stalking his next victim as we speak." Her mind went to the DMV database. Maybe it was time to try another search.

"I don't know what you want me to say. The sarge and chief aren't going to risk a potential lawsuit for defamation of character or something else the guy might concoct."

"So they'd rather another innocent person be murdered?"

"We're closing in on him, but we need to give it a little more time."

"I'm not good with waiting or with patience." Her inner child stomped her foot, while her adult self had to swallow the situation. "The question we need to answer is why he targeted Laura and Heather? Why two women from different walks of life? Different marital statuses?"

"Your guess would be as good as any I'd come up with," Terry said.

Madison pulled into the parking lot for Rachel's building. It was rundown and in a poorer area of the city, with no security. They let themselves inside, and it smelled musty with a hint of fabric softener. Madison didn't have to look hard to find the entrance to the laundry facilities. It was close to the main door and next to ten mail slots. She had just spotted *Clayton* by the last slot when her phone rang.

She barely got her greeting out when the police chief cut her off. Just hearing his voice made her cringe in the same way cracking knuckles did, or nails scraping on a chalkboard. "Chief," she interrupted his tirade, "we're working the investigation from a few angles right now. Actually, we were just talking about putting a picture in the paper—"

He cut her off again and raised the same objections Terry had.

She let him tire himself out, then said, "Yes, I knew that's how you'd feel... I'll call you when we have any real news." She clipped the phone into its holder, and she just got it there when it rang again. "You've got to be shitting me!" This time she read the caller ID, and it was Winston. Without hesitation, she threw the phone at Terry, and he caught it on reflex.

Madison shrugged and set out in search of apartment ten, which in this odd little building, she found on the third floor. She could hear Terry's voice coming up through the stairwell.

"Yes, sir... I know you want to talk to Knight... Yes, I know it's her phone..."

Madison waited for Terry on the third-floor landing. When he got there and wrapped up the call, he threw the phone at her.

She caught it with a raised arm to the side of her head.

"You're not funny," he spat.

She laughed, tears beading in her eyes. "Hey, I did say next time he called it would be for you. As it is, I think he's called me a few times since then, so..."

"Don't paint it as if as you've done me a favor," Terry snapped.

She composed herself and approached apartment ten. Muffled voices were coming from inside. Either Rachel wasn't alone or she was watching TV. Madison knocked and footsteps came toward the door, accompanied by frantic whispers. The door opened, and two people were standing there: a twentysomething woman with blond hair pulled back into a clip, a few stray ringlets lining her face, and a man in his thirties. The man they'd met before, but this time he was in a state of partial undress; the top three buttons of his collared shirt were undone, and it hung over his pants.

"Mr. Hampton?" Madison said, barely able to hold back her astonishment.

"This isn't what it looks like." Hampton worked to tuck in his shirt.

Joel from Wow F/X had said Rachel took care of personal errands for Heather, but how far did those errands go? And for a man who had claimed Heather had been his entire world… She'd get back to him shortly, but the sight of him tossed her stomach as memories of her own past betrayal came to mind. Madison held up her badge and addressed the woman. "Are you Rachel Clayton?"

"Yes."

"We're Detectives Knight and Grant. We're investigating Heather's murder, and we have a few questions. Can we come in?"

Clayton stepped back. "Sure."

Madison and Terry entered the tiny apartment, and Clayton closed the door behind them. The living room was immediately there, and an assortment of toys were spread out on the floor. Madison wasn't an expert on kids, but she'd guess they belonged to a toddler.

"We can sit in here…" She led them to the couch, but there was only enough seating for two.

"I'll get a couple of dining chairs," Hampton offered and headed toward an alcove.

As they waited on Hampton to return, Madison wondered if Hampton was the father of Clayton's child, though that might be a huge reach.

Hampton set out the chairs, and he and Clayton sat on the couch together. Madison and Terry took the chairs.

"How long have the two of you been involved?" Madison asked, pulling no punches.

Hampton flinched. "I'm sorry, Detective, but I don't see how that relates to the case."

No denial. Interesting...

Clayton started crying into her hands, shaking her head, and mumbling something indiscernible.

Hampton ran a hand through his hair, pinched and twisted his lips for a second. "It's not a good time right now."

"Should we come back in five minutes, or will you be finished in two?" Madison dished out.

Hampton glared at her. "This is ridiculous. You can't come in here—"

"We have questions we need answered by each of you."

Hampton handed Clayton a tissue, and she blew her nose and then spoke through clipped breaths of air. "I loved Heather. She... She gave me...a break when I had nothing."

"How's that?" Terry asked.

Clayton looked at Terry. "The job market wasn't the best when she hired me, and I was desperate to get a job. It would be one thing if it was just myself, but I need to take care of Dillan."

Madison leaned forward. "Who's Dillan?"

"My son. And he's not Kev's," she tacked on.

Madison nodded. "You said you loved Heather..."

"I did...I do." Clayton shrugged. "Not sure how I'm supposed to phrase it now."

"We spoke to some of your coworkers," Madison began, "others who reported to Heather, and they felt a lot differently about her."

"She wasn't the greatest boss in the world," Clayton admitted, "but she was a good person in here." She laid a hand over her heart.

"People mentioned that Heather seemed to have been losing her mind lately. How do you feel about that? Do you agree?"

"Honestly?" Clayton glanced at Hampton. "I'm sorry to say this, Kev, but I think she *was* losing it."

Hampton's brow pinched, and he shook his head, as if he'd been betrayed somehow.

Clayton took a deep, staggering breath. "I don't want to speak badly of her. Especially not now…" She bit on her bottom lip. "But last week when she got back from lunch, she rushed inside with a look of pure panic on her face. She began telling me over and over, 'He's out there again.'"

"He who?" Madison asked.

"I don't know, and I never saw anyone. She'd tell me to look, but every time I did, no one was there."

Madison took out a picture of Photo Guy and handed it to Clayton. "Does he look familiar to you?"

Clayton shook her head, and Hampton looked away.

"Like I said, I never saw anyone." Clayton handed the photo back to Madison.

Disappointment sank in Madison's gut. She'd hoped that Clayton had caught even just a glimpse of him at some point. She stuffed the picture back into her pocket. "How long did Heather claim to have a stalker?"

"Not too sure. Two, maybe three months. Possibly longer. Time goes so fast."

Hampton was sitting there with his hands clasped in his lap, letting Clayton do all the talking. He hadn't even raised an issue with the picture of Photo Guy or asked if he was still a suspect in his wife's murder.

Madison addressed Hampton. "Do you know anything about Heather having a stalker?"

Hampton frowned, and when he spoke, his voice was gravelly. "I gave her such a hard time about it. Told her she was crazy for thinking someone was following her, watching her." He sniffled, his eyes glazed over, then matched his gaze with Madison's. "And despite what you might think, I did love her, Detective. I still do. It's just she'd go on a tangent about how she was being watched, but whenever I looked, no one was ever there." He glanced at Clayton. "It quickly wore on my nerves. We were fighting a lot about it in recent weeks." His face paled, and his eyes fell to the carpet. "And now it's probably that sicko who killed her."

"We don't know that for sure," Terry said.

Hampton nodded, hopefully, but he didn't seem reassured. In fact, his heartbreak was a tangible entity in the room, and Madison was having a hard time reconciling that with him cheating on his wife. Time to move on from the stalker for now.

"We have a question that you should be able to help us with," she said, snagging Hampton's attention. "Do you know where she got the pendant she wore and what the inscriptions on it meant, including the letters on the outside?"

"I'm going to look like a horrible husband again," Hampton began.

Well, you're certainly not the husband of the year…

Madison bit her tongue.

Hampton continued. "Heather never told me what the pendant was all about, and it wasn't because I didn't try to find out. She had it before we were a couple and told me that it was incredibly personal and she didn't want to talk to me about it."

If Heather had the pendant before she'd met her husband, there was no way the acronym stood for Heather Olivia Hampton. Still, Hampton's not knowing anything about the pendant called into question Hampton's claim about being close with his wife—and if that didn't, the apparent affair did.

"But you were close," Madison said with a sarcastic tone.

"I couldn't force her to tell me," Hampton snapped.

Madison glanced from Hampton to Clayton. She was staring at his profile, and the odd tear was falling down her cheeks.

"You told us you went grocery shopping Sunday morning about six," Madison said.

"I did."

"You also told us you would never do anything to hurt her." Madison couldn't help the accusation that seeped into her voice, the implication was he was doing just that by being an adulterer.

"I wouldn't."

Clayton reached for his hand. "You should probably just tell them. I think they know anyway."

"I was here," Hampton blurted out and his confession seemed to suck air from the room.

So, he was here screwing around on his wife while she was being murdered. "That's true?" Madison asked Clayton.

She nodded.

"And you would go on record to that effect?"

"It's the truth," she said, "so, yes, I would."

Madison regarded the two of them. They appeared to be telling the truth, but appearances couldn't always be relied on. In fact, there was something in Hampton's eyes that said he was holding something back. Was it about Heather's murder or something to do with the pendant? She'd inquire further about that later. "In all the time you were married, you never peeked inside the pendant, not even once, to read the inscription?"

Hampton pursed his lips and nodded. "Once. She was usually always wearing the thing, but one night we went to a social gathering, and we drank a little too much. She passed out when we got home, and I took a look. Don't think she ever knew I saw it. I felt guilty as hell."

Guilty about looking at his wife's pendant but not about cheating on her. Some people...

"Do you know what it meant to her?" Madison asked.

Walls went up and his body stiffened. "Detective, I loved my wife, I still love her, I will always love her, and I will not tarnish her name by making assumptions as to her emotional condition."

Madison shared a look with Terry, then said, "Mr. Hampton—"

"No, I will not elaborate. You're detectives. Go investigate," he said, his voice raising with each word. "You'll probably find out what it actually means and not just my best guess." He rose to his feet and directed them to the door. "Now, if you would both leave."

CHAPTER THIRTY-TWO

Madison was at her desk at the station, holding both Laura's and Heather's photographs and studying them. The differences in their appearances were obvious. Laura was blond, and Heather was brunette. Laura's hair was long, and Heather's was short. Laura was Caucasian, and Heather was Asian. Outside of their looks, Laura was single, and Heather was married. Really, only two things they held in common were their age range and being physically fit. There was likely a third similarity, too: they had the same killer. What else linked the women and motivated their killer to target them?

Madison's cell rang, and she picked up without glancing at the caller ID. It turned out to be Richards asking her and Terry to pay him a visit at the morgue. She and Terry quickly headed out the door.

As they walked into the morgue, Richards lifted a white sheet off Heather Nguyen. "Thought you'd want to see this for yourself." He pointed to a large bruise on her cheekbone. "Assigning a timeline to bruising is not an exact science, but since it didn't show up until now, it tells me it happened peri-mortem or near the TOD. I'd say it has the markings of being made by a direct blow, possibly a fist."

Madison rounded the table. "So the killer binds the first victim with handcuffs, but sucker-punches the second to the face. Wow." It didn't seem the killer was satisfied with just strangling his victims anymore; he wanted to inflict further pain prior to doing so. Or maybe it was just how he'd subdued Heather. It could also be that after he knocked her out, he took the time to look at her pendant. Still, why risk being caught by prolonging his time with the victim? There had to be something about the pendant that drew his eye. Did the killer know what the acronym meant?

Richards's words broke through her thoughts. "And none of her facial bones were broken. He only hit her hard enough to knock her down." Richards looked at her. "Maddy, you have this look about you. Are you hearing anything I'm saying?"

"Oh, I'm hearing everything." A slight lie, but she'd heard enough. She addressed Terry. "We've got to get this guy before he gets to his next victim."

"You're assuming there will be another one."

"I have a very strong feeling there will," she defended. "We need to figure out who he's going to target next."

Terry pressed his lips. "Unless you have a crystal ball…"

She shook her head. "I'm at a loss. For the first time—"

"I wouldn't go that far," Terry jested. His face then turned serious. "We'll figure it out. It's still rather early in the investigation."

He was doing his best to encourage her, but his words fell on unreceptive ears. It killed her that she didn't have it figured out already, and technically, she didn't consider that they were in the early stages of the investigation. Laura's murder had been over two weeks ago. How could she silence her conscience when it was telling her it was her fault another woman was dead?

Madison and Terry left the morgue and went back to their desks.

"Where to next?" she asked.

Terry tapped a pen against the arm of his chair. "Let's take another stab at searching the DMV—"

"We've been down that road, and it was a dead end."

His eyes widened suddenly. "I've got it!"

"Keep talking," she prompted.

"I can't believe you never thought of this. My, I'm a sheer genius."

"Spit it out already, *genius*, I don't have all day."

"No, I have to savor this moment for a while."

Madison narrowed her eyes.

"Fine. Were you filtering by registered plates?"

"Yes..." She tried to remember all the parameters she had in place, then said, "Oh."

"Yeah, *oh*. I mean if the killer was driving that Honda, why would he care about a valid plate?"

"But if his plates aren't valid, surely he would have been pulled over by now." She wasn't ready to hand her partner too much credit just yet.

"Not if he rarely drives the car. He could only take it out to kill people."

"Sick thought, but he'd be taking a big chance of getting caught," she countered, scrambling to her defense, but she could feel any efforts falling short. While in the morgue, she had been thinking that the killer had been careless taking the time to look at the pendant. By extension, maybe he showed the same stupidity by driving a car with expired plates.

"Maddy, assume that guy's the killer," Terry said. "Do you think he's worried about risk? I can see that you're just being stubborn and don't want to admit that it's a great idea."

"Fine, you have me. I think it's a brilliant idea, and I'd like to take credit for it."

"But you can't. It was my idea. Mine, mine, mine."

Oh, he was almost unbearable to be around when he was right about things. She brought up the DMV and made sure to search Honda Accords with letters AVL in the plate— both currently registered and expired. She limited the search to the state.

Madison's desk phone rang, and Officer Ranson informed her that Heather's parents were there to speak with her and Terry.

"Sure, we'll be right up," Madison said. "Anyone in the soft interview room?" It was set up for comfort with a couch, coffeemaker, and small fridge.

"No. You're good to use it." With that, Officer Ranson hung up.

"That was Ranson," Madison informed Terry, who was looking over at her. "Heather's parents are here and want to talk with us. I wonder why."

He shrugged. "I guess we'll find out."

They met the couple at the front desk, and Madison introduced herself and Terry.

"I'm Brad Nguyen and this is my wife, Jenny. We're Heather's parents…or were. *Are?* Guess we always will be."

Jenny started sobbing, her entire body quaking as she tried to get enough air. Her husband stepped closer to her and put an arm around her.

"Her death…her *murder*…has been quite hard on us," Brad explained.

"Of course," Madison replied as she ushered them to the privacy of the soft interview room. Once they were all inside, Terry shut the door and offered them a drink. Both Nguyens declined and sat on the couch.

"I'm sorry for your loss," Madison said as she sat in a facing chair, Terry beside her.

Jenny pulled out a crumpled, worn-out tissue from her purse and dabbed her nose. "My baby girl," she whimpered on an exhalation.

Madison was craving a Hershey's bar—*now*. She imagined herself pulling one from the stash in her desk drawer and chomping off a huge bite.

Brad put an arm around his wife and rubbed her arm. He spoke low and soothingly to her. "They will help us," he said, then turned to Madison. "We don't know everything. Please tell us what happened to her."

How could they not know? Surely, Kevin Hampton would have told them. By obligation, she and Terry only needed to inform the next of kin, which was Hampton. "You don't—"

Jenny sniffled, and Brad said, "All we know right now is what's in the papers."

"Then you know that Heather was strangled, and her body was found in Mitchell Park this past Sunday morning," Madison said, running on an assumption that they did.

Jenny sucked in air and resumed crying.

Brad put his gaze on Madison. His eyes were brimming with tears and indignation. "That son of a bitch."

Madison's heart fluttered. "Who?"

He flailed his arms in the air. "Her husband," he spat as if it should be a foregone conclusion.

Jenny cleared her throat and pierced her husband's profile with a glare. "It's not Kevin's fault. It's yours, Brad."

Madison looked back and forth between husband and wife. Who was to blame—and for what? Were they on the topic of the murder or something else?

"How can you blame me for any of this?" Brad bristled. "Though, it's typical. You always had too soft a spot for that girl when all she did was talk back." His voice cracked, but he pushed through. "She caused you pain, baby." His eyes softened as met his wife's gaze.

"We could have worked through it as a family, but you didn't want to." Her grief morphed into rage. "You made me lose her. You took my baby from me." Her body shook, and she freed herself from her husband's hold on her. "Don't touch me."

"Please, Jenny, you're being—"

"Don't touch me!" Jenny rose to her feet.

Brad also stood and moved toward his wife.

Jenny's face darkened, and her body was quaking almost as badly as a seizing epileptic. "No, no, no." Her protests gave way to crying again, and she ended up falling into her husband's embrace. They stood there hugging each other, and Madison and Terry gave them a few minutes.

"What happened to your daughter is inexcusable," Madison tiptoed, and the Nguyens parted from their embrace. "And her death is no one's fault except for the person who did this. And we plan on finding out who that was. You have my word."

The Nguyens sat down again.

"I'm so sorry that you had to find out about your daughter in the paper," Madison said. "You don't have a good relationship with your son-in-law?"

Brad shook his head. "Not really, but we reached out to him when we heard, and he refused to speak with us. He just said if we wanted to know more, we were to contact you."

The size of the rift between Hampton and the Nguyens had to be large—and probably with a long-standing history—for Hampton to refuse to speak with his in-laws about their daughter's murder. Nothing was more final than death, after all, and it should disintegrate any disagreements. "Can I ask why he wouldn't tell you any more than that?" Madison asked, knowing she was treading on delicate ground.

Brad glanced at his wife, then said, "He didn't like us, and we didn't like him."

"Okay, but still… It's too bad your differences couldn't be pushed aside, considering the situation," Madison said. She wasn't completely buying that it was a matter of simply not liking each other; something had happened.

Her words had sat out there for some time before either Nguyen spoke. It was Jenny who broke the silence. "It goes back a long ways."

Madison leaned forward. "Mrs. Nguyen, it may be important for us to know why you and your son-in-law don't get along."

Jenny glanced at her husband. "I'm not sure it's of relevance." She blew her nose and stuffed the well-used tissue back into her purse.

Madison fought the urge to say something; in this case the power of silence might be the best way to go. She was pleased when Jenny spoke again.

"Back when Heather was a teenager," she said, her husband eyeing her, "she got into a lot of trouble with boys. She had a lot of them."

Didn't the Saunderses say practically the same thing about Laura?

Jenny continued. "Once, there was no going back. She got herself in too deep and wound up preg—"

"She needed to be taught a lesson, Jenny," her husband cut in.

"She was young," Jenny said, speaking over him. "She made a mistake, but we could never forgive her." She glowered at her husband and added, "Brad was busy in our church."

Madison looked at Jenny, then Brad, back to Jenny. From what she knew, Heather hadn't had a baby—and what did the Nguyens' religion have to do with all this? "I'm not sure why…"

"He didn't want others speaking badly about us and our illegitimate grandchild," Jenny said.

"You make it sound so horrible," Brad seethed. "We loved her, Detectives, but she needed to be accountable for her actions. At some point, you have to show tough love."

Is that what he calls abandoning his daughter in her time of need?

Madison could acknowledge there were times tough love was needed, but in this instance, it was a hard pill to swallow. "So—what?—you kicked her out?"

"She was sixteen…" Jenny's words parted off into a sob, but she composed herself quickly. "And, yes, we kicked her out," she hissed and glared at her husband again. "We left her all alone in this world with a baby."

Hearing Jenny actually say "baby" made Madison's mind go to Heather's pendant and Hampton's claim she'd had it long before he came along. The pendant was related to something incredibly personal. Maybe Heather's parents had given it to her?

"Do you know anything about a heart-shaped pendant your daughter wore?"

Both Nguyens shook their heads and disappointment snaked through Madison. "Did you ever talk to Heather after you…after she left?"

Jenny cleared her throat. "I couldn't find any way of reaching her for the longest time, and by the time I did, years had passed, and she refused to talk. I thought about showing up and approaching her in person, but I'm too much of a coward, I suppose. We ended up hearing that she got married, and I was happy that she was settling down. Her child would have a father, too. We used to think that Kevin was the father, but now we don't think so."

"Why is that?" Madison asked.

Jenny shook and tears streamed down her face. She pulled out another crumpled tissue from her purse and dabbed her nose.

"We don't know for sure…" Brad balled his hand into a tight fist and covered his mouth. "But we did hear that she gave her baby up for adoption." A tear slid down his cheek, and he wiped it.

Madison could feel the pain emanating from him; he was a broken man full of regret over a decision he had made years ago.

"We tried to find our grandson," Brad added, "but he had already been adopted by the time we found him."

Madison wanted to say something comforting, but words were failing her. Instead, she took a well-traveled and familiar path. "Heather's body should be released this week. I can let you know."

"Not that that bastard will let us see her," Brad countered. "He'll probably make sure we're banned from the funeral." He put an arm around his sobbing wife.

Damn, I could use a Hershey's bar right the F now!

"We could take you down to see her," she told them softly.

"Please," Brad said, and Jenny nodded.

The Nguyens fell completely apart at the sight of their daughter lying on the gurney. Tears were flying, and Jenny had wailed hauntingly for a long time.

Watching them had stabbed Madison's heart like it did every time she delivered "the news" to a family. No amount of training could steel her emotionally when witnessing the sheer heartbreak of the loved ones left behind. Eventually, this emotional toll of the job might devour her alive, but no matter how she tried, she couldn't force herself to become a robot.

After the Nguyens left, she and Terry checked on the progress of the DMV search. Her eyes widened as she verbalized the findings. "Almost five hundred results."

"Whoa, what parameters did you put in?"

"The letters AVL in the plate, Honda Accord, currently registered and expired, and had it run for the state."

"The state?" He gasped. "Is this your first day?"

She narrowed her eyes at him. "You remember I'm the senior detective here?"

"Well, there's no way we're going to get the results we want that way. You're lucky you only got back five hundred matches."

"Then, what do you suggest, *genius*?"

"Narrow it down to the city of Stiles."

"We don't know he's from here."

"We don't know he's not, and it's a place to start. I'm sure you'll get back a lot less than five hundred results, too."

"Huh."

"Just key in the new search parameters and let me take you for the dinner I owe you."

He stood in front of his full-length mirror, not admiring the view of his reflection but contemplating the next step, the final step. His primary target had only moments to live. The thought, as it surged through his mind, caused him a moment's joy—and joy was such a hard thing to come by these days. He had to savor it while he had the opportunity. Though he was also pleased with the moniker attributed to him in the *Stiles Times*: the Stiles Strangler.

He smiled at himself, knowing tomorrow was the day he'd mete out his final justice. He'd do it right now if he could, but the timing had to be perfect. He couldn't allow himself to give into his rage. Rather, he needed to keep it tightly reined—even if that was proving more difficult with each passing day.

He looked at the tie had around his neck. It was another beautiful G&C number that would be sure to do the trick, as all the others had done. He ran his hand down the length of it. Such beautiful fabric, such a beautiful design, and such a beautiful purpose he had for it. He connected eyes with himself again in the mirror and saw his weaknesses rising to the surface. His apprehension and his possible regret over the last kills threatened to immobilize him.

It was Heather's locket that was really haunting him. When he'd seen those three letters on the outside, he felt compelled to look inside. The inscription only angered him further. After all, who the hell did she think she was? Did she think a few artfully contrived words etched into a piece of jewelry would compensate for past sins? Did she stop to consider for one second all the pain she had caused?

Unlikely! And that was why both Heather and Laura had gotten what they deserved. He had nothing to feel guilty about. Now, the woman who had started everything in the first place—it was her turn to die.

CHAPTER THIRTY-THREE

Madison was in the passenger seat while Terry drove to Sammy's, Stiles go-to place for Greek food. "Okay, so first you pick where we're going," she said, though she'd never say no to Sammy's, "and then you insist on driving. You know how nauseated I get when I'm not the driver."

"You really think I buy that?" Terry looked at her and quirked a brow.

Nothing escaped her *genius* partner, and she laughed. "I don't understand why you wouldn't."

"Uh-huh."

He pulled into Sammy's parking lot.

"So, do you have coupons?" She butted her head toward the restaurant and had a hard time not smiling again, but her attempt to act serious was flawed from the start.

"Oh, I might." Terry made a show of pulling down his visor and shuffling through some papers that were there.

"How could I have guessed?" She knew she shouldn't push it; he was buying her dinner. "Your little lady have you on a budget?"

Terry shot her a look that shut her down. She'd gone one jest too far.

Apparently, mention of his wife was a sore spot. His face softened as he said, "You should have spoken up if you'd rather have gone somewhere else, but I said I'd take you for dinner, not a fancy gourmet meal at an award-winning restaurant."

The glint in his eyes told her that all was forgiven. Besides, he likely knew just the thought of dining in a fine restaurant made her uncomfortable. She was a simple meat-and-potatoes kind of woman, and she didn't have caviar dreams and champagne wishes. The only reason she was in the city at all was to pursue her career. Thinking of that made her curious whether the DMV results had come back. Was the killer's information on her desktop right now?

She let the thoughts go; she'd get there in due time. Her mind needed a bit of a reprieve, and she was so exhausted she'd love to sleep for a month after they caught this killer. She didn't even want to think about the fact that there'd just be another one to hunt down.

They went inside the restaurant, and only five people were in line. Not anywhere near as busy as she'd seen it before. Maybe she'd be back at the station faster than she'd thought.

They placed their orders and waited at the counter for them to be prepared and then took a booth next to the front window.

He pointed at the Greek salad she was eating. "So…what? You're getting all healthy on me now?"

"I thought I'd take it easy on your wallet," she teased, waving her fork over her meal. But the truth was by the time she got to place her order, she was more tired than hungry—and she wasn't about to admit that she had a Hershey's bar after the Nguyens had left.

Terry rolled his eyes and stuffed a large forkful of food into his mouth. He swallowed it before speaking. "I was going to pay you back, too. Make good on our bet."

"No way!" She gasped.

"Nope, you just blew it. Blew it goodbye."

"Oh really? You don't want me to get hostile on your ass, do you?"

"Oh, I'm scared." He pretended to quake.

She laughed, and people were starting to watch them. One woman smiled at Madison, and she got the feeling the stranger thought Madison and Terry were a couple. How absurd that would be! Terry was the brother she never had.

They both went about eating their meals, and Madison wanted to ask about Annabelle, but thinking back on the reaction she'd received upon mentioning her in the car, it was probably best to say nothing. Still the words tumbled out, "Are you and Annabelle going to be okay?" She winced, wishing she had better control of what she said sometimes. She expected she was going to get a lecture about how it was none of her business again. Instead, Terry looked right through her, his expression revealing nothing.

"Couldn't let it go, could you?" Irritated. "Guess I should have known you'd pry."

Madison swallowed roughly and felt her cheeks heat, but she remained silent.

"I'm sorry. I know I'm being a jerk lately. It's just that…" He paused, seeming to search his mind for the right words. "Maddy, you're my favorite girl save my wife, and things are rough right now. *Real* rough."

Now, she really wanted to ask if Annabelle had cheated on him.

"She's not cheating on me, if that's what you're thinking," he said, reading her mind as usual and stabbing at his souvlaki with a fork.

"Well, you never know. I mean, look." She gestured at him. "See what she has to live with." She was teasing to lighten the air.

"Hardy-har. You should quit your day job and be a stand-up." His eyes drifted to his food, then back up to meet her gaze. "We're likely going to break up."

"Why?" The one-word question squeaked out.

"She wants kids. I don't."

"I didn't think either of you guys wanted them."

"We didn't. Now it's only me who doesn't." He slurped some soda. "I thought everything was going great, but she tells me she wants…more."

"Two beagles aren't enough?" She was trying to lighten the mood again, but his brow tightened and tugged downward.

"Seriously? At a moment like this, you're dragging my dogs into it?"

Madison didn't know how to backpedal out of this one, and stress was settling into her chest…until he smiled.

"I'm giving you a rough time now," he admitted.

"Well, stop it."

"As for the dogs, nope, not enough. She's now set on having a *human* baby."

She felt the pressure for Terry and set her fork down. "Oh."

He pointed to the salad left on her plate. "You going to eat that?"

Guess the personal conversation's over…

She looked down at the remaining food and shook her head. "No."

"You mind if…" Terry nudged his head toward her plate.

She pushed it toward him. "Knock yourself out."

"Don't mind if I do." Terry dug in, and her phone rang.

She took the call, and when she was finished, Terry was looking at her expectantly.

"So…" he prompted.

She felt the smile spread her lips. "Cynthia confirmed that the photo of Laura and Photo Guy was photoshopped. Her picture had been taken from the one of her with her aunt and uncle."

"Really?" Terry stamped out. "Why the heck? Assuming he's the killer, he's got to be the dumbest criminal in the history of mankind."

"Yet, we still haven't found him," she said, hating the admission.

Madison should have gone home after dinner, like Terry had. He'd warned her that she could be facing hours of digging, but she had stubbornly insisted on going back to the station. After all, how could little, obsessive-compulsive Madison sleep without having at least one peek at the DMV results? And now, instead of sitting on her couch staring mindlessly at HBO, she was fishing through the results.

And Terry had been right—not that she'd tell him as much. There were far less than five hundred matches, but there were still fifty. She'd have to work through each plate, one by one, and bring up each and every associated driver's license photo. Just hoping she'd get lucky.

She yawned and looked at her wristwatch. *11:03.*

She ran both hands down her face, wishing she'd wake up, but her vison was starting to blur from exhaustion and staring at the computer screen. She pinched her eyes shut, hoping that would help, but it only made her want to close them until morning. Still, she pushed on, clicking away, until finally just after one in the morning, she couldn't keep her eyes open anymore.

She called it a day then, trying to justify it with the thought nothing could be accomplished at such an hour. But that was ludicrous. Justice knew no bounds, had no curfews and no time restraints. Unfortunately, her body did.

CHAPTER THIRTY-FOUR

Madison walked into the bullpen the next day at one thirty in the afternoon.

She found Terry at his desk. "Why didn't you call or wake me up?"

He opened his mouth to speak, but snapped it shut when Toby Sovereign came sauntering toward her.

"How nice of you to come in today, Knight," Sovereign said.

"What's it to you?" she shot back. She'd crawled into bed this morning when she got home and passed out. She'd only come to less than an hour ago, and when she did, she'd showered and rushed here.

She ignored Sovereign, but he failed to take the hint. He walked over.

"Looking especially lovely today. Must be late because you put extra effort in. It's like you knew you'd see me."

God, she hated this man and wondered what she ever saw in him. He stood before her, not one wrinkle in his white shirt or pressed pants, and he was smiling at her with a smile she used to find charming. Maybe if she ignored him, he'd go away. She turned to her partner. "What are you working on, Terry?"

"Now you're ignoring me?" Sovereign winced. "Come on, Knight, why are you so cruel to me?"

Do you really need to ask?

She grimaced and stared blankly at Terry's monitor, doing her best to squeeze Sovereign's existence from her awareness.

Terry looked from her to Sovereign and back again, but didn't say anything.

Good thinking, partner…

"Well, Vixen, guess we'll talk another time." The words came off Sovereign's lips flooded with flirtation. "Just tell me when you want to meet up at the range."

She didn't look at him, but said, "As long as you're willing to be the target."

She heard footsteps moving away and turned to see Sovereign's retreating figure.

Finally! And what nerve asking me why I'm cruel to you!

Her heart sank, and she hated that she was feeling any conflict. She couldn't stand him, couldn't stomach what he did to her, and yet now guilt threatened to set in for being rude to him. She was pathetic.

"Vixen?" Terry chuckled.

"Not another word." She tapped him on the back of the head.

"What the—" He rubbed where she had hit him. "Now you're hitting my head? Are we starting something new now that my shoulder's been well tenderized?"

"You're such a crybaby." She chose to ignore that Terry seemed to know about her past relationship with Sovereign.

"Keep it up, Miss, and I'll start hitting back."

"Idle threats, Terry. We both know that." She smiled at him and put her gaze back on his monitor; this time actually looking at what was on the screen. It was her DMV results. "What are you doing?"

"I thought you'd be happy."

Maybe she should be happy, but her initial reaction was irritation. "I was here until after one working on that, and you just run with it as if you were already on it?"

He shrugged. "I just thought I'd help out. It is *our* investigation."

"Then where were you last night?" she tossed back, instantly feeling like she might be acting a tad possessive.

"And where were you this morning?"

She groaned. "Fine. We are partners. Working on this together."

"Right. Really, what's the big deal?" He started pecking at the keyboard and clicking with the mouse.

Had this man learned absolutely nothing in married life? "Fine" for a woman didn't mean everything was hunky-dory, it meant simply that—*fine*. Today the translation literally meant: *I'd love to fight about this, but I don't have the energy right now.*

A picture came up on Terry's monitor, and her heart raced. "Oh my God," she exclaimed. "That's Photo Guy."

She read the details to herself.

Ethan Younge, 9238 Elmwood Boulevard, Stiles.

She looked closer at the file. The plate had expired ten years ago and had originally been connected to an '87 Ford Mustang.

She pointed to the monitor. "Print that guy's photo and information," she said and bounced impatiently in front of the printer. "Warm up, you stupid thing. Why does this thing always need to warm up?"

"Maybe because it's female." Terry was grinning, and she might have decked him if the printer hadn't chosen that moment to spit out a sheet.

She snatched it before it hit the tray and looked at the photo. "That's definitely him." She passed the printout to Terry.

"Ow." He pulled his hand back and sucked his fingertip. "Paper cut," he hissed, then held out his finger to inspect the damage.

"This is our guy," she repeated, overlooking her partner's complaint. "Look at his vehicle history. Any Hondas, by chance?"

Terry consulted the report on his screen. "A '98 Honda Accord."

"Color?"

"Silver."

"Leaving now." She turned toward the exit, knowing Terry would follow; he always did.

CHAPTER THIRTY-FIVE

His heart was beating faster than advisable. This was the moment he had waited for. All the years and all the planning would not be wasted. They would come to fruition today. See what all the papers would say about him now—and he'd walk away from all of it. He had a backup plan. He knocked on the front door, and not long afterward, the door opened. "Hello, Mother."

She backed into the house and motioned for him to follow. He closed—and locked—the door behind them.

"What are you doing here?" She studied his face. "It's the middle of the afternoon. Shouldn't you be at…" Her words trailed off as she peered into his eyes, and something in hers flickered. Her mouth gaped open.

He lunged toward her and put his hand over her mouth. "I wouldn't think of it."

She bucked beneath his hold, trying to bite his hand, but he kept it flat. She said something, but all he could discern was mumbles.

Ah! The satisfaction that came with that. It was his turn to talk; her turn to listen.

"I'm going to let you go," he said. "I want you to sit on the couch and shut up. Not one word." He spoke so closely into her ear she could probably feel his spittle.

She nodded in silence.

He let go of her, she screamed, and he cuffed her across the face. "Mother, I'm so disappointed. Look what you made me do. Now, your beautiful face is marred." He fought off the sinister smirk he had growing inside—just waiting for the happiness, the joy, and the elation that would come when she drew her final breath.

She dropped onto the sofa and put a hand on her cheek, tears streaming down her face. "Wh-why are y-you doing this?" Her voice cracked and stuttered.

There she was distressed, and he was on top of the world! Seeing her grief, her fear, made him feel alive.

"You brought this upon yourself." He sat down on the coffee table in front of the sofa and leaned in toward her.

"You're scaring me," she whimpered.

"*I'm* scaring you? Wow, and I'm not trying." His tone was dry, riddled with sarcasm. "Life is about justice, and today I will create my own."

She bit her bottom lip, her chin quivering like a fish fillet frying in oil. "I'm sorry for…" Her breath hitched, and fresh tears fell.

He didn't say a word, and he refused to allow hers to affect him. It was far too late for an apology, anyway. Who the hell did she think she was? He summoned courage to follow through on his purpose, while years of pent-up emotions battered him. But he couldn't allow himself to become weak. It was too late to turn back now.

"Why are you doing this?" she beseeched him, her voice so low he barely heard her.

He refused to look at her, and a single tear slid down his cheek. He quickly wiped it with the back of his hand, disgusted at his sign of weakness, and he hoped she hadn't seen it. But she leaned forward, reaching out a hand toward him. He moved in closer still.

He gripped her by the wrist. "Don't think of touching me. You have no damn right to touch me!" He rose and pulled her up by the hair, forcing her from the couch.

"Please, don't hurt me, Ethan. You leave now, and no one has to know about this. About you coming here."

Hearing his name coming from her lips slowed his heart rate and his breath. A sense of calm blanketed him as it had just before he'd executed the other murders.

She screamed again and started to run.

He easily caught her, grabbing her by the back of her T-shirt. He yanked her back so hard she fell to the floor. He got on top of her, pinning her body beneath his, her arms overhead, her wrists clamped by his hands. She tried to lift her arms and squirmed in an effort to free herself—but to no avail. He wasn't going to budge; he'd waited too long for this moment. And looking down on her, he felt nothing except the hunger for revenge. Adrenaline pumped though him, blood rushed in his ears, and a feeling of euphoria set in. She would finally pay for her actions, for setting his life on the course it had gone.

After a few minutes, and for seemingly no reason at all, she lost her fight. She became motionless, no longer crying. Her eyes were frozen on the tie around his neck.

"You killed those girls," she whispered.

He smirked at the recognition of his work, feeling immense pride. He said nothing as he yanked the tie from his neck.

"Why…why did you do it?"

"You don't need to know everything."

She started to fight against him again, and it was apparent he would have to restrain her in another manner so that he could get the job done. His gaze fell to the welts on her cheek, and he had the solution. He released one of her hands and punched her, as he had Heather when she'd raised her Mace sprayer. As his fist was in motion toward Mother, she rushed out the words, "I loved you," but it was too late to stop the momentum. His blow knocked her out—her eyes rolled back, and her head fell to the side.

He pulled her arms down and pinned them under his body and proceeded to wrap the tie around her neck. As he did, her words haunted him: *I loved you.* Sadness welled up in his throat, and he choked back the urge to cry.

This murder was more personal than he'd anticipated; the others easier by comparison. After all these years of convincing himself that she deserved this fate, he now second-guessed himself. His gaze fell to the sight of her unconscious form.

He could walk away without seeing this through, disappear and leave everything behind. No one ever had to know. No one ever had to know. He dismissed the stupidity. Of course people would know! She wouldn't keep her mouth shut, and she'd proudly see him fall.

He pulled the necktie tight, tighter, and tighter still. Her eyes sprung open, bulging wide, her fate written in them. She tried to move but was powerless to stop him. He continued to work the tie, her body convulsing beneath him—until all movement stopped.

CHAPTER THIRTY-SIX

Madison couldn't get to Ethan Younge's residence fast enough. She weaved through traffic, lights flashing and sirens wailing. Her phone rang, and she answered as she rushed through an intersection. Upon hearing her caller's news, she screeched to a halt and performed a U-Turn.

Terry grabbed for the front dash. "What the hell are you doing?"

She slapped her palms on the steering wheel. "We're too late. There's been another victim."

"Number three. So we're looking for a serial killer."

"I'm afraid so."

She drove to the address given to her by dispatch, which turned out to be a neighborhood well outside of Madison's financial bracket. The only way she'd ever be able to live there—if she even wanted to—was if she won the lottery, but her chances were nil as she didn't play.

Two cruisers were out front when she and Terry arrived, and an officer stood at the door. He nodded a greeting to them.

Terry addressed him. "What have we got?"

"A DB, female, sixties, name is Evelyn Younge. Spelled with an 'e' on the end. Her son found her."

"Younge?" Madison squeaked out. Her heart galloped. Could the son be Photo Guy? She grabbed the officer's arm. "You're sure about her last name?"

"Positive." The officer's brow pinched, seemingly not understanding why she was having a hard time accepting that. "Anyway, the son's still in there. The vic was found lying on the floor, a huge welt on her face, and a tie around her neck. Officer Weir is there, too. We were the first at the scene."

Madison bolted past Terry and into the home.

Inside, it felt more like a museum or gallery, not a residence. An oriental, oval-shaped area rug sat on top of marble flooring. The ceilings were double-story and vaulted, and a large staircase with maple banisters wound up the right wall and ended at sizable landing that overlooked the entrance. In front of Madison, there was a round table with a black marble top that had a three-foot-tall urn full of Boston ferns sitting on it.

Beyond that, an oil painting hung on the wall, a picture light mounted over it. Three arched doorways came off from the entry. One went to the back, beside where the painting was, one went off to the left, and the other to the right. The doorway at the back led to the kitchen and its maple cabinetry. She peeked through the door to the right to find an intimate sitting room.

"In here, Detective," a man's voice called out from the room through the door on the left.

She entered, finding herself in another massive room. The ceilings here weren't double-story but easily ten-feet high, and the flooring was maple hardwood. A fireplace with a custom-built mantle was the centerpiece of the room on the back wall. A faux fur rug sat on the floor in front of it, a maple coffee table on top of that. On each side of the fireplace, two more oil paintings were displayed with more lights above them. There was also an antique bar cart in the room with an assortment of crystal decanters full of amber liquid.

Daylight flooded in through a bay window at the front of the house, and the curtains were drawn open.

In full view of the road…

Yet that hadn't stopped the killer. He was continuing to escalate, and Madison wondered how many more victims there would be.

She finally looked down at the victim. Evelyn was lying on the floor, her arms to her sides. Her eyes weren't clouded over but marred with petechiae. The murder had happened recently, and Madison could imagine Evelyn's chest rising with air.

Madison stared at the tie around Evelyn's neck. The tag on the back of the tie was visible. Another G&C.

Something else stood out to Madison: Evelyn hadn't been posed. Had the killer been in a hurry to leave—or to call it in?

"Detective Knight," a man said from the doorway, and Madison turned to see an officer with a man next to him.

She stared at the man, at first unable to move. It was Photo Guy, mere feet away from her. He was as handsome in real life as he was in a photograph. His complexion, tanned like a roasted almond, offset the dark hair sprinkled with gray. Now face-to-face with him, it was hard to imagine him as a killer—but she knew better.

Madison moved to him. "You're coming downtown for questioning."

The officer next to him stared at her in confusion, began to say something, but Photo Guy, a.k.a. Ethan Younge, beat him to it.

"Why would I need to do that? My mother was killed, and I found her."

Are you sure you *didn't kill her?*

"Why are you here?" she asked him.

"She called me," Ethan rushed out and looked around the room from Madison to Terry, back to Madison. "Why are you looking at me like I had something to do with this?"

"I don't know," she said nonchalant. "Did you?"

Ethan stiffened. "I will not dignify that with an answer."

"Okay, so your mother called you. Why?" She'd play along for a little while.

"She said that the toilet was backing up, and she needed me to come over, shut off the water, and fix the problem."

Madison couldn't hear any running water. "Did you turn the water off?"

His eyes widened. "Crap, I…I forgot all about it once I saw her lying here…" He made a move like he was about to leave the room.

Madison stepped forward and held up a hand. "Mr. Younge, you to stay here." She told an officer to check on the situation, but then realized the house probably had several bathrooms. She turned to Ethan. "Which bathroom?"

He shook his head and raised his shoulders. "I don't know, but there are three of them." He went on to tell the officer where each one was.

The officer left, and Madison faced Ethan. "Let's assume you're telling the truth…" *Fat chance in hell…* "Why would she call you to fix a plumbing problem?"

"Dad's not much of a handyman."

Madison crossed her arms. "And you expect me to believe that?"

"Why wouldn't you?"

"For one, it seems like a hokey story to me. And two, I think you killed her and then called in her murder. All you're trying to do now is look like you innocently stumbled over the body."

Ethan jutted out his jaw. "I don't care if you don't believe me." He pointed toward the cordless phone that was on the coffee table. "Pick it up, redial the last number. I called emergency services from my cell phone."

"I can't touch that phone until the scene's been processed,

but you have my word that we will check the caller history."
She moved closer to him. "Like I stated earlier, we're going to
need you to come downtown with us and—"

"Ethan!" A woman yelled from the entryway, her steps
coming closer. "Oh my God." She stopped, her hands going
to her mouth as she took in the dead woman on the floor.
"Evelyn, oh my God. Ethan…" She ran to him and flung her
arms around him.

*How the hell did she get by the officer guarding the crime
scene?*

Madison stepped in front of Ethan to block him, but the
woman moved around her. Madison shot a look at Terry to
reprimand the officer outside. This was a murder scene, and
she didn't care if the president showed up, he shouldn't be
allowed in.

The woman pulled back from her embrace with Ethan
and looked at him. "Are you okay?"

Ethan pinched the bridge of his nose and shut his eyes.
When he opened them, he was looking directly at Madison.

She repeated her earlier request with added weight. "You
can come willingly, or we can use force. It's up to you."

"Are you mad?" the woman exclaimed.

"We need to question him in regard to his mother's
murder, and you need to leave immediately." Madison
gestured for an officer to escort her.

"I'm not going anywhere." She shirked out of reach when
the officer went for her arm.

"Who are you?" Madison asked, though it didn't matter
who she was; she needed to leave.

"I'm Brooke Younge, Ethan's wife." She stared Madison in
the eye.

"I'm going to have to ask you to step aside." Madison
pulled out a set of handcuffs.

"I'm not moving until you tell me what this is about." She
put hands on hips.

"Very well, you can come with—"

"Get your hands off me," a man said, and Madison turned to find another trespasser on scene; this one an older gentleman, and he was struggling with the officer who should have been watching the front door. Instead, the officer released the man and stood in the doorway, looking like an ape. He should have his badge stripped or, at the very least, a formal reprimand and a note on his file.

"Evy." The older man lurched forward, about to get down on the floor next to the dead woman, but Terry stopped him.

The man turned on Terry with eyes that were full of pain. "I'm her husband...Frank."

"I'm sorry, but you can't touch her," Terry told him.

Frank shrugged Terry's hand off his shoulder and lamented, "Evy, my baby, what happened to you?"

"You need to clear this scene, Officer," Madison seethed.

"Sorry..." The officer went to reach for Frank, and Madison walked over to Ethan.

"So which is it?" she asked. "Willingly? Or we cuff you?"

Ethan stepped forward and dipped his head in consent.

"What are you doing?" Brooke pleaded, tears falling down her cheeks.

"It's all right, baby," Ethan assured her.

"What the hell are you doing?" Frank snarled, tugging on the officer who now had a hold on him.

"We have some questions we need to ask your son."

Frank's eyes darted to Ethan. "Don't you say anything, you hear me. Nothing. Nothing at all. I'm getting you a lawyer."

CHAPTER THIRTY-SEVEN

Madison had Photo Guy behind bars, but now she couldn't talk to him. He'd requested a lawyer when they hauled him in, and it was taking a bit of time for the Younges to round up a defense attorney. That meant Ethan spent the night in holding—and in a way, so did she. All she wanted to do was start questioning him about the murders. Before he'd requested representation, he'd calmly said that everything would work out. She felt the same way. By the time this was over, the victims' families, including his own, would have justice served. Still, she'd gone home and had a fitful night's sleep. It was probably only made worse by how well Ethan was handling the accusations against him, especially for someone with no criminal background.

With the light of a new day, she was beyond ready to get some answers, and Ethan's lawyer was on his way. While she waited, she placed a courtesy call to the Nguyens to let them know that Heather's body had been released, but they'd have to get in touch with their son-in-law for the funeral details.

"Detective Knight," Winston said from behind her, and she turned to face him. "Blake Golden's coming in the front door." He just dropped that and kept on walking.

Strange…

Madison headed toward the front counter.

"My favorite detective," Golden greeted her. He was wearing a power suit—overpriced, no doubt—with a red tie.

She wished she could counter with something snide, but she had nada. "What can I do for you?"

"I'm here to represent Ethan Younge."

Wonderful!

"You seem to be speechless." His mouth twitched like he was fighting off a grin.

"Why would I be?" She reached for the gold necklace she was wearing and squeezed it between her fingers. "Come this way."

She led him into interrogation room two, ordered Ethan to be brought up from holding, and went in search of her partner.

Fifteen minutes later, Ethan was in with Golden, but she hadn't been able to find Terry, and his phone kept ringing straight to voice mail. She even had him paged in the hopes he might be somewhere in the building.

She watched through the one-way mirror as Golden introduced himself to Ethan.

"Blake Golden?" Younge's eyes lit in recognition of the name, and he smiled, showing a large dimple in his right cheek. "You're that guy from TV. '*Guilty, not guilty, we don't care. But whichever it is, choose us for the best representation. Don't take a chance on your future.*'" Ethan sang the words to the commercial jingle, making Madison want to puke.

Golden nodded.

"Leave it to Frank to get me the best," Ethan said.

She turned the mics off and let Golden confer with his client.

Terry finally entered the observation room fifteen minutes later.

"All right, I'm here, let's go," he said.

"Really? That's it? No explanation as to where you've been?"

"You my keeper now?" He scowled and brushed past her.

They entered the interrogation room.

"So, now that everyone's acquainted," she began, "let's get to the point. We'll discuss your mother's murder first." She was watching Ethan, trying to read his facial expressions and body language, but the most she got from him was indifference. It was hard to know if it sprang from grief or guilt. "Why were you at your mother's?" she asked.

"I thought we covered this yesterday. She asked me to come over."

"And why did she do that?"

"I told you. Her toilet was backing up." Ethan glanced at Golden, and Madison figured Golden had coached him. Ethan added, "I didn't kill my mother or those other women."

Golden took a deep breath.

"What other women?" Madison jumped on that.

"Do you think I live under a rock? Two other women were killed recently, both strangled."

"Why would you assume we suspect your involvement with those murders?"

"Well, don't you—"

Golden put his hand on Ethan's forearm and said to Madison, "Unless you have evidence that implicates my client, Detective Knight—"

"Mr. Golden, I can assure you we have reason to suspect your client, but one thing at a time. I'd like to revisit my first question, Mr. Younge. You said that she called you because of a backed-up toilet?"

"That's right."

"I'm finding that hard to believe given that there was no evidence of a plumbing problem. No water damage, nothing. You had said you forgot all about the matter when you *found* your mother." She put "found" in finger quotes and then looked at Terry. "Do you remember any water damage being reported?" Her partner shook his head, and they turned their gazes back to Ethan.

Ethan paled. "I know she called me about the toilet. Did you check her recent calls?"

"We did." She gave birth to a pregnant pause. "The last number dialed from your mother's phone was to FYI Inc."

"There you go." Ethan flailed his hands. "That's where I work."

"It doesn't mean that your mother placed the call," she countered.

Ethan's chest heaved, and he glanced at Golden.

Madison continued. "You could have made the call to cover your tracks."

"Why that and not do something to the toilet, then? Huh, tell me that?" Ethan asked, a little on the hysterical side. No more Mr. Calm.

"We spoke to the company's receptionist," Madison started, unaffected by Ethan's emotional reaction, "to see if she remembered the call from Evelyn. She explained that they had two numbers. See, I had to hit zero to speak with her when I called the one your mother did. The receptionist explained that the line was connected to a twenty-four-hour automated answering service, a back-door line."

"So she punched in my extension," Ethan said.

"Where were you before heading over to your mother's?" Madison asked, ignoring what Ethan had said.

"I was at work—FYI Inc.—where I am every weekday from eight to five."

"So why didn't she call your father?" She'd asked him this at the crime scene but wanted to see if his answer would be the same in the light of a new day.

"Dad isn't good with home repairs—electrical, plumbing, whatever you name it. Not to mention when mother did silly things, which she did fairly often, Dad would never let her live it down. Once she poured grease down the kitchen sink, and it sealed up tight. Dad teased her for months about it."

"And yesterday she called about the plugged toilet," she said in a conversational manner.

He nodded. "I can't explain why it didn't make a mess. I know I didn't deal with it. I had forgotten all about until you asked why I was there."

"Or perhaps it was a matter of there being nothing to forget about."

"Get to the point, Detective," Golden said.

Madison sat back and crossed her legs. She played the power of silence for a few seconds. "Here's *the point*. We believe your client, Ethan Younge, killed Laura Saunders, Heather Nguyen, and his own mother, Evelyn Younge."

Ethan's eyes were widened pools, staring past her.

Madison fanned out crime-scene photographs of all three women, including that of his mother.

Ethan looked at them, and when his gaze landed on his mother's photo, he picked it up and sat there studying it.

"How do you feel when you see your mother like that?" Madison prompted.

Silence.

Is he feeling remorse?

She was having a hard time reading him. "Mr. Younge?" she prodded, hoping he'd say something, no matter how minimal.

A few tears fell down his cheeks.

"Mr. Younge," Madison repeated.

He sniffled, blinking away more tears as he matched his gaze with hers. "I feel pain."

"Why did you do it?" she said gently.

"Do what?" he spat, "Murder those women? My own mother?"

"Yes."

"I didn't."

He was so put-together. Maybe he had MPD, multiple-personality disorder. Maybe his evil self carried out the murders, while his good side was repressed and knew nothing about it. She went on and asked him where he had been at the time of Laura's murder.

He leaned forward, letting his forehead fall into his hands. Seconds later, he raised his head. "I don't know. That was, what, over two weeks ago now?"

She pushed the photograph of Laura closer toward him but said nothing.

Golden spoke up. "You need more than his lack of an alibi, Detective."

"I'm sure we'll be able to place him there, but we'll leave that until a little later." A good start would be getting his DNA, and there was a warrant for it already in the works.

"Why don't we try a date a little more recent?" she began. "How about this past Sunday between five and eight in the morning?"

"I can barely remember yesterday. And I don't want to remember yesterday."

"So, you have no alibi for that time period on Sunday?" she pressed. He met her gaze again, and Madison would swear he knew exactly where he had been. "Mr. Younge?" she prompted, tiring of sounding like a broken record.

"Please...Ex-excuse me." He got to his feet and paced, his face pale.

"Mr. Younge,' Madison snapped. "Please sit—"

Ethan held up a finger and quickly turned away from everyone.

Then he vomited.

"We're done here." Golden put his hands on the table to get up.

"No, I'll be fine." Ethan spoke from behind a hand.

"You're fine?" Golden said, incredulous.

Ethan nodded.

The stench was quickly filling the room. If they were going to continue the questioning, it would have to be somewhere else. "We'll have to get into another room," she said.

"Good idea," Golden agreed. "And when we switch, I want my client given a bathroom break and something to drink."

Madison wanted to say, "This isn't the Hilton," but she needed to get out of there. She nodded and hurried from the room.

CHAPTER THIRTY-EIGHT

Madison paced outside a new interrogation room, waiting for Ethan to clean himself up, the stench of vomit wedged in her sinuses. She just wanted to get back to questioning Ethan, especially considering how strong his reaction was to her question about his whereabouts on Sunday morning.

Terry was walking toward her with a coffee, not that it was for her. But she took it anyway and inhaled deeply, praying the aroma of the brew would clear smells like coffee beans did. Then she took a sip.

"Hey!"

"Thanks, buddy." She handed the cup back to him.

He scowled. "My coffee."

"Oh, stop being a baby. I'd make that sacrifice for you. It's not like it's great coffee here, anyhow."

"Then why steal it?" he mumbled. "And I'm sure you wouldn't."

She shrugged and turned away. He was probably right. After all, coffee was sacred, even if it was from the bullpen and potentially hours old.

Ethan was escorted by an officer past Madison and Terry into the room, and they followed. Golden was bringing up the rear.

Everyone took a seat except for Terry who remained standing.

"We'll try this again, Mr. Younge. Where were you last Sunday morning between five and eight?" she asked, trying not to think about the consequence last time she'd asked the question.

Golden reassured his client. "You don't have to answer that if you don't wish to."

"There are other means of determining where you were, Mr. Younge," Madison said. "Do you own a silver '98 Honda Accord?"

Ethan shot his lawyer a look, then answered. "No."

"No? I find that curious as the DMV records show you do. And you also have a license plate number AVL34A." Madison intentionally phrased it as if the plate was still valid.

"I just sold it, the Accord."

No word about the plate, but she carried on. "When did you sell the car?"

"Monday."

"This past Monday?"

"Yeah."

"That was the day after Heather Nguyen's murder. You knew you were spotted and needed to get rid of the vehicle," she accused.

"Speculation." Golden put a hand down heavily on the table.

Ethan went on as if Golden hadn't said anything. "That's ridiculous, Detective. And for the record, the '98 Honda was my *wife's* car. I bought her an updated model. Check your records again." He crossed his arms.

"You haven't countered my suggestion that you got rid of the car because you'd been spotted, Mr. Younge."

He opened his mouth but stalled, appearing as if he didn't know where to start.

Golden said, "He doesn't have to respond to your *suggestion*."

She ignored the lawyer. "Mr. Younge, were you at Mitchell Park between five and eight Sunday morning?"

He hung his head briefly, then looked up. "I was there."

Adrenaline coursed through her body at the admission.

"Between five and eight?" She wanted to make absolutely sure.

His facial expression went vacant.

Madison pressed her lips. "I'll take that as an affirmative."

"Absurd. You can't presume my client's guilt by omission of an answer."

Again, Madison ignored the lawyer. She pulled out pictures of the neckties as they were photographed in the lab. "And what about these, Mr. Younge? Do any of them look familiar?"

Ethan placed his hand on the photo of the tie that was used to strangle his mother. He let his eyes wander over the others and then nervously at his lawyer before leaning in to whisper something to him.

Golden was the first to pull back. He straightened his own necktie. "What my client says next is to be kept in the proper context. Go ahead, Mr. Younge."

"I recognize all three."

"All three of them? You're sure?"

Ethan nodded.

"These were the murder weapons used to—"

"I didn't kill anyone," Ethan rushed out.

"Why do you recognize them, then?"

Ethan glanced briefly at Golden. "They're all G&C. I only wear that make of tie."

"So, *that's* why you recognize them? No other reason? Not because you used them to strangle the life from your victims?" With each question, her pitch became higher, and the lawyer simpered.

"If we could please bring this questioning down to a respectable level," Golden requested.

"Respectable?" Madison fixed eyes with the lawyer, and then moved on to Ethan. "Was it a respectable act when you took three women's lives?"

"I didn't do it," Ethan pleaded, but Madison wasn't persuaded.

"And your own mother?" Madison added.

Golden's face pinched, and his brows lowered, warning her to back off.

She'd give it a moment's reprieve and approach things from another direction. "So, you claim to only wear G&C, and that's the reason you recognize them?"

"That's right. I own the same ones."

"Then you wouldn't object to our searching your home for them. If they're there, I mean unless you had two of each, we should find them." Madison was working to call Ethan's bluff, but she also wanted permission to get inside his home. A warrant would be approved, but it would take a little longer to get than occupants' consent.

"I see what you're trying to do here, Detective, but I must insist that you obtain a warrant if you want to snoop around my client's house."

"Fine enough. I don't think any judge would have a problem authorizing one."

"Based on some circumstantial evidence?" Golden scoffed. "You really think—"

"*Strong* evidence," Madison corrected.

"Apparently you haven't shared everything with us, if that's the case."

Madison clasped her hands. She'd hardly scratched the surface with Laura's case. He couldn't remember where he had been, and then she'd jumped ahead to Heather's murder. "Laura Saunders, who was murdered over two weeks ago— on a day your client can't recall where he was. We have good reason to believe he was with Laura."

"Absurd," Ethan interjected, "I don't know who this Laura—"

His lawyer held up a hand to silence him. "And why is that?"

"Mr. Younge was spotted by people approaching the victim in a bar named The Weathered Rose and leaving with her." Madison looked at Ethan, but there was no sign of recognition on his face. Regardless, she continued. "Your car was also spotted in Laura's driveway the night of the murder."

"There's no way. No way."

"Well, not long ago you confessed to owning a Honda."

"There are a lot of people who own Hondas, Detective," Golden stated.

Madison tossed the photograph of Ethan and Laura across the table. "Then there's this. You knew Laura. This was by her bed."

Golden put a hand on Ethan's arm and directed him not to say anything.

With the silence, the atmosphere in the room changed.

"Ms. Saunders was found naked in her bed," Madison added. "In the least, you had an affair with Laura, but why kill her? Did she threaten to tell your wife?"

"Sounds like you're reaching again, Detective," Golden warned.

"I didn't do it," Ethan repeated as if locked into a chant.

She'd talked herself into a corner, really, because there was no DNA evidence to prove sexual intercourse, but maybe she could turn things around. "Did you have a vasectomy, Mr. Younge?"

Golden admonished his client, "You don't have to answer that."

Ethan's eyes snapped to Madison's, but he didn't say a word.

"I could subpoena your medical records. Shouldn't take any more than twenty-four hours, and I'd get my answer."

"I did," Ethan practically whispered.

"Excuse me?"

"I did have it done. About three years ago now, just after Meg was born. Brooke doesn't know. Please don't tell her."

Madison knew from his file that his daughter's name was Megan. "You kept that from your wife?"

His face fell into his hands.

"What else are you keeping from her?" Madison pressed him, trying to evoke a guilty conscience and a confession.

"That's enough," Golden barked. "Relevance? What more would you like from my client?"

"We want his DNA."

Golden leaned back in his chair. "Let's see a warrant."

She tossed the signed warrant for his DNA across the table. It had come through while Ethan had been taking a break. Golden's lips parted slightly, clearly not expecting this turn of events. "And you can be certain we'll get some solid results," she added with confidence.

For once, Golden was speechless. He faced his client, silently inquiring if he should be told more.

Madison moved back and looked under the table at Ethan's feet. "I'm curious. What size shoe do you wear?"

"Oh, yes, the common-sized muddy shoeprint from the Saunders's murder," Golden said. He must have remembered discussing it when Layton had been interrogated. "It could belong to anyone."

"Then let's rule your client out since you seem so adamant that he's innocent."

"Size twelve," Ethan offered.

"Now was that so difficult?" She smiled smugly at the attorney.

"You mentioned a license plate—AVL34A," Ethan said. "I haven't used that in a long time, and I believe it's stored in the garage."

"We'll make sure to look for that when we search for the neckties and the shoes. That is, if they're there to be found."

CHAPTER THIRTY-NINE

Terry got out of the car at the Younges' and addressed Madison. "So, let me get this right. We're searching for something we don't expect to find?"

"Yeah." Madison knew he'd see it as a waste of time. "We don't have a choice but to check it out. We're waiting for the DNA results to come in, anyhow. Not to mention we might find something that helps our case. It's also an ideal opportunity to speak to Mrs. Younge about her husband." Madison rang the doorbell.

Brooke cracked the door, opening it only wide enough to allow the width of her face through. Her body was rigid.

Madison remembered her from the crime scene, and the defensive stance she had taken for her husband. "Mrs. Younge, we're here to search your residence." She held up a signed warrant.

"Ethan called. I'm not sure what you expect to find. And I want to make something very clear to you. My little girl is inside, and I don't need you upsetting her." She then opened the door wider and moved out of the way to let them inside. "My husband didn't do what you're accusing him of."

No one liked to think their loved one was a killer, but it didn't change the truth. "It seems your husband may be connected to the murders of three women, Mrs. Younge," Madison told her.

"That's absurd. Ethan wouldn't hurt anyone. He's a gentle man. Quiet."

"It's often the quiet ones who are hiding something."

"I would know if he was," Brooke snapped. "You seem to have your mind made up against my husband. You think he did it. I can read it in your eyes."

"I'm not going to lie to you. The evidence points us in that direction." Madison paused, looking around the small house. "Do you know what his relationship was like with his mother?"

Brooke sniffed and shook her head.

"Is there something you should be telling us?"

Brooke took a seat at the kitchen table and gestured for them to join her. "I can't accept that he did it. I never will."

"It sounds like you might think he did."

"I'm not saying that." Her eyes snapped to Madison's. "Their relationship had its problems. The biggest one being his mom couldn't see her son as a grown-up."

Madison could relate when it came to her own mother sometimes. "They'd argue about things?"

Brooke nodded. "His father owns a company here in town named FYI. You probably know that by now, but Frank is getting ready to retire. Ethan wanted to take over the business, but his mom had other plans."

"His mother didn't want him having it?" Terry interjected.

"No, and it made Ethan so mad. But he wouldn't have killed her over it."

Madison leaned forward, meeting Brooke's gaze. "Are you sure of that?"

Brooke diverted her gaze and said, "They fought a lot about it—I can't believe I'm going through this. That we're going through this. It's like a bad nightmare."

"Mrs. Younge, how escalated were these fights?" Madison asked, trying to reel Brooke back on topic.

"They'd raise their voices, but that was pretty much it."

Terry angled his head. "Why didn't she want him taking over?"

Brooke looked at Terry. "She said that it would interfere with him being a good father to Megan. Personally, I think she was crazy. Ethan was all about his family. At least, until now."

As much as Brooke put on the front of believing in her husband's innocence, there were cracks, and Madison had to keep prying at them. "When was their last fight?"

"Just this past Sunday. We were over there for dinner, like we are every week. And just like every week, the topic of the business came up. Frank got so frustrated he said he was never going to retire. He'd keep the business himself. All Frank wanted was to keep the peace."

"How did Ethan react to that?" Madison asked.

"I just remember he was quiet when we came home that night. The more I think about it, he's been a little different for a while now, and I'm not sure why. I thought he was busy at work. I never thought he was killing people." Brooke's lashes soaked with tears, and a few rolled down her cheeks.

Madison and Terry were back at their desks down at the station. The search of the Younges' property had confirmed that Ethan Younge certainly had an interest in G&C ties. His closet was full with different colors and patterns, but none of them matched the ones used in the murders. Something that wasn't in his favor.

"Just one little thing bothers me," Terry said. "The guy in the bar—"

"Ethan."

"Okay, we'll assume Ethan. He left behind a towel soaked in blood."

"Yeah."

"Well, wouldn't you think if the guy got into the altercation described, there'd be some physical evidence left over to that effect?"

She thought back to Ethan's appearance and couldn't recall any cuts or bruising.

"Then again, never mind me. Maybe the guy heals quickly, or maybe he's an easy bleeder." Terry tapped his pen against the desk. "Yeah, never mind. I'm thinking out loud."

"Well, it *has* been over two weeks." She hoped all this told them was Ethan was a fast healer. After all, he had been seen by eyewitnesses at the bar, and he was in a photo in Laura Saunders's home.

"Good work, you two," the sergeant said, parking next to her desk, the police chief beside him.

McAlexandar's clenched and unclenched his hands, not striking her as impressed at all. "We should get this guy locked away. Now." He stabbed a finger downward.

"We're working on it." Madison wanted to say so much more but shut her mouth.

"I'm not sure why the delay. He killed three women."

"Do you want us laying charges before we know with absolute certainty?"

"Nothing's absolute."

Oh, you are an infuriating man!

She said, "No, but things can be more definitive than they are now."

McAlexandar's entire face went red. "I'll be watching you interrogate the son of a bitch once you get the DNA results back."

"Fine." The single word came out relatively harmless on its own, yet it carried attitude, and the sergeant fixed his gaze on her. She made no attempt to backpedal, and her phone rang.

Saved by the bell again!

"Knight," she answered, turning away from her superiors. She sensed them staring at the back of her head, but with the news she was receiving, she couldn't have cared less. She hung up and rose to her feet. "DNA results are in."

CHAPTER FORTY

Golden pulled out on his tie. "I'm sure you wouldn't want to waste any more of our time, Detectives."

Madison let his comment go and addressed Terry. "Should I tell them, or do you want to?"

Terry held out his hands. "Go ahead, by all means."

Ethan's face paled.

"Well, let's start with the search results," Madison said.

Golden ran his hands down the lapels of his suit jacket and turned to his client, giving him a reassuring nod.

Ethan seemed to attempt a smile, but it was more of a facial twitch at the corner of his lips—they rose and fell so fast. His attention focused on Madison. "You find the ties?"

Madison played the power of silence for a few seconds, then shook her head. "No, we didn't. And we didn't find the license plate or the shoes that match the prints at our crime scene, either."

"I don't understand."

"What don't you understand, Mr. Younge? You murdered—"

"Wait…" He let his words trail off. "A couple of months back…" He appeared to be calculating what he would say next. His eyes shifted to the table and then up. "Yeah, it was a couple of months back now…"

"What was?"

Ethan glanced at his lawyer, who splayed his hands giving him the go-ahead to talk. "Well, Brooke thought someone had been in the house."

Don't tell me this guy is going to say his ties were stolen.

"Elaborate," she said with very little patience.

"She told me that when she got home from work, the front door was unlocked. She said that the house felt different, like it had someone else's presence in there. I figured she was getting carried away and must have forgotten to lock the door before leaving the house."

"Did you report the incident?" Madison asked, not swayed an iota by his tale.

"Like I told you, I thought she was being paranoid." He was shaking his head. "I believe her now. Someone stole my ties."

He had a lot of ties, so she could believe some could go missing without his knowledge, but still it was a reach. "And a pair of shoes that would implicate you in a murder?" Skeptical.

"What shoes? You never mentioned them before."

"Just everyday runners. Cheap."

"I don't buy cheap runners. Only brand names."

Madison did her best to hide her honest reaction. Given his gravitation to designer neckties, and his elaborate collection of them, she tended to believe that statement. She'd divert. "What about your license plate? It wasn't in your garage. Someone steal it, too?"

"I don't like your innuendos," Golden cut in.

Madison ignored the lawyer's interjection and kept her eyes on Ethan. "Let me get this straight. You didn't believe that you had a break-in before, but now that some ties are missing that implicate your involvement in three murders, you think they were stolen? Along with a pair of shoes and an old license plate? Were any electronics or jewelry stolen?"

Ethan shook his head, and Madison let out a laugh.

"Please, tell me why someone would break into your home and steal three neckties, a pair of shoes, and an old plate."

"I don't know." Ethan hitched his shoulders. "The ties are worth a lot."

"Those ties showed up on three murdered women."

"One being my mom." His shoulders sagged. "Has her body been released?"

"Not yet."

His eyes glazed over.

Madison looked at Golden. "You wanted hard evidence… well, we have the results of the DNA testing." She glanced at Ethan. "Yours was a match to physical evidence found at both murder scenes."

Ethan opened his mouth as if to speak, but Golden silenced him. "*Both*? I thought you suspected my client of three murders?"

"Forensics connected him to Ms. Saunders and Mrs. Younge. Eyewitnesses connect him to Ms. Nguyen." There was one thing Madison wasn't going to share right away—Ethan didn't match the prints from Heather's locket or any prints lifted from Laura's crime scene. But he could have worn gloves.

"So forensics matched what, specifically?" Golden pounced.

"This is crazy!" Ethan exclaimed. "I didn't do it. How could it match? How could I—"

Golden reached out a hand to calm Ethan, but Ethan shrugged out of reach.

Madison continued. "Mr. Younge has confessed to his love of G&C ties and his closet attested to that claim. Your client left some epithelial behind on the one tie that strangled Ms. Saunders."

"My client says that tie was stolen from him," Golden interjected. "Some epithelial doesn't prove he killed her with it."

"Your client *says* it was stolen," Madison emphasized.

"I'm telling you the truth," Ethan croaked. "And I didn't kill her."

"Your DNA is also a match to skin taken from Ms. Saunders's fingernails."

"Impossible," Ethan mumbled.

"Then there's Heather, Ms. Nguyen. You might have improved by not leaving behind implicating physical evidence, but where you messed up was allowing yourself to be spotted leaving the scene."

Sweat was beading on Ethan's forehead. "I found my mother. I called nine-one-one. I was only at her house because she called me there."

"We've been through this, just because the last number dialed from your parents' phone was FYI doesn't mean your mother made the call. You could have just as easily."

"Were my prints on the phone?"

"You could have worn gloves."

"Did you find gloves at the scene?"

Golden put a hand on Ethan's arm, no doubt trying to get him to stop playing his own defense.

"It doesn't mean you didn't discard them before we got there," Madison shot back. "A lot of murderers will call in the find."

"But she called me over there."

"That's enough," Golden barked. "Lay charges against my client or release him."

"Just one more thing," Madison said, moving her gaze from the lawyer back to Ethan. "Did you touch her when you found her?"

"No, I didn't."

"Not even a kiss or a hug? Try to resuscitate her?"

"I could tell she was dead." Ethan frowned. "And I knew enough not to touch her."

"Huh. See, the evidence says otherwise. A trace of your saliva was found on your mother's forehead." Madison stood and directed Ethan to stand.

"I didn't do it!" Ethan's cry resonated off the walls of the small room as she forced him to his feet and pulled his arms behind him. She snapped on the cuffs and rattled off his Miranda rights, then cited the charges against him.

An officer entered the room to collect Ethan, and he struggled against him and called out, "I didn't do it!"

"They all say that, Mr. Younge," she said.

Golden left the room with a nod toward Madison, passing by the sergeant and the chief as they came inside.

"Guess you'll sleep tonight," Terry said to her.

"You should know me better than that by now. I won't rest until it's been passed by the DA and the guilty verdict comes in. There are a couple things niggling at me. One is we have possible motive for him to kill his mother, but why Laura and Heather?"

"We might never know."

CHAPTER FORTY-ONE

The door was opened to the visiting room and Brooke walked in with two officers. She wasn't looking at her husband. Instead, she had her gaze fixed on the chair across from him.

Ethan rose to hug her, but she simply sat down across from him.

"Tell me you didn't do it," she said.

"I didn't."

She looked at him now. "You're insulting my intelligence. Is this why I got a new car?"

"Don't be absurd."

"Why do you go to Mitchell Park that Sunday for a morning run, Ethan? You never do that."

"I always run there," he defended himself.

"Not on Sunday mornings. Why that day?"

He must have been insane to think she would support him through this. He only prayed the cops hadn't made it sound to her like he was having an affair with this Laura lady. It was bad enough his vasectomy would be coming out.

"Three women, including your own mother…" Her chin trembled. "My God, Ethan, your own mother!" Tears rolled down her face, dripped off her jaw.

"I didn't do it, Brooke. Please believe me." He extended a hand toward hers, but she pulled back.

She scanned his eyes, probing them. Somewhere in hers, he could tell she wanted to believe him, but she didn't.

"They talked to your dad, Ethan. And me. They know about everything." She continued through heaves for air. "The business. How your mother wouldn't let you take it on. Did you kill her for it?"

He felt like he'd been betrayed by his best friend. "What do you think, Brooke? You think I'd risk everything for this?"

"I don't know." She pulled out a tissue from her purse and blew her nose.

"What about my dad? Does he think I did this?"

Her gaze drifted away from him, and he had his answer. His dad hadn't come to see him yet, and Ethan didn't think he'd be getting a visit from him anytime soon. His chin quivered as he struggled to suppress his grief. "They'll realize they were wrong."

"But are they? What am I supposed to tell our daughter?"

"Tell her that her daddy will be home soon."

She laughed derisively. The tears had dried up. "You think everything's going to be all right? I know everything, Ethan. I know about…about the girl. Were you sleeping with her? Never mind, I don't want to know." She sniffled and met his eyes. "I found out about your independent decision to…fix things." She waved her hand toward his lap.

"I can explain that."

"There's not enough time." She stood. "I've got to go."

"Brooke, please!" He made a fast movement toward her, and both guards rushed to hold him back. She only stopped long enough to shoot him a look before leaving.

She never made a single effort to comfort him, to touch him. She hadn't come to console him. She had come to pass judgment.

As the door closed behind her, all he could do was sob like a child. He was more scared now than when he'd found his mother's lifeless body. His mother's existence had threatened his career goals, but now he stood to lose his entire family. If only he could turn back time.

CHAPTER FORTY-TWO

"Tell me you're sleeping a full night by now, Maddy."

Sometimes Terry's attempts at small talk amused her. They were sitting across from each other down at the station.

"Why are you so concerned with how I sleep? Has Younge had his pretrial?"

"You can be moody when you're sleep deprived."

Ah, so his concern is more about him…

She looked at her desk and considered her choice of weapons, then spotted the perfect one. It was a rubber band—blue and thick. It would pack a sting. She'd aim right between his eyes, quiet him up. She pulled back on the elastic, ready to fire, then changed her mind and let her hands drop.

He nudged his head toward her hands. "Impressive, you're learning self-control."

"Keep pushin'," she dared him.

Terry smiled. "About Younge. There's nothing to worry about. Two days from now, he'll be at his pretrial. We're *this close.*" Terry pinched his thumb and index finger together.

She'd play along. "That close doesn't count unless it's—"

"Horseshoes," Terry popped out with a smile. "Yeah, I know the saying, and I don't like it. And maybe you should use this little bit of in-between time to clean that mess of a desk you've got going."

"That *I've* got?" she scoffed, but it was a losing battle. His desk was bare except for his phone and paper tray, which had about a one-inch stack of paper and a folder or two in it.

Papers were strewn all over hers. A few file folders had been scattered at various angles, and the tray was a haphazard stack. Most of it represented something she had grandiose plans of accomplishing, but there was plenty she could simply file.

"Okay, I'm messy." She gathered the papers and folders and added them to her tray. She didn't bother straightening it.

"How is that cleaning it up?"

"Hey, don't tell me how to tidy." She kept the papers moving.

"You're not doing anything except moving things from one pile to another."

"See, that's how little you know. One neatly arranged stack is better than several."

"Uh-huh. Lazy man's way."

She was about to correct him, when he did it himself.

"Excuse me. Lazy *woman's* way. You're such a feminist." He rose from his chair. "Going to get a coffee. Want one?"

"Sure, I'll have a Starbucks."

"I wasn't going to go there." He jacked his thumb toward the machine in the bullpen.

"Yeah. No." She shook her head. "But I'll have a Starbucks." She smiled at him, trying to manipulate him. Besides, Starbucks wasn't that far of a walk from the station. "Please, I'm working so hard here. Throw me a frickin'—"

"Bone. Another stupid saying." He turned to leave, shaking his head and mumbling.

"Hey, now you know what you normally sound like," she called out to him, not sure if he'd hear her, but it still gave her some satisfaction. Her gaze went back to her desk.

With the papers moved to one side, the small collection of pens and highlighters were more obvious. She had the perfect place for them, too: the top drawer of her desk.

She opened it, planning to shovel everything in, when she noticed what had already made it in there. The printout of the photograph of Laura and Ethan. It was looking a little worse for wear, having been placed in and out of numerous pockets and scrunched into a ball.

To think that she'd carried the killer around with her for weeks, and now he was finally behind bars and would pay for his crimes. That was satisfying, even if there were still some lose ends to stitch together, such as the towel they'd collected from the bar. They never did get the results back from the third-party lab.

She studied the photo, trying to search for answers. Ethan may have had motive to kill his mother, but what had Saunders and Nguyen done to warrant his attention? Maybe she would never know, but the "not knowing" still niggled at her.

As she kept looking at the photo, a thought struck: Laura had been superimposed on another photo, so what's to say someone hadn't done the same with Ethan? Maybe Evelyn's murder and Ethan having found her was nothing more than a coincidence. *Shit.* Did they have the wrong guy?

But that was crazy. Ethan's DNA was a match to the Laura Saunders case and the Evelyn Younge case. He had to be the man in that photograph—his image undoctored. But still, she had some doubts slithering through her body, more questions. She hated it, but it was true. What would have pushed Ethan to murder—assuming three times over? He didn't seem to prone to angry outbursts. He had no criminal background. He held a steady job, and he had a wife and a daughter.

She sat back in her chair and blew out a loud breath. Why did she always have to second-guess herself? It didn't matter if a case was closed; she'd been known to question things even after a conviction. Terry teased her that it was a sickness.

As she scrutinized Ethan's face, she noticed how he seemed to be forcing himself to pose for the camera. He had a disgruntled look hidden behind the smile—an underlying anger. His eyes were glazed over, hardened, but as she traced his face, she noticed a few discrepancies that momentarily stole her breath. They were small enough that she could excuse herself for not noticing sooner, but she wasn't looking for a cop-out.

"Hey, whatcha doin'?" It was Toby Sovereign.

She looked up at him as he stopped at her desk. "What is it, Sovereign?"

"Just passing by."

"Looks like you're standing, not passing." She put her attention back on the photo.

"Heard you got the guy."

Does this guy not pick up on body language at all, or is he so insensitive that he just doesn't care?

"The strangler case," Sovereign went on. "Good job."

"So people keep saying."

"Hey, that's his photo, isn't it?"

Madison sighed in exasperation. "Yes." She waved him off, while dreaming of giving him the finger.

"Fine, I get the point. Have a nice one, Knight."

"Uh-huh."

Before the interruption, she had seen something potentially monumental. When she focused back on the photograph, she realized she hadn't imagined it. Everyone was going to kill her, but she didn't have any other option.

She rushed down to the jail cells and demanded to see Ethan Younge.

"You can't ask him any questions without his lawyer present," the officer cautioned her as he unlocked the door leading into the cell area.

Madison glared at him. "I fully realize that, but I need to see him."

"Okay." The officer followed along with her. "Fifth door on the left."

As soon as she reached Ethan's cell, he stood up from the cot where he'd been sitting. "You find the real killer yet?"

She remained silent as she studied his face, absorbing his facial features. All this time, she wondered how Ethan could have been stupid enough to put his own photo by Laura's bed. Now, she didn't think he had.

CHAPTER FORTY-THREE

Madison knew she couldn't talk to Terry about her suspicions. At least not yet. She went to the one person who might listen to her.

"What do you mean you don't think it's him?" Cynthia asked. "You have a bad habit of doing this. And every single time, I'm here for you." She leaned against a table in the lab. "But—"

"Please don't say you're not this time."

"I can't keep supporting this obsession of yours. You never feel a case is over. You always think there's more to uncover."

Madison shared her new discoveries with Cynthia and pointed out the inconsistencies she'd found in the photo.

Cynthia shrugged. "It could have been added." She raised her eyebrows. "You ever think of that? The photo was forged. Maybe he added those tiny differences to toy with you?"

"The case still isn't coming together all nice and neat. Doesn't that bother you?"

"Just leave it alone." She reached into one of the pockets of her lab coat and pulled out a pack of cigarettes. "Time for a break. You can come outside with me if you want to." She smiled at Madison.

"Yeah, no thanks." The invitation reminded her that Terry would have been back a while ago with her coffee. "I've got to go, though."

"Leave it alone," Cynthia called out behind her.

Madison found Terry at his desk and on the phone. He gave her a disapproving look. Was it because she made him go to Starbucks and then wasn't around when he got back, or did it have to do with Annabelle? Maybe he was on the line with her, having another argument.

He hung up, and his scowl became deeper. "Why were you down to see Ethan Younge?"

Wonder who the snitch is…

"What do you mean?" The options were to feign innocence and diffuse a fight or counterattack.

"Don't play stupid, Maddy. I know you were. What I don't understand is why. We've got the guy. Let it rest."

"Are you absolutely positive about that?"

"The DNA is a match."

"Fingerprints weren't, and what's his motive? Doesn't that bother you even a little bit?"

"With his mother, she didn't want the family business transferred to him."

"It doesn't explain the others." She handed the photograph to him. "Look closely at that. Notice anything?"

He took it from her but barely grazed his eyes over the picture. "What is it?" he asked, impatient.

She pointed to the discrepancies she'd found.

He barely considered them before tossing the picture to her side of the desk. "Big deal. It was a forged photo, anyhow."

He sounded like Cynthia. Madison picked up the photo. "But why go to that trouble?"

"For this exact reason. To cast doubt."

"So he planted a photo of himself but changed those particular features?" She sighed, hardly believing she was going to share her theory with Terry. "What if Ethan was framed?"

Terry let out a laugh. "Framed? But his DNA was in Laura's bedroom, he was spotted leaving the area where Heather's body was found, and he finds his mother. Yeah, it doesn't sound like a frame job to me."

She remained silent.

"I'm begging you to leave this alone," he added.

"Closing the case might be the most important thing to you, but finding out the truth is more important to me."

"Well, then let me know how it goes in the unemployment line." He stood up and pushed his chair in.

"Where are you going?"

"I'm going home, and so should you. We've already logged enough overtime on this case." He spun around and headed toward the exit.

Why didn't anyone else understand the situation? She sat there staring into space and thinking, not even taking in the people moving around her, as she mulled everything over.

"HOH," she said out loud. The letters from the pendant. If they didn't serve as initials for Heather's name, they had to stand for something else.

She opened an internet browser and typed in the letters. Over four million results in point two three seconds. Apparently HOH stood for a lot of things, none of which seemed helpful to the case. There was a Native American tribe, a rainforest, and apparently a disease that had those initials. This was useless—until her gaze went to a result that just might make sense to the case.

"I'll be damned."

CHAPTER FORTY-FOUR

Madison was beating herself up over not figuring out the connection between all the victims before now. The link had been right in front of her. She still wasn't entirely sure how it had resulted in their murders.

She was driving to Terry's house as fast as she could, but traffic wasn't being cooperative in that respect. Neither were the streetlights that seemed to turn red just as she'd approach an intersection.

She finally got to her destination and pulled into Terry's driveway. She immediately regretted her timing.

Annabelle stormed out the front screen door with such force, the door hit the house and bounced back.

Terry hurried behind her. "Anna."

His wife spun to face him. "I've had enough, Terry. Enough." Annabelle rushed down the stairs. "I'll be at Mom's."

If only I could become invisible…

Annabelle glared at Madison as she rushed by, and Madison hustled back to move the department car onto the road so Annabelle could back out of the driveway.

Madison watched Annabelle drive away, gave it a few seconds before getting out of the vehicle. She huffed it up the front steps of the house, and the door shut in front of her. She flung it open and followed Terry to the kitchen.

His two beagles, Todd and Bailey, came over to her and were sniffing her like crazy. She tried shooing them away, but they weren't having it, their tails wagging furiously.

"What are you doing here?" Terry opened the fridge, took out a beer, snapped the top off, and guzzled it back until the bottle was empty.

"I should probably come back," she offered, but didn't make a move to leave. The news, the link between the victims she wanted to share, was too monumental to wait.

"You think?" He set the empty bottle on the counter, opened the fridge, and had another by the neck when he asked, "You want one?"

She shook her head.

"Right, you're the little freak who doesn't care for beer." It didn't stop him from nearly draining a second bottle.

He kicked the fridge door shut with his foot and headed toward the living room. The beagles followed, and so did she.

He settled into an armchair, his hand with a tight grip on the beer bottle. The dogs curled on the floor at his feet. Madison took a seat on a facing couch.

"I see your offer to come back wasn't sincere." He lifted the bottle to his lips.

"I need to tell you something."

"Oh, God, don't tell me it's about Ethan Younge. Shit, Madison, let it rest."

For Terry to use her full name and a swear word, he was in genuine pain—and extremely angry. Most of it wasn't directed at her, even if she was the punching bag.

She leaned forward and asked, "You going to be okay?"

He drained the rest of his beer and set the bottle on the table beside him. "What is it with you women? You think if you pitch a fit, things will turn out in your favor. You bat your little eyelashes and expect men to cater to your every whim."

Madison wasn't sure exactly what to say to that. "She'll be back."

He shrugged his shoulders in such a way it stripped away any pretense and revealed the depth of heartache. "We'll see."

This time she remained silent. There was nothing she could say that would make the situation better.

"Okay, let me have it. What did you find?"

"I pulled a deep background on Evelyn Younge. It turns out she was married to some guy before Frank. The guy would beat her. She wound up pregnant about the same time the marriage ended. Her record shows that she gave birth to two sons, thirty-two years ago. The boy's names were Ethan and Evan Frost. She gave the boys her maiden name, disowning them from their biological father. One was given up for adoption. Where that was is locked."

"So you want me to believe Ethan has an identical twin? We have the wrong one?" He lifted his bottle but put it down when he realized it was empty. "Are you being serious right now?"

"What's so hard to believe about that? Maybe this kid found out about his twin, was jealous of his lifestyle."

"So he framed him for murder?"

"We've come across stranger situations."

"You've got to let this go, Maddy. It doesn't prove anything. So what? Evelyn gives a baby up, we still don't know where, or how it connects to the other victims."

"Here's the thing. Remember Heather's parents said that they found out their daughter gave a baby up for adoption? Her background shows a birth record at the age of seventeen. I did a background on Laura, and she gave birth when she was sixteen. She also put her baby up for adoption."

"So you think somehow they were all connected?"

"Evan was in the system. Our vics gave up their babies." Madison went to get off the couch. "And I found out where for one of them. I made a call. The Nguyens did all the searching years ago. Haven of Hope. HOH, the same—"

"Letters on the pendant," Terry finished.

"Correct. We just need to see if Evelyn's son, Evan, and Laura's baby were connected to this orphanage. I asked the Saunderses, but they refused to discuss it. They confirmed her teenage pregnancy but said Laura had come to terms with it, and so had they."

"What do you suggest we do now?"

"We go to Haven of Hope."

"Oh, Maddy—"

"No, hear me out," she cut in and then reminded him of the discrepancies she'd noticed in the photograph.

"If, and I add *if*, that is even a remote possibility, it's going to be hard to prove," Terry said.

He was still wanting to debate what was right in front of him, but she wouldn't rest until she knew for sure they had the right man behind bars. "What part of this don't you get? Ethan is not Photo Guy."

CHAPTER FORTY-FIVE

"Haven of Hope is a three-hour drive away." Terry buckled into the passenger seat of the department vehicle. "It's just after three now. We won't get there until after six. How do we even know they're going to be open?"

"It's an orphanage. Someone's going to be there twenty-four hours a day. By the way—" she pulled out a piece of gum "—chew this. Beer breath is disgusting. And, as you said, it's a long drive. It would be more pleasant without all your whining."

He stuffed the gum into his mouth. "Think of just calling the place?"

"I did, but they wouldn't give me any answers. Said I needed a warrant."

"And you have one?"

"No."

Terry threw his hands up in the air. "I don't get why we're going, then."

"If I'm standing right in front of them, they won't turn me away. I can be persuasive."

"Well, you might be able to nag them to the point where they'll concede." His tone started off bitter, but then he laughed.

"Oh, shut up." She pointed to the laptop in the car. "If it's not too much to ask, pull a background on Evan Frost."

"You said Frost?"

"Do you listen to anything I say? Yes, that was Evelyn's maiden name."

She tapped on the steering wheel. "What are you waiting for? Type it in."

Terry turned the laptop to face him and keyed in the name. "Okay, Evan Frost…"

Madison swore she could hear the system grind away. "Why does everything take so long?"

"Just to piss you off."

"Oh, shut up." She smiled at him, and the system let out a small beep. "Okay, share." She held her next breath, waiting for the results.

He met her gaze. "You can't have it both ways: shut up *and* share."

"Terry," she prompted.

"Fine, here it is. Evan Frost, son of Evelyn Frost, father unknown. No criminal record."

"Just means he hasn't been caught." She bobbed her head, wishing for him to continue. Seconds of silence passed. "What is it?"

"Beyond that, his information only goes up to a few years ago, and then he falls off the grid."

"What do you mean 'off the grid'? Did he die?"

Terry shook his head. "Not according to the file. Give me a minute…" He clicked more keys. "Okay, the file on Evan Frost stalled a few years back because he changed his name."

"Terry?" She leaned over.

"Eyes on the road."

"You can be so bossy."

He started keying something. "I learned that from my partner."

"In your words, hardy-har." Besides, why did she have to keep her eyes on the road? There wasn't another soul out here except for the occasional tractor that slowed her down. She didn't see any of those right now. "Terry, what do you have?"

He stopped typing. "I can't believe it. I mean, you're likely going to, but I—"

"Terry!"

"He changed his name to Ethan Younge." They matched eyes.

"It's all coming together," she concluded. "Evan could have seen Ethan as having everything he wanted. A life he'd never have."

"All speculation."

"But possible. After years of feeling unloved and rejected, rage and jealousy built up until he could no longer control his emotions. He was willing to risk everything by trying to claim what wasn't his." Her thoughts ran to a conclusion, and she glanced at Terry. "What's his address?"

"Dame Avenue in Stiles."

"Guess we know where we're headed next."

"*Next*? Why not straightaway?"

"Let's get our facts together first. See what we find out at Haven of Hope."

Terry bobbed his head left and right. "Probably one of the sanest things you've said since you showed up at my house. One question for you, though. If Evan was motivated by jealousy or revenge, as you theorize, why not just kill his mother and possibly his brother? Why the girls?"

Leave it to Terry to stump her.

CHAPTER FORTY-SIX

Haven of Hope was house in a colonial mansion that sat in the middle of landscaped gardens and manicured lawns. Its presence was overwhelming, and Madison could only imagine how intimidating it would be to small children.

"Remember we need to tread lightly," Terry said.

Madison rolled her eyes. "I realize that, Casanova. You always have to point out the obvious?"

"Casanova? You can stop that nickname right here and now."

Madison laughed.

They entered the building and explained to a woman at the front desk that they needed to speak with someone in charge. She may have gotten the impression that Madison and Terry were there to make arrangements to either adopt or leave their expectant baby there. When the woman set off to get a Connie Miller, Madison turned to Terry.

"I look pregnant?" she gasped.

"You're not fat," Terry assured her.

"But she thought I—"

"If she thought you were pregnant, she must have thought you were just inseminated. Maybe you have a glow about you."

"Urgh. Just shut your mouth; you're not helping." The thought of a baby growing inside her body was nauseating. The thought that someone would even imagine Terry being the father, even more so. He was good-looking but he was like a brother to her. Not to mention, he was married.

A woman walked toward them. Her hair was pulled back tightly into a bun, making her facial features taut.

"Connie Miller?" Madison asked, and the woman nodded. Madison went on, gesturing to Terry, "This is Detective O'Malley, and I'm Detective Rodriguez." Madison felt Terry's glare burning through the side of her head. She ignored it and smiled at Connie, but the woman was too busy looking at Terry, her eyes slightly dilated.

"Do you have somewhere we could talk in private?" Madison prompted.

Connie didn't take her gaze off Terry. Madison hid her amusement, but she'd be able to work Connie's attraction to their advantage.

"This way," Connie said, looking over a shoulder and smiling at Terry. The woman also seemed to put an extra swing in her swagger.

Madison looked over at her partner, who rubbed his knuckles against his chest, trying to indicate he was "hot stuff." She rolled her eyes, but at least he'd picked up on the woman's interest in him.

"O'Malley and Rodriguez?" Terry whispered to her. "Couldn't come up with something more original?"

Connie led them to an office with mahogany walls. She sat behind an ordinary desk and gestured for them to sit in two chairs positioned in front of it. She put her gaze on Terry. "What can I do for you?"

Madison gestured for Terry to answer.

"We're working on an investigation and could use your help," he said.

Connie leaned forward, crossed her arms, and rested them on the desk. "Unfortunately, without a court order, we're not supposed to release any confidential information."

"Miss Miller…or is it missus?" Terry began.

"Miss." Color touched Connie's cheeks.

"Well, *Miss* Miller, if you could help us at all, we would be grateful."

Connie's gaze drifted briefly to Madison, but when it returned to Terry, he smiled at her.

"I would be grateful," he added.

Maybe Terry was a bit of a Casanova, after all.

He leaned forward, tilted his head to the right, and plastered on the charm. "Could I convince you to make an exception just this once? It would mean a great deal to me."

Connie pulled back, her face hardening. "I could lose my job."

Terry winced. "But if you don't live on the edge once in a while, life's not worth living. Come on."

Seconds passed, and Connie's cheeks were becoming quite red.

"Come on," Terry petitioned.

"I could lose my job for doing this," she repeated.

Terry raised his hands in the air. "Then we're sorry to have bothered you." His words threatened to leave, but he made no move to do so.

"Stop—" she let out a small nervous laugh "—you're right. Life needs to be lived. And it wouldn't hurt to hear what information you need."

Madison and Terry briefly connected eyes.

"I need you to look in your records and see if you show a baby in there by the name of Evan Frost," Terry said.

Connie's face paled, and Madison feared she might be losing her nerve. Getting to the truth hinged on this woman's cooperation. There'd be no way she could get a signed court order, not with Ethan already charged with the murders. Not to mention that he'd face a judge at his pretrial hearing tomorrow. There was no way she'd jeopardize everything at the chance Evan was the guilty party—unless she knew for sure. If the pursued a warrant for the adoption agency, it would cast doubt on the entire investigation and be a defense attorney's wet dream.

After an agonizing few minutes, Connie said, "I'll help you."

Madison let out the breath she'd be holding.

"Thank you." Terry smiled at her.

"Well, don't thank me yet." She smiled at him and pulled out her keyboard tray. "Do you have an approximate year?"

Terry gave her the exact year.

"Okay, should only take a second."

The silence in the room while waiting for the results sounded as loud as thunder.

"Here we are." Connie leaned in toward the monitor. "Yes, we show an Evan Frost for the year you mentioned."

Terry and Madison looked at each other.

"One more," Madison stated.

Connie's gaze went to Madison, her brows tugging downward as if she were an intrusion.

"Please," Terry said, taking Connie's focus again.

"Not sure I should. I've already told you about one."

"Only one more. I promise." Another charming grin.

"All right, one more."

"Do you happen to show a mother by the name of Laura Saunders giving up a baby in…" Terry moved his finger in the air as if figuring out math, and then shared the resulting year with Connie.

"Let me see." She clicked on the keyboard and nodded. "Yes."

Madison's heart galloped. Now they could connect Laura, Heather, Evelyn—*and* Evan—to Haven of Hope. The women had all given up their babies, and Evan had been a child. Terry had brought up a good point on the way here, and she still didn't have an answer. If Evan was motivated by jealousy or revenge, why not just kill Evelyn and possibly his brother?

"Miss Miller, thank you so much for your help," Terry said, standing to his feet.

"Actually…" Connie's gaze became inquisitive. "Can I ask why you needed that information?"

Terry smiled at her. "I'm sorry, but that's confidential. I hope you understand."

CHAPTER FORTY-SEVEN

"You've got to stop the hearing," Madison pleaded with Winston. She'd made it to the parking lot before making the call. "We've got the wrong guy."

"Knight." Only her name, and the sergeant's agitation was clear. "You're not doing this to me—"

"But I can tell you, it will all line up. You've got to trust me." She went on to explain, in the amount of detail he would listen to, how the DNA in identical twins can be similar. He seemed disinterested. She told him how the man's facial features in the photo weren't a perfect match to Ethan's. She pointed out the fact the fingerprints left at the crime scenes didn't match Ethan. She even told him that Ethan had claimed his tie had been stolen, and that alone could explain his epithelial on the one used to strangle Laura. And she stressed their most recent conclusion: Evan had a commonality or a connection to all three women.

"I trusted you last time," Winston said. "I don't want to hear another word about this. Ethan Younge is going away for three murders."

"But, boss…"

"Not another word." The line was disconnected.

"Dammit, he hung up on me." She smacked the steering wheel. "The sarge isn't going to cooperate, so we go this alone. We're going to get Evan and pull him downtown, prove without a doubt that he did it."

"And how do you propose we do that? I think this is the point where I want out." He waved his hand at her, and she turned to give him *the look*. "What did you expect, Maddy? Ethan Younge's been charged. Are we just supposed to barge in and claim he's innocent now? We have nothing on Evan." She opened her mouth to speak, but he continued. "Ethan will have a case against the department. We'll be called into question. We could lose our jobs."

Madison felt her earlobes heating with rage. "Isn't the truth more important?" she spat. "And I think Ethan would prefer to regain his freedom, his name, and his family, don't you?"

"Fine. I'll stick with you but if, or should I say *when*, the crap hits the fan, I'll be pointing the finger at you."

"Wow, thanks."

"Don't mention it." He paused for a moment. "I'll probably regret saying this, but you could be right about all of this."

Madison kept her eyes on the road. "Geez, thanks for the vote of confidence."

The three-hour drive back to the city felt longer than the ride there. Maybe it had something to do with their arriving after ten at night. The sun had long set, and darkness blanketed the city with the exception of the city lights.

"Ah, the smell of exhaust." Terry inhaled. "I'll take it any day over manure."

Madison laughed.

She pulled into the parking lot of the apartment complex indicated for Ethan Younge, the former Evan Frost, and it was a dated structure much like the building Heather's assistant lived in.

After knocking about ten times and announcing themselves as being with the Stiles PD, the door of a neighboring apartment opened.

"He's obviously not there, assholes," a guy shouted and then slammed the door shut.

Madison moved toward the apartment, ready to pound him, but Terry pulled back on her arm.

"Let this one go," he said.

"Fine," she spat and turned to leave the building. "I thought we had him, Terry."

"I know."

Well, Evan had to be somewhere. She tried to put herself in his mind. *Where would I go if I had killed three women and framed my brother? If I was obsessed with the life I didn't have, to the point of changing my birth name, what would be my next logical step?*

She stopped walking and turned to Terry. "I know where he might be."

CHAPTER FORTY-EIGHT

He stood outside the front door, eagerly anticipating the reception he might get while at the same time fearful of it. He didn't know how to approach it—ring the bell, make her think a stranger was at the door, or let himself in? He had a key, after all. He opted for knocking. It would make for a more dramatic reaction.

He heard shuffling on the other side of the door. The curtain was pulled back, and the front light came on, then the door opened.

"Ethan?" Brooke's expression was a mixture of emotion—happiness, shock…anger. He hadn't expected that one.

He forced a smile. "I'm out on bail." He brushed past her, walking into the house. She stayed at the doorway.

"Bail? Well, why wouldn't Mr. Golden have informed me?" She closed the door and followed him into the kitchen.

He disregarded her words. He noticed the soft glow seeping from the other room. It must have been the television. "Where's Megan?"

"You ignored my question," Brooke said with heat.

"I have already explained it to you. I'm out on bail. I don't know why Mr. Golden didn't call you."

As he spoke, she watched his face, his expression, but she noticed something different about his eyes. They were like peering into a void, but it was probably just his time behind bars that had changed him, hardened him.

"Megan. Where is she?" he repeated his question, irritation licking his tone.

"Don't you think we should talk first?" There was so much she needed to know, so many questions she needed answered.

He paced, sticking his head through doorways of a bedroom and the living room as if he was looking for something.

"What are you doing?" she asked.

He came to a stop in front of her, inches from her face. "I'm looking for Megan."

A tear slid down her cheek, and it unsettled her. It wasn't prompted by elation or happiness to see her husband; she found herself fearing for her and Meg's safety. Her husband looked the same, but there was something different about him. And it wasn't just his eyes. She didn't remember the freckle under his right eye. And when he smiled a moment ago, a small dimple formed on the left. Wasn't Ethan's dimple on the right? Not that this made any sense. She must be losing her mind. Had it been so long since she'd seen him that she forgot her own husband's face?

He kept moving.

She didn't know whether to go along with his quest to find Meg or fight against it. But something told her to cooperate. "Meg's in bed, Ethan." She had intended his name to sound more convincing, but it came from her lips with the believability of a B-movie actress.

Something flicked across his eyes, and he lunged toward her and grabbed her arms. She gasped and struggled against him but forced herself to stay quiet for her daughter's sake. Whoever this man was, he certainly wasn't her husband.

"Where is Megan?"

Ethan never called their daughter by her full name. It was either Meg or Princess.

A bedroom door creaked open, followed by, "Mommy?"

The man put his hands around Brooke's neck, and she fought for breath, clawing at his hands. Tears streamed down her face. "Please…please don't do this."

He tightened his grip, and she stood taller, shifting to her tiptoes, hoping to alleviate the pressure on her throat. But nothing was working.

He whispered into her ear, "Never did it with my bare hands before."

Her heart was thumping hard, and she couldn't breathe, but all she could think about was Meg. "Ple…ease…."

Meg padded toward the living room, and the man finally released his grip on Brooke.

Brooke's hands instinctively shot to her throat as she gasped to get air.

Meg stepped into the room, rubbing her eyes with balled fists. "Daddy!" She ran toward the man. "You're back!"

"No, honey…" Brooke intercepted her daughter. "He's tired, baby." She sniffled. "Go back to bed."

"You crying, Mommy?"

"A little, baby—"

The man wrapped his arm around her and squeezed her side. She winced, and fresh tears fell. She worked to compose herself. She had to convince her daughter everything was okay. "I'm just happy to see Daddy, that's all. Go back to bed."

God, please listen to me, Meg!

The man released his grip on Brooke and got down on his haunches. "Let her come to me."

Brooke stepped to the side, attempting to block her daughter, but to no avail. Meg moved past her and put her arms around the man she thought was her father.

Brooke tensed, maintaining a vigil stance as this stranger hugged her daughter. What Brooke noticed now came unexpected. The man's eyes were wet as he cupped Meg's face and kissed her forehead.

A moment of weakness Brooke might be able to use. "Come on, sweetie," she said, "let's go to bed. We'll visit with Daddy in the morning."

"Okay," she sulked and trudged off to her bedroom, dragging her feet the entire way. Brooke heard the door close behind her.

"All right, now where were we?" The man's hands were back on Brooke's neck faster than she could move. "Ah, yes, here we were."

She detected the smile in his voice. "Who are—"

His calloused hands had a firm grip on her, but they weren't tightening. Maybe if she could keep him talking… "I know you're not my husband."

She felt his grip slip a little before tightening once again.

How did she know? Was it the way he was treating her, or did he just radiate not quite good enough? He tightened his hold on her.

"Why are—"

Tighter still as he summoned everything from inside of him to go through with this, to finish taking everything away from Ethan for good, but he couldn't do it. He hadn't slept in more than two-hour intervals since Evelyn…*Mother.*

Her last words were singed on his psyche like a branding iron marks livestock. "*I loved you.*"

He knew in that moment that his mother had recognized him. He inhaled deeply, and everything within him liquefied. His legs weakened. He released his grip altogether and stepped back.

Brooke was dizzy and in a daze. He'd let her go, and all she could think about was killing him or knocking him unconscious. She looked around for something she could strike him with, and her eyes settled on a wrought-iron candlestand, the one Ethan had always insisted stay out on display.

He was standing there, covering his face with his hands. She had an opportunity to make a move, but she'd have to be quick. In a swift movement, she grabbed the candlestand, and took a swing at him.

His hands dropped just before impact, shielding himself from her blow that ended up being just shy of his head. He squeezed her wrist, and her hand released its hold on the would-be weapon. She shrieked.

He pulled her against him. "Quiet, or you'll wake the little girl." He smiled smugly and tossed her onto a nearby sofa, handling her like a twig. He moved his body over hers.

"Please, no…" She squirmed and fought to keep his hands off her neck.

Then all of a sudden, he stopped and stood to full height. "You called the cops?"

"Wha-what," she stuttered and tried to rise to her feet, but he was still holding her down. She could see colored flashing lights shining through the front door's window into the living room.

Her heart lightened.

"When…why?" he pleaded.

"I never did…" And Brooke was telling the truth. She hadn't been out of his sight the entire time.

There was loud banging on the front door, followed by, "Stiles PD! Open up!"

Brooke let out a deep breath. She and her daughter were saved.

CHAPTER FORTY-NINE

Madison was good with how everything had worked out, but it would have been even better if they'd gotten to the Younges' a little sooner. She wasn't giving herself any grief over it, though, because she'd listened to her gut.

She'd placed an anonymous call, reporting a disturbance at the Younge residence. If Evan was there and other officers actually arrested him, Madison and Terry would have their guy but not have to face the wrath from the sergeant and the chief for getting involved.

Brooke Younge decided to press charges against Evan. She felt her life was in danger, and if they hadn't arrived when they did, he would have killed her. Madison had no doubt Brooke was right about that. They'd found another G&C necktie in Evan's pocket. So, as opposed to an assault charge, Evan would be looking at attempted murder. That on top of murder charges for the deaths of Laura Saunders, Heather Nguyen, and Evelyn Younge.

They did end up obtaining a warrant for Evan's DNA, and it came back at a higher-percentage match than it had to Ethan's. Concreting the evidence was the fact that Evan's fingerprints were a perfect match to the ones on the cuffs, the photo, the wineglass, and the locket.

"And I see that you own a '95 Honda Accord." Madison watched him from across the table of the interrogation room.

Evan Frost had refused his right to an attorney. He had claimed something about needing to cleanse his soul. "Yeah."

"So why did you do it?" The one question that needed a solid answer.

Silence.

"I can tell you what I think," Madison began.

He gestured with his hands as if to say, *go ahead*. He tried to appear more laidback than Madison believed he was. Maybe he didn't think she noticed how his leg was bouncing up and down underneath the table.

"You felt abandoned, unwanted. You were shuffled from foster home to foster home. Never adopted." Madison made a wincing face. "That must have hurt."

Evan started rocking back and forth.

She continued. "Rejected by your own mother and repeatedly by strangers. No one accepted you. You were an outcast."

He stopped rocking, hunched forward, and shook his head. "I'm not. I'm not."

"Is that you trying to convince yourself? Because what *I* see is an outcast. I can understand how all this would make you hold your mother accountable for all your suffering."

"No, she wasn't…"

"She wasn't, Mr. Frost? She put you in that home. *Abandoned you*," she taunted, waiting for him to break.

Rage burned in his eyes and flared his nostrils. She was finally getting to him.

She kept pushing. "You killed your own mother."

He lowered his gaze to the table, fanned his fingers through his hair, and shook his head.

"Your *own* mother," she stressed.

He sobbed, gasping for breath.

Madison carried on. "She didn't know your full potential, or she would never have given you up and chosen Ethan over you."

He lifted his gaze, tears rolling down his cheeks, and he chewed his bottom lip.

"You saw the life Ethan had and wanted it for yourself. So you seized the opportunity." Madison sat back and clasped her hands. "But what I don't get is why those other women? What did they do to you?"

The crying stopped, and his eyes turned dark. "Those women deserved what they got. They left their babies in the hands of strangers! They walked away without any care about them. They left them to rot!"

"We know they were left at the same orphanage as you, but how did you find out about them?"

He let out a puff of air, looked up at the ceiling and then to Madison. She didn't know whether he spoke to God in that brief time or was trying to decide whether to continue.

"Guess it doesn't matter now, does it?" He laughed.

His laugh chilled her, but she pushed through. "What doesn't?"

"How I knew about them," he said matter-of-factly. "I mean, I assume I'm about to be charged with murder."

"Three counts, in addition to the attempted murder of Mrs. Brooke Younge."

He didn't give the impression he was affected at all by his fate. "I wanted to know who my mother was, so I broke into the orphanage office."

"When was this?"

"Does it matter?" he snapped.

"Years ago?" Madison asked calmly. She would bank her curiosity as to why he'd killed now, after all these years.

"Yes," he hissed. "The files for Laura and Heather were on top of the cabinets, unfiled. Their babies were abandoned within the last day or so, and I imagined their wailing cries echoing off the walls, a dire reminder that we weren't loved." He'd listed off the details devoid of emotion, but when he continued, his voice quivered. "It was the same day I found a picture of two boys. Both their heads were circled, the names Evan and Ethan scrawled on the photo. That's how I found out I had a twin."

"Must have been rough on you." Madison acted like she wasn't moved at all by Evan's story, even though there was a small part of her that ached for him. Also, by extension, for his victims. If he'd had a better childhood, maybe Laura, Heather, and Evelyn would still be alive. "But why wait so long to kill Laura, Heather, your mother?"

"I tried to fight my urges, but in the end…" He dragged a hand under his nose and sniffled.

"In the end, you couldn't anymore."

"No," he barked. "I wanted those women to know pain. And how was it fair that my brother was out there living a normal life with a family that loved him?"

"How did you know he wasn't dead?"

"I hunted him down."

"And you wanted to take everything he had away from him," Madison surmised. "Including his wife and daughter, if you could."

"No, I would've never hurt the girl. The rest of it is a case of two birds, one stone, Detective. In this case, three birds."

"You wanted to frame your brother. That's why you left that photo on Laura's nightstand?"

His lips curved into a subtle smile.

"You also wanted us to find your brother after you killed your mother…" Her words trailed off as she matched eyes with him. "You made your mother call Ethan at work."

Evan smiled proudly. "Yes. Everything was going perfectly—until you got involved." He glared at her, but his eyes softened when he said with the trace of a smirk, "I thought…what would be more fitting than using the face and DNA God gave me to carry out my payback?"

"Don't pull God into any of this," she snarled.

His smirk grew, but she was about to kill it real quick.

"You're actually the one who messed up, Evan. You wanted to frame Ethan with the face God gave you, but you failed to realize you and your brother have slightly different facial features. He has his dimple in his right cheek, you the left, and there's a freckle under your right eye and none under

Ethan's eyes. You used *your face*, Evan, and that's why you're going away for a long time." She motioned to the nearby officer. "Book him."

As she and Terry left the interrogation room, her phone rang. "Knight."

"Hey." It was Cynthia. "You know the phrase 'better late than never?'"

"Yes."

"I have the results on the bloody towel."

"About time."

"Now, now."

"What were the results?"

"I guess I don't really need to tell you…"

Madison's chest swelled with hope. "Seeing as you called, let me— Actually, hold on a second. Tell Terry." She handed her phone to her partner, even though he wouldn't take it at first. He must have feared it was either the sergeant or the chief.

"Hello?" he said with hesitation.

She watched as her partner's trepidation morphed into a smile.

"Bye," he said and handed the phone back to Madison. He started to get up.

"Terry?" she prompted.

He laughed.

"Come on. Just say it once. Say it with me, 'You were right, Maddy.'"

"Nope. Not gonna do it." He shook his head, a smirk in place, and walked toward the door.

"Terry." Her begging made her laugh. She didn't need to hear him admit it. She had been right, and he knew it.

CHAPTER FIFTY

Madison wanted to apologize to the Younge family on behalf of the Stiles PD, but she was limited as to what she could say by the legal department. To admit they'd made a mistake would be tantamount to admitting the department was incompetent and open it up for a lawsuit.

"Thank you, Detective," Ethan told her while holding his wife's hand. His daughter Megan stood in front of her parents, and Frank Younge was present, too. "You gave me my family back," Ethan added and smiled at Madison.

To Madison, Ethan represented resiliency. He had been through hell and back and seemed to have come out on the other end much stronger.

"If you want to meet him," Madison started, "I can take you to him." She referred to Evan.

Ethan shook his head. "After what he put me through?" He looked at his wife. "After what he put *us* through? As far as I'm concerned, I don't have a brother."

Madison noticed a mild twitch in his cheek that belied his words. Maybe someday he would be back to see the man who was related to him by blood. "Good day, Mr. Younge."

"That it is." He kissed his wife on her forehead. Megan held her grandfather's hand.

Madison watched them walk away a family reunited, the little girl doing her best to keep up as she swung her grandfather's arm. She'd heard that Frank had his faith restored in Ethan and was transferring the business to him. Maybe there is such a thing as a happy ending.

An opening door caused her to turn, and she came face-to-face with Blake Golden. The sergeant and the chief filtered out behind him, passed her a cursory glance, and kept moving.

The lawyer stopped in front of her.

"Are you going to make yourself more famous by suing the department?" she asked. Why poke the bear, right? But sometimes she couldn't help herself.

"Kind of tough to do when you didn't do anything wrong." Golden smiled at her. "You had every reason to believe Ethan Younge did it, and the DNA evidence to back it up. Besides, Ethan doesn't want me to pursue legal action against the department. Or you."

"DNA evidence or not, I'm sure you'd have used your magical lawyer powers to manipulate the situation." She'd aimed for sarcasm and hit flirtatious.

"Magical lawyer powers?" Blake laughed. "Wow, how I'd love to get myself some of those."

She laughed despite her better judgment. "Yeah, well, given your line of work they'd come in quite handy."

An awkward moment of silence passed.

"There is something that does need to be discussed, though." Golden's voice had turned serious.

She felt herself stiffen, ready to defend herself. She had followed everything by the book. She could feel her earlobes getting warm. "If it's about Layton's harassment charges, you can discuss that with my superiors."

"No." He smiled. "See, the guy can't afford me. My charity's been used up. And the partners were not too happy about it in the first place."

"Your charity?"

"Sometimes I can feel bad for the underdog."

Madison had wondered how Ethan Younge managed to keep Golden after the father wanted nothing to do with him, but it had been a brief passing thought. It also confirmed her suspicion about how Layton had afforded Golden, as well. Maybe this particular lawyer wasn't all that bad... "How sweet, a lawyer with a conscience."

"Have a drink with me," he said.

She nearly choked on her saliva. "You're serious?"

"Yes, Detective Knight, I'm always serious."

Madison laughed.

EPILOGUE

Months Later, Christmas Eve

"So are you going to let me in or what? It's freezing out here." Madison stood on the front steps of Terry's house, bouncing to keep warm.

He continued to block entry, letting the warm air heat the chill of winter, looking over and around her. "Where's Blake?"

Madison scrunched up her face. "Not here."

"But I thought you two were a hot item."

"Oh, Lord." She brushed past him, giving up on the etiquette of waiting for him to invite her inside.

"Hey, I didn't say you could come in."

"Technically, when you asked me for drinks and dinner, you did." She let out a small laugh.

"Fine." He closed the door behind them. "But you didn't answer my question."

"Oh, I didn't?"

Terry shook his head.

She had been seeing the lawyer in the months following Younge's release. In a single moment of weakness, she had agreed to a drink, and it had gone on from there. One date had turned into two, three, then several. She'd lost count. She would like to blame it on the love she saw between Ethan and his wife. After all, it made her realize she might be missing something in her life. But she wasn't going to give her heart blindly and get hurt again. This time, she'd play things slow and cautious.

Terry kept looking at her with big eyes like a hound. Speaking of...

"Where are Todd and Bailey?" she asked, feigning interest in the canines. Anything to take the focus off her relationship status.

"Don't sidestep my question about Blake with another question."

"Why not?" She smiled when she realized she'd just done it again. Terry was smiling as well, but his eyes revealed a growing curiosity. "You seriously want to know?" She gave it a few seconds and then continued. "The simple truth is we're not at that point in our relationship yet."

"What point is that?"

"The point where we spend Christmas with each other's families."

Her explanation silenced him, then a huge smile engulfed his face.

"What?" She must have missed something.

"You think of me as family." He moved to hug her, but she punched him in the shoulder. He pretended to be in pain.

"Here, take my coat and purse, would you?" She tossed them at him, and he caught them, putting them in the closet.

"Huh, and to think Annabelle and I have a gift for you. I'm not sure if you deserve it now."

"We agreed...no gifts." They had discussed it at length. It was to save each other the regret of buying something inferior and getting into a lengthy competition in the following months, trying to best each other. "Besides you have a baby on the way. You'll need your money. I don't need anything, anyhow."

Terry and his wife had made up not long after Ethan Younge was exonerated of all charges. Terry had left in a hurry that day because he'd realized how short life is—and the unexpected turns it can take. He didn't want another moment wasted on the we-should-haves or we-*could*-haves.

"Come on, don't deflate me like that. Besides, it didn't cost too much."

It was then that she caught a glimpse of a puppy peeking out of the doorway from the seating area. A chocolate lab, if she was right, and he had a red bow around his neck.

Terry turned, following her gaze. "Ah-ha, speaking of your gift…"

Her chest tightened. The responsibility, the hair, the—

Terry kneeled and said, "Come here, buddy." The pup walked over with a wagging tail. Terry scooped him in a blanket that was hung over the banister. "Here, he's all yours." He held it out to her, and she had no option but to extend her arms or let the little guy fall.

"Oh, you shouldn't have…" The pup was so tiny in her arms now, but don't these dogs get huge? She had just a small apartment. Her inclination was to set the dog down and run—fast and far away—and this from someone who hated running. The door was right there. "I don't know what to say," she added.

"You could say 'thank you.'" Terry grinned.

You'd be waiting a while….

"Oh, and don't worry about him getting hair on you. We brushed him before you came. And he won't mess up your dress while he's wrapped in the blanket."

Yeah, her dress. Another thing she'd done tonight that was outside her comfort zone. She hated dresses almost as much as running—maybe about the same. She looked down at the pup and realized how he'd settled into her arms, and it served to melt away some of her apprehension. But it was when the pup tilted his head back to look at her that she softened. She pet his ears, soft as velvet. She was starting to understand what Terry might see in these animals—at least, until a little pink slip came out of its mouth and licked her chin.

"Oh…" Madison wanted to add *gross* but didn't want to hurt Terry. Still, the thought of dog's spit all over her face made her shiver. "Maybe we should put him down for a bit, let him explore." She bent over, freeing him from the blanket.

"So you like him?" Terry was grinning—again, still? Hard to say.

Madison didn't know how to respond. She had mixed emotions.

"I know he's not what you'd expect, but hopefully, he'll grow on you," Terry said.

"Yeah, I'm sure he will. Don't these dogs get to be a hundred pounds or something?" She could feel her chest constricting.

"Eighty at the high end."

"Oh, so…"

"I know this is probably a bit overwhelming, but you're going to love him, I promise. To help you out, I took one responsibility off your shoulders."

Madison raised her eyebrows.

"I named him."

You named my dog? She was in too much shock to verbalize her thought.

"I'm sure you'll like it."

Well, if she didn't, she could always change it. "Just don't say it's Fred—"

"Hershey."

She was speechless. She loved it, and it was so fitting, and it wasn't a person's name. She smiled.

"I trust that's a dog's name," Terry added as if reading her mind.

"Yes, that's a dog's name. Who calls an animal a human name, anyway? I'll tell you who. Crazy people who are too attached to—"

"Oh, we're not getting into this again."

Both their gazes went to Hershey, who was scrunching down. Madison didn't realize the implication at first, but Terry moved quickly.

"Bad, Hershey, bad." Terry hurried to pick him up, but it wasn't in time.

"He peed in a shoe. Yet you wonder why I've never had one."

"You only think it's funny 'cause it's my shoe."

"It's yours?" She burst out laughing, and then snatched Hershey from the floor and stroked the top of his head. "Good boy. Yep, I think I love this dog already." She squeezed Hershey extra tight, and he let out a bark.

Terry mumbled, "Brat."

A ringtone coming from the closet reached both their ears.

"It's my phone." She went for the closet door.

"Please don't answer it," Terry begged. "Let someone else get the call tonight."

She continued pushing coats aside until she reached hers. She matched eyes with Terry as she rummaged through her purse that hung on the hanger with her coat.

"Please…" He held out his hand. "Think about how much it would piss Sovereign off to have his Christmas interrupted."

She held the phone in her hand and locked gazes with her partner. But, unfortunately, no matter how much satisfaction it would give her to inconvenience Sovereign, she had a job to do. She answered and watched as Terry let out a sigh of defeat. He likely anticipated what her next words would be, and if so, he would be correct.

"We'll be right there," she told her caller.

Catch the next book in the Detective Madison Knight Series!

Sign up at the weblink listed below
to be notified when new Madison Knight titles are available
for pre-order:

CarolynArnold.net/MKUpdates

By joining this newsletter, you will also receive exclusive
first looks at the following:

Updates pertaining to upcoming releases in the series, such
as cover reveals, book descriptions, and firm release dates

Sneak peeks of teasers and special content

Behind-the-Tape™ insights that give you an inside look at
Carolyn's research and creative process

There is no getting around it: reviews are important and so is word of mouth.

With all the books on the market today, readers need to know what's worth their time and what's not. This is where you come into play.

If you enjoyed *Ties That Bind*, please help others find it by posting a brief, honest review on the retailer site where you purchased this book and recommend it to family and friends.

Also, Carolyn loves to hear from her readers, and you can reach her at Carolyn@CarolynArnold.net.

Upon receipt of your e-mail, you will be added to her newsletter mailing unless you express your desire otherwise.

Keep on reading for a sample of *Justified*, book 2 in the Detective Madison Knight series.

PROLOGUE

He had to do it. He had no choice. Pushed into an unpleasant corner, he had no other option. How could he allow himself to be walked all over, manipulated? All that he had sacrificed for her, laid on the line.

It was pitch-black, the wind moaned, and small flakes dared to precipitate. It was a bitter cold, the type he felt through to his bones.

He knocked on the door.

He had chosen the back side of the house for added seclusion. If the cover of the night wasn't enough, surely this approach would diminish the possibility of a curious neighbor trying to play the hero. He didn't need any cops showing up. This was to be a private visit.

He knocked again, harder and more deliberate. A light came on inside followed by one on the back porch. Finally, he was getting some attention.

She opened the door the few inches the chain would allow. "What are you doing here?"

"Trying to reason with you." The chills left his body and a calm, radiant heat overtook him.

The door shut. The chain rattled. The door reopened. "You can't just show up whenever you feel like it." She let him in, more likely for her own comfort given the way she was dressed. Arms crossed in front of her chest, an act of modesty over a lacy piece of lingerie. He had seen it before. Shivers trembled through her, and she gripped her arms tighter. "What is it?"

He disregarded the tone in her voice, the condescending overture it carried. He ignored the body language that screamed for him to leave. He went to touch a ribbon that served as a strap.

She stepped back. "Please don't—"

"Claire, we're meant to be together." His lack of control surprised him; his voice had risen in volume with each word.

"You should leave."

There was more to her words. And the way she was dressed. "You move on already?" He took steps forward, heading for her bedroom.

She grabbed his arm and pulled him back. She didn't deny his accusation, and she refused to look at him when she did speak. "It was your choice. I gave you the option."

He swore her eyes misted over. "Not really much of one."

"You should go."

He shook his head as if it would bury the jealousy. But the fact there was someone else here, lying in her bed, waiting on her to come back…

He would do what he came to do, regardless. He had too much to lose.

CHAPTER ONE

The coffee came up into the back of her throat, and Madison Knight swallowed hard, forcing the acidic bile back down. This was a messy crime scene, the kind she did her best to avoid. She knew Weir, the first officer on the scene, was speaking, but the words weren't making it through. Despite her revulsion, her eyes were frozen on what was before her.

The victim lay on a crimson blanket of death, wearing nothing but a lacy camisole. The blood pool reached around her body in an approximate two-foot circumference. The blood had coagulated, resulting in a curdled, pudding-like consistency. The kitchen floor was a porous ceramic, and the blood had found its way to the grout lines and seeped through it like veins. Arterial spray had splattered the backsplash like the work of an abstract painter who had fanned a loaded brush against the canvas.

Cynthia Baxter was hunched close to the body taking photos and collecting shards of glass that were in the blood. She was the head of the forensics lab, but her job also required time in the field. She looked up at Madison, nodded a hello, and offered a small smile. Madison knew her well enough as a friend outside of work that the facial expression was sincere, but the scene had dampened it from reaching her eyes.

Weir stood back at the doorway that was between the front living room and the kitchen. "Such a shame, especially on Christmas Eve."

Terry Grant, Madison's partner, braced his hands above his holster and exhaled a jagged deep breath.

"What's her name and background?" Madison asked Weir with her eyes on the victim.

"The vic is Claire Reeves, forty-three. Lived here alone. No record of restraining orders or anything out of the ordinary. Nothing noted as her place of employment. Her maid, Allison Minard, found her. She's over at the neighbor's. Officer Higgins is over there with her."

Madison managed to break eye contact from the body, glanced at Terry, and settled her gaze on Weir. His words came through as though out of context.

"Detective Knight?" Judging by the softness in his tone of voice, Weir must have read her reaction to the scene. His eyes inquired if she was okay, but the silent probing would have been squashed by the wall she had erected. He continued. "The maid's pretty shaken up."

Madison could understand that. She had experience in processing murder scenes, and she could barely handle this one. She did her best to keep eye contact with the officer, but her fear, her distaste for blood, kept pulling her attention to the dead woman.

Claire Reeves. That was her name before she had been reduced to this. To be killed in this manner pointed toward an emotional assailant. Her lack of clothing was an indication that she likely had an intimate relationship with her killer.

Madison scanned the room. There was no sign of a struggle, no overturned chairs or broken dishes. The only thing standing out was a tea towel bunched on the floor in front of the stove as if it had slipped off the front bar. "Any evidence of forced entry?"

Weir shook his head.

"She let her killer in." Madison's gaze returned to the victim.

She was someone's daughter, someone's best friend, someone's lover. Normally Madison didn't have an issue with separating herself from crime scenes and keeping them impersonal. Maybe it had something to do with all that blood and the fact that Claire had been murdered just before Christmas.

Claire was on her back, albeit slightly twisted, from the fall to the floor. Her legs were crumpled beneath her. A large slash lined her neck, and based on the angle and directionality, her killer had come at her from behind. Logic dictated the killing method as typically belonging to a male, but something about the maid finding the body didn't make sense.

"The maid was scheduled to work on Christmas Eve?" Madison asked.

"Supposedly she got a text message from Claire. She called us right after she—" Weir pointed toward the vomit at the far entrance to the kitchen.

Madison had noticed it on the way through. She took a shallow breath, hoping to cleanse her focus despite the stench of the crime scene having transformed to a coating on her tongue. "Did you see this text message?"

Weir shook his head. "She couldn't produce it. Said she must have accidentally deleted it."

"Anyone think to check Claire's phone?"

"I'll go check on that now." Weir's cheeks flushed. "Anyway, Higgins is with her, and Richards should be here soon." He excused himself with a wave of a hand.

Cole Richards was the medical examiner.

Cynthia rose to her feet, picked up her kit, and addressed Madison. "What are you thinking? Love affair gone wrong?"

"It looks like it could be but rarely are things that straightforward."

"Isn't that the truth? But I know you'll figure it out."

"Hey, I'm here, too," Terry said.

Both women smiled.

"Okay, *both of you* will figure it out."

"Better." Terry smiled.

Cynthia left the kitchen in the direction of a hallway that led to the bedrooms. Based on the vic's attire, it would be a reasonable progression to search there.

Madison moved toward the body. "Wonder where her underwear is."

"Maybe they were of the edible variety." Terry gave her a goofy smile.

"At a time like this, you're going to bring out that horny grin of yours?"

"I'm only a man."

"Uh-huh, that's your excuse for everything." Her gaze drifted to the backsplash and then the floor around the victim. She was looking for any cast-off blood spatters that could have come from the weapon or for any voids. "She was standing in front of the sink taking a drink when her killer came up from behind her. He would have wrapped his arm around her, holding her steady, when he slashed her throat." Madison glanced back at the body. "It looks like the cut went from right to left." She swallowed hard. Periodically, the smell of the blood hit in intensive waves equal in scale to tsunamis.

Terry nodded. "We're looking for a left-handed killer."

"Someone call?" Richards entered the kitchen.

"Are you a left-handed killer?" Terry teased and received a mild glare from the medical examiner.

"Hey." Madison smiled. The man's presence had the ability to make her happy—ironic given his job description. Too bad he was married.

"There's my favorite detective." He returned the smile. His dark skin contrasted with the brightness of his teeth, which were a pure white.

"Nice to see you, too," Terry said.

"I was actually referring to Knight."

"Ouch. She always gets the spotlight."

Madison laughed. "Oh someday, Terry. Someday, when

you grow up, you can be a—"

"Ah quiet. You and I are not even talking right now." Terry continued the show with a dramatic crossing of his arms.

"Moody like a female." Richards shook his head.

"Excuse me? Moody…like a female? Are you implying that we're moody? That I am?" Madison challenged him.

"Never." He waved his hand in a gesture of making peace.

"Uh-huh." She laughed, but it faded fast. Small talk was often used to ease the intensity of a scene, but doing so here caused her a few seconds of guilt.

"Hey, I'm with Richards on this. Only thing is, he's afraid of you, Maddy, whereas I'm not. If anyone can attest to the mood swings of a woman—"

"I know you can," Madison began, "and only you can get away with that comment right now."

Terry's wife was two months pregnant, and according to him, she was somewhat temperamental.

"I should be a good husband and dispute what you're implying, but I can't. She's driving me nuts. Drove all around town the other night looking for black cherry ice cream only to come home and be asked what took so long."

"Nice to know they're all the same." Richards's joviality ended abruptly as his focus went to the victim. "It's pretty safe to conclude COD was exsanguination. Based on the amount of blood loss, her carotid artery was severed."

His comment drew Madison's attention to the red expanse on the floor. Her coffee threatened a repeat showing.

Richards continued. "The blood pressure in her brain would have dropped so rapidly that she would have lost consciousness pretty much immediately. She would have bled out in less than a minute. The blood separation testifies to the fact that it had left her body some time ago. She's also coming out of rigor, so it puts time of death over twelve hours ago. But I'd estimate closer to fourteen or sixteen. Somewhere between two and four this morning. Of course, I'll take her temperature and conduct other means before I verify with certainty."

Richards bent down beside the victim, put a rubber-gloved hand on her face, and continued. "The killer was no professional, I can tell you that." He traced a finger along the jagged edges of the slash. "He was hesitant." Richards carefully turned the body over, handling it with care as if it were a priceless china doll. "Lividity shows she was killed here." He pressed fingers to the skin, and even under the touch, it remained a bluish color. "This also confirms that she's been dead for over twelve hours."

Madison had to step back from the body just for a few seconds. She moved to the doorway near the vomit, a normally potent scent, yet all she could smell was blood.

She looked out the window in the back door. The walkway was buried under eight to ten inches of snow, but that wasn't what had her attention. It was the boot prints leading to the door. She knew Weir had said something about which entrance the maid had used, but her focus had been on the blood at the time. "Did Weir say which door the maid came in?"

"The front," Terry answered.

She stepped aside to let Terry see out. "Let's put it this way. Either the maid's lying or we know where our killer came in."

CHAPTER TWO

Sam Thompson and his wife Linda owned the home next to Claire. Although a man of easily six foot four, his height seemed to buckle under the intense glare of his wife. She stood in the doorway of a neighboring room where numerous people went about their evening conversing with light chitchat and laughter.

Madison and Terry were in the dining room with the husband.

"I promised Linda this won't take too long."

Madison could imagine him wiping his forehead, as if sweat formed there, or flexing his fingers on a temple to ease the concentration of his wife's controlling stare. Madison glanced at her again. The scowl, the arch of her brow, and her narrowed eyes, said it all: *Our dinner is ruined.*

The table was set for eight with full place settings. A carved turkey sat in the middle of the space on an antique platter, possibly passed on through generations and only brought out for special occasions. Mashed potatoes, stuffing, and cranberry sauce were set out in three bowls. They had all the fixings of a perfect holiday dinner. Yet despite the spread of food, all Madison could smell was the blood that was lodged in her sinuses.

"Where is she?" Madison was referring to the maid, Allison Minard.

Thompson directed them to another side room and gestured with his head, *In there.*

"I promise we'll be as fast as we can."

"I'd appreciate it."

A woman was on the couch, leaned back, arms crossed, and head shaking. Her long, black ponytail swayed with the movement. She stopped and looked at Madison and Terry.

An officer was in the room with her and sat braced on the edge of a recliner. He quickly rose to his feet when he saw them.

Madison sat where he had been, but Terry hung back and leaned on the doorframe.

Seconds passed in silence, but words weren't always needed. Energy, body language, and facial expressions usually communicated plenty. Allison's chestnut eyes weren't puffy and her cheeks and nose weren't red, so she hadn't been crying. If she did feel bad about her employer's death, it hadn't physically manifested yet. The head shaking could have been in response to several things—recounting her shock of discovering Claire dead or in reaction to something the officer had said.

"Allison Minard," Madison began, breaking the silence.

Allison matched her gaze to Madison's, and while her looks could have pegged her as midtwenties, the wisdom in her eyes spoke to late thirties, maybe even early forties.

Madison went on. "You're the one who found Claire Reeves?"

"Yes." She exhaled, sinking further into the couch and crossing her legs. "I've been through this with the other officers." She twisted a wrist, looked at her watch. "And I've got to go." Her crossed-over leg bobbed up and down, fast, without a set rhythm.

"You have something more important to do?"

"Actually, yes, I do." She offered no further explanation and her posture stiffened.

"I'm sure that whatever your plans were, they can be postponed a little longer—"

"Always whatever Claire wants. Even in death she's a conniving bitch." Allison crossed her arms tighter, adding height to an already well-endowed bosom.

"Why were you working tonight?"

Allison remained silent.

"Claire is dead. She was someone who you knew, Miss Minard, someone with whom you had regular contact. And if you take it from our viewpoint, short of a spouse, the last person to see someone alive or the first person to report the find is the first suspect—"

"I'm not the killer!"

Madison leaned forward like the officer had, yet she was not anxious to leave; rather, she was desperate for answers. She placed two hands on her thighs. "Prove it to us. Help us by reconstructing everything as you found it."

Allison broke eye contact and looked around the room. "I don't see why I have to go through it again. I have a party to get to."

Madison couldn't help but contemplate how selfish and single-minded people could be. If anything came up to interfere with their agenda, the mentality was, *How dare it?*

"I'm sure they'll wait on you to get things started." Madison's disgust over the woman's priorities couldn't be masked. "A woman's dead—"

"Like I said, I had nothing to do with it."

"Miss Minard, Claire Reeves was murdered." Madison placed emphasis on *murdered.* "I would hope that you could find it within yourself to see the bigger picture."

"Maybe you should know the *full* picture. Any number of people would have wanted her dead."

"Were you one of them?"

"I'm not going to answer that."

"I'll take that as a yes."

"I didn't kill her. Why would I? She gave me a job when I had nothing."

Quite the contrast to *she's a conniving bitch...* There was something hidden deep within Allison's eyes, something she was holding back. Guilt perhaps? And if so, on what scale?

"You don't seem really shaken up by her death. Maybe more by what you saw," Madison ventured.

"Do you think you can read everyone?" There was a flash of defensive anger in her eyes. "You can't read me."

"On one hand, you give me the impression you didn't like Claire, and on the other, you seem to have a soft spot for her, saying that she helped you out when you had nothing. What made you resent her despite the fact she helped you?" Madison glanced at Terry. "Normally I admire those who help me out—"

"Well, she was a very anal-retentive person. Meticulous. She had a way she wanted things done, and you had to do it by the book. She had a list of what she wanted cleaned weekly, monthly, and bimonthly. She'd leave it on the kitchen table and expect that I work through it, checking off the items as I went along. Like I was an idiot."

"So that's why you hated her?"

Silence.

"You said a number of people would have wanted her dead. Who specifically?"

"She made a lot of enemies—" she loosened her crossed arms, then retightened "—but I'd start with Darcy Simms."

"Who was she to Claire?"

"Her best friend."

Madison and Terry shared a look. "Her best friend wanted her dead?"

"Hell, I wouldn't put anything past that woman, but there's more. Claire was very active. Sexually." The last word came out tagged with disgust. "Although, I'm sure your CSI people have already confirmed that. I was always cleaning up used condoms from the wastebaskets."

It was possible Claire was caught in the crossfire of a love triangle...

Allison continued. "Let's just say Darcy wasn't as good a friend as she portrayed herself to be. I know her well enough."

"How do you know Darcy?"

"Claire recommended my services to her, and I ended up cleaning for her once. She made up a reason to fire me after what I saw."

"Which was?"

"She was sleeping with one of Claire's men."

"Do you know his name?"

She shook her head, her ponytail swaying the way it had earlier. "Not going to say. All I know is Darcy will sleep with anything that has a pulse. Male or female."

With the last word from her mouth, Allison had erected a barrier. The energy was tangible, and they wouldn't be getting any more from her right now. But Allison had already said plenty and brought up the possibility of a love triangle. Darcy could have confronted Claire—or the other way around—and things got out of hand. But that didn't fit with the lack of evidence to indicate a struggle or the kill method typically belonging to a man.

Madison pulled out a notepad and pen for Allison. "Please write your name and phone number here."

"Don't see why I should have to."

Madison kept the notepad and pen extended.

Allison let out a heavy breath, scooped the pen from Madison, and scribbled down the information.

Madison observed which hand she used: her right.

"Now may I go?" Her head tilted to the side.

"One more thing. Where were you between two and four this morning?"

Allison stared blankly. "I was at home."

"Can anyone else verify that?"

She avoided eye contact as she tossed the notepad onto the coffee table in front of her. "Want anything else, talk to my lawyer." Allison rose to her feet and snatched her purse from the couch cushion.

"Why a lawyer? Guilty of something?"

Allison stopped moving and faced Madison. "The smart ones get a lawyer, Detective."

"Thanks for your help," Madison muttered sarcastically to Allison's back as she left the room. Madison picked up the pen and notepad and said to Terry, "Well, I guess she *could* be innocent. She's right-handed, unlike our killer, but she does seem to be holding something back."

Terry nodded.

Sam Thompson came up beside Terry in the doorway. "Detectives, I'd like to talk with you."

"Sure."

The man's hands clasped and unclasped. He twisted his wedding band. "I saw someone at her back door in the wee hours. About two or so."

That was the estimated time of death. He could have seen the killer. "What did they look like?"

"Her light back there is bright enough to illuminate a football stadium. And that's what woke me up." He was dancing around the meat of his discovery.

"You said you saw someone?"

"Well, I didn't see anyone at first. Figured the light was one of those motion-sensor ones and triggered by a cat or something. I just got back into bed only to have the damn light come on again. I threw the sheets off and looked out. That was when I saw someone."

"A man or a woman?" Madison didn't know whether to laugh or scream. She struggled for control. *Please get to the point.*

"Not too sure, but they walked like they were in a hurry. But at the same time, they took deliberate steps."

"So this person was in a hurry but deliberate?" Not intended, but her tone mocked his message. "And you're not sure whether it was a man or a woman?"

"I'm only telling you what I saw."

"At the time you saw this person, didn't you say the light was on?"

"The surrounding area was quite dark, and the glare from the light made it hard to see clearly. The person was more of a hazy silhouette, but they wore a puffy jacket." He mimicked the bulge with cupped hands pulsing from his shoulders.

"Which direction were they going, toward the house or away?"

"Toward."

It could have been the killer, and it would explain the boot prints in the backyard. She wanted to verify the view, and she was also curious how a bright light hindered clarity. "Show us this window."

He directed them to the bedroom, pointed toward the window, but stayed in the hallway.

Madison and Terry looked outside. A CSI worked in Claire's backyard but physical distinction was hard to ascertain. It was only due to their size and mannerisms that she could identify the investigator as Mark Andrews. The light was just as bright as Mr. Thompson had said. "So we have a witness who could have seen our killer but can't identify them. Still no further ahead." When she turned back to look outside, the CSI was gone.

Also available from
International Bestselling Author
Carolyn Arnold

JUSTIFIED

Book 2 in the Detective Madison Knight series

She could feel her life draining from her body, but there was nothing she could do except wait until it was all over...and for the darkness to descend upon her.

The **brutal murder of Claire Reeves**, a successful entrepreneur, darkens Christmas Eve for **Detective Madison Knight**, who is assigned the case. Claire was found stabbed in her home, and her intimate attire would suggest her killer was someone close to her, but Madison knows things aren't always as they appear.

As Madison investigates, **the lies and secrets pile up** and reveal a long list of people who aren't shedding any tears that Claire's dead. Friends, lovers, and former business partners—they're all suspects. After all, Claire's love was money, and **she thought nothing of betraying even those closest to her**. No one can be trusted, but if there's going to be justice, Madison will need to determine who had the most motive to pull off the crime. **But just when Madison thinks she's getting closer to finding the truth, there's a deadly twist she never saw coming.**

Available from popular book retailers or
at CarolynArnold.net

CAROLYN ARNOLD is an international bestselling and award-winning author, as well as a speaker, teacher, and inspirational mentor. She has several continuing fiction series and has many published books. Her genre diversity offers her readers everything from police procedurals, hard-boiled mysteries, and thrillers to action adventures. Her crime fiction series have been praised by those in law enforcement as being accurate and entertaining. This led to her adopting the trademark: POLICE PROCEDURALS RESPECTED BY LAW ENFORCEMENT™.

Carolyn was born in a small town and enjoys spending time outdoors, but she also loves the lights of a big city. Grounded by her roots and lifted by her dreams, her overactive imagination insists that she tell her stories. Her intention is to touch the hearts of millions with her books, to entertain, inspire, and empower.

She currently lives near London, Ontario, Canada with her husband and two beagles.

CONNECT ONLINE
CarolynArnold.net
Facebook.com/AuthorCarolynArnold
Twitter.com/Carolyn_Arnold

And don't forget to sign up for her newsletter for up-to-date information on release and special offers at CarolynArnold.net/Newsletters.

Made in United States
Troutdale, OR
01/02/2025

27479800R00184